THE $TRIP

THE $TRIP

A NOVEL

E. DUKE VINCENT

BLOOMSBURY

New York   Berlin   London

Published by Bloomsbury USA, New York

All papers used by Bloomsbury USA are natural, recyclable products
made from wood grown in well-managed forests. The manufacturing processes
conform to the environmental regulations of the country of origin.

LIBRARY OF CONGRESS CATALOGING-IN-PUBLICATION DATA

Vincent, E. Duke.
The $trip : a novel / E. Duke Vincent—1st U.S. ed.
p. cm.
ISBN-13: 978-1-59691-615-9
ISBN-10: 1-59691-615-X
1. Television producers and directors—Fiction. 2. Extortion—Fiction. 3. Gangsters—
Fiction. 4. Mafia—Fiction. 5. Las Vegas (Nev.)—Fiction. I. Title. II. Title: Strip.
PS3622.I527S77 2009
813'.6—dc22
2008037168

First U.S. Edition 2009
1 3 5 7 9 10 8 6 4 2

Typeset by Westchester Book Group
Printed in the United States of America by Quebecor World Fairfield

For the *boyus* . . .

It is no secret that organized crime in America takes in over forty billion dollars a year. This is quite a profitable sum, especially when one considers that the Mafia spends very little for office supplies.

Woody Allen

AUTHOR'S NOTE

In the late seventies, in an attempt to wrest the Las Vegas casinos from the hands of organized crime, the FBI launched an investigation that became known as Strawman. The result was the beginning of the end of Vegas as a Mob town. While *The $trip* is a novel, the background and the references to historical characters—their relationships and how and when they were involved—are accurate.

CHAPTER ONE
LAS VEGAS. LATE OCTOBER, 1980

THE SIGN READ 2:36—103—20. It was the first thing Nick noticed when he drove out of the Desert Inn's parking lot. Time—temperature—humidity. An electric wink pulsing on a billboard next to the Frontier Hotel.

Christ, those were August numbers. Vegas was sweltering in an off-season heat wave and you were telling yourself it was okay because of the parched air.

Bullshit. It was hot!

It was the vicious sun. The top of the Firebird was down, but even Nick's dark shades couldn't prevent him from squinting against the glare and glitz bouncing off both sides of the Vegas Strip.

Midday in Sin City. Tourists scurried, horns blared, and the air reeked of false hope and cash.

Nick turned right on Flamingo, took another right on Industrial Road, and pulled up to a large warehouse. A small sign out front read:

THE $TRIP
SAM ALTMAN PRODUCTIONS
15015 INDUSTRIAL ROAD
LAS VEGAS, NEVADA

The thirty-thousand-square-foot building contained the permanent sets for a new smash-hit television series on United Television Broadcasting that starred Hank Donovan as a tough Vegas PI.

Nick Conti was its creator, head writer, and executive producer. Normally he worked out of the production offices in the Desert Inn.

He'd been called to the set because there was a problem.

Today they were working a split day-night schedule. The crew call was for the warehouse at 10:00 A.M. Therefore when darkness fell they would go to exterior locations for night shots until the end of their twelve-hour day at 10:00 P.M.

A Harley roared up as Nick got out of the car. It skidded to a stop a few feet away and the rider grinned at him. He wasn't wearing a helmet. Johnny Johansen was the costar of the series—a handsome nineteen-year-old kid who played Hank Donovan's sidekick. A shock of blond hair drifted over his green eyes and his cleft chin conjured a very young Kirk Douglas. He was a teen heartthrob.

Nick slammed the Firebird's door. "Where's your helmet?"

Johnny dismounted—still happily grinning. "It's too hot for a helmet."

"You like working here?"

Johnny nodded.

"Good. Your contract states, 'No dangerous activities.' That would include skydiving, bull riding, and Russian roulette. Can you think of anything else it might include?"

Johnny looked sheepish. "Not wearing a helmet on my hog?"

"Good guess, Johnny. Get a helmet."

Nick whacked the kid playfully on the arm, smiled, and headed into the warehouse. He liked Johnny. He was a good kid. This was not the problem he'd come to solve.

A wall of cold air blasted Nick as he stepped through the front entrance. A pair of megaton air-conditioning units were battling heat that radiated from 103-degree outside air, ten-kilowatt arc lights, and a crew of sixty, plus cast and extras. The unit's efforts dropped the temperature twenty-five degrees but sweat still glistened on grunt-type crew members.

"Hi, boss." Snuffy Benton, the star's stunt double, raised a hand in greeting. He was talking to a gorgeous extra wearing spikes, tights, and feathers.

Nick returned the wave in passing. "How goes the war?"

"It goes . . ." Snuffy smiled but never took his eyes off the girl.

The $trip was an action-adventure show. Brawls, shoot-outs, and car chases were de rigueur. The last thing you needed was the star in traction because of a misguided punch or a freak accident—hence Snuffy, stunt double for Hank Donovan, *The $trip*'s star.

Hank played the PI—Zack Taylor—and he looked every inch the part. Although not traditionally handsome in the Hollywood sense, he was tall, well muscled, and had a rugged, chiseled face that still bore a hint of his Cherokee heritage.

Hank was never a problem.

Nick saw him chatting with Brad Tilden, a local actor who played an LVPD detective, and Lori Donner, the actress who played Zack's secretary. Lori was a dimpled cutie who was a perfect contrast to Hank's smoldering PI.

Neither of them were problems.

Continuing across the warehouse floor, Nick passed several sets, stepped across a warren of cables, and exchanged greetings with a myriad of crew members—from set dressers to prop men, gaffers to grips.

He finally arrived at the brightly lit active set, a replica of a backstage dressing room at the Copa Room in the Sands hotel. Basically it was two rows of opposing tables and chairs with mirrors ringed by makeup lights. Costumes—mostly sequined and scanty—were hung on rolling pipe racks. It was peopled by a dozen statuesque extras in various stages of undress. They were all showgirls from Strip hotels—and all as exquisite as the girl being hit on by Snuffy.

Part of the current episode's plot was that Zack was temporarily dating one of the Sands showgirls in order to infiltrate a cocaine operation. The scene they were shooting was between Zack and Bridget—the showgirl.

The showgirl was the problem.

A portly man wearing shorts, a Hawaiian shirt, and a beard spotted Nick coming up behind the camera and padded over on sneakered feet. Rodney Lang was a highly touted, exceptionally talented director who had little patience for actors with attitudes or opinions. This was television—not feature films with their auteurs and inflated egos. In television it was simple: *Hit your marks and say your lines—time is money and budgets are tight.*

And here was the problem.

Rodney threw up his hands in frustration and pointed at the girl playing Bridget. "She won't do the scene. She doesn't see how she could be jealous of Lori!"

Lori's character was a fresh-scrubbed beauty of the girl-next-door variety. Bridget was a blonde of the bombshell variety—she'd never been jealous of a girl next door in her life.

Nick walked over to Bridget and smiled. "Hi, Laura . . ." That was her stage name—Laura. Her real name was Greta.

Laura/Greta/Bridget jumped on her high horse and held forth.

"I just don't see it! It's not in character! Bridget would never say that! She'd never say she was jealous of another women—especially not that woman! Look at us! She's Doris Day! I'm Marilyn Monroe!"

She'd been holding up shooting for close to an hour. Nick assumed a warm tone and an understanding smile.

4

"You certainly are, Laura . . . And everyone assumes that because you're playing an exquisitely beautiful showgirl who could launch a thousand ships faster than Helen of Troy, she's shallow . . . She's not. What the character is showing here is her vulnerability. We are exposing her hithertofore unrecognized inner warmth and sensitivity. When it comes out here it gives her character depth . . . and dimension . . ."

Total bullshit, but Nick didn't want to rewrite the scene.

Attentiveness, confusion, understanding, and acceptance all crossed the girl's face in a six-second span, and she beamed.

"Ohhh . . . I see it . . . It's wonderful . . . She has depth! Thank you, Nick . . ."

Nick patted her on the arm, turned back to Rodney, and nodded.

Rodney grunted and signaled the first assistant director, who cupped his hands around his lips.

"Okay—first team! This is a take! Put us on a bell!"

Nick went back to his office.

Another barnacle removed from the ass of progress.

CHAPTER TWO

NICK CONTI'S FIFTEEN-HOUR day had been crammed with script conferences, production meetings, the Bridget problem, arguments with the network, and a trip to the night location shoot. It ended with an orgasmic romp in the sack.

The rompee was a showgirl from the Tropicana's *Les Folies Bergere.*

When she heard the midnight banging on his door, the girl screamed, "Christ, it's the house dick!" launched herself out of bed, and took the sheet with her. Her incredibly long legs propelled her to the bathroom in three strides, and then disappeared behind an angrily slammed door.

Nick let out an exasperated sigh, got out of bed, and wrapped a towel around his waist. He could handle the internal fuzz. He wanted to call out her name and tell her, but unfortunately he couldn't remember it.

The showgirl was picking up some additional cash, kicks, and contacts working as an extra on *The $trip.* Earlier that night they'd been introduced on the fly by his eager-to-please casting director at the end of the show's dinner break. It was a quick hi, a mutual spark, and an agreement to rendezvous.

The set had wrapped at ten in the evening, and after returning to his suite at the Desert Inn they'd only remained vertical for a quick drink before hitting the sack for a horizontal rumba.

Nick certainly understood the girl's panic. It was hotel policy all over Vegas, albeit weakly enforced, that unregistered women were not allowed in the rooms. This was to ensure that the burgeoning hooker trade was being aggressively thwarted by management.

A great public-relations ploy, but as effective as a eunuch's dick.

Nonetheless, there was the occasional late-night raid for cosmetic purposes. Nick's current playmate obviously had thought this was one of those occasions and panicked. If it had been, she knew that the apprehended offendress would be blacklisted and not allowed into any of the Vegas hotels. Obviously that meant she wouldn't be allowed back into the Tropicana—which in turn meant she would be fired from *Les Folies Bergere* and thus never again allowed to parade her fabulous tits in front of a gawking audience.

Horrifying.

But not as horrific as the bloody nineteen-year-old kid who was shoved into Nick's face when he opened the door to his suite. The towering hulk that shoved the kid into the room was over six three and topped three hundred pounds. Wordlessly he looked at Nick, then vanished down the hall like a fat tree with a bouncing ponytail.

The kid was Johnny Johansen—costar of *The $trip*.

CHAPTER THREE

THE $TRIP WAS produced by Altman Productions— Sam Altman, owner, president, and resident genius. Many would add *tyrant* and *asshole*.

When Sam turned sixty in 1980 he was reigning as one of the most successful producers in Newton Minnow's vast wasteland of television. Mind candy was his king and jiggle his queen. All producers did it, but no one did it better. Ideas sprang from his head like exploding kernels from a popcorn machine, and the networks clamored for his talent. Altman was at the top of his game—a mogul who stood astride his sprawling Hollywood empire like a colossus. In the soaring pantheon of his television megahits were eight series on a single network: UTB.

Sam was in Hollywood heaven. Articles, profiles, photos, and interviews splashed across newspapers, magazines, radio, and TV talk shows. They couldn't get enough of him and he never got enough of them. He never had. It was his addiction—his drug of choice.

8

The opposite was true of Nick. He equated the limelight with a root canal. In his three years with Altman, Nick had only done five unavoidable interviews—print and radio—none for TV. He treated paparazzi like bipedaled piranha. He was reputed to be intimate with some of Tinseltown's most desirable leading ladies, but his swarthy, handsome face always seemed obscured by a turned head, sunglasses, or a strategically placed hand. At a well-preserved forty-two, Nick's 190-pound, six-one frame was as elusive as smoke.

Howard Hughes would have loved him.

Sam *did* love him—as a talent. In its first month on the air *The $trip* had soared to number one in the Nielsens and was expected to stay there, a cash cow that was paying off faster than a rigged slot machine. But that wasn't all. It wasn't just that Nick could prevent, solve, or handle anything to ensure the continued success of Sam's latest megahit. Although Nick was its talented creator, head writer, and executive producer, there was another reason Sam had picked Nick to honcho *The $trip*.

It was the skeleton in Nick's closet that Sam had uncovered. Nick was the perfect choice to run *The $trip* because he was uniquely familiar with the organized-crime families who were the hidden owners of the Las Vegas casinos.

Nick Conti was born Nicolo Condini, and his family was part of the Kansas City Mob.

CHAPTER FOUR

AN HOUR BEFORE the violent banging on Nick's door began, Carlo Strozzi had jerked Johnny Johansen out of his car and thrown him onto the roadside. One of the kid's Gucci loafers popped off, and he was planted face-first in the sand.

Johnny groaned and rolled over.

It was after midnight. The freak heat wave was causing radiation to rise off the Mojave, and a stiff wind blew tumbleweeds across the wasteland. The air smelled of dust.

Two huge men shambled out of the car's front seat and were framed by the glittering lights of Vegas four miles to the north. The radio was pounding out the Bee Gees' "Stayin' Alive."

A morbid fluke? Hopefully not a prophetic one, thought Johnny through his pain.

The men positioned themselves on either side of Strozzi, dwarfing their five-foot-six boss, and hovered over their victim. All three wore suits. The larger of the two, Fats Arnheim, resembled Ernest Borgnine's

Fatso Judson in *From Here to Eternity*. His bulk was misleading. There was muscle beneath the layers of fat and he had the power of a locomotive. Fats blew his nose and dropped the Kleenex on the kid's formerly handsome face.

The kid sputtered something that sounded like *P-plizz* through a split lip and was rewarded with a vicious kick from Strozzi's pointed boot.

Strozzi had a narrow, pinched face with sunken cheeks and pock-marked skin. He was a sadist whose normal facial expression was a sneer. If he were an animal he would have been a ferret.

"Pick 'im up."

Fats hauled Johnny up by his shirtfront and half the buttons popped. The kid groaned and the crotch of his bell-bottom jeans darkened.

The second gorilla, Angie Angelino, grunted his disgust. He was thirty pounds lighter than Fats but equally formidable and sadistic as his boss. He'd been branded a probable retard in grammar school and by eighteen was riding with a Hells Angels motorcycle gang. His face was marred by a droopy left eye and a harelip, his graying hair worn in a ponytail.

He thrust five powerful fingers into the kid's wet crotch and vise-gripped his balls.

Johnny screamed.

Strozzi cut it off with a backhand to the kid's face—leaned in and sneered.

"You really wanna die?"

"N-no . . . I . . . I'll . . ."

"You'll what? Talk sense inta your boss? Convince him I'm serious? That what?" Strozzi leaned in over Johnny's face. "'Cause if ya don't convince Conti I'm serious, your next ride out here's gonna be your last. Lemme me hear you're straight on that."

"I-I'll talk to . . ."

"I *said* let me hear you say you're straight on that!"

Blood trickled out of Johansen's mouth. He coughed and tried to focus.

"I'm—I'm straight."

Strozzi gently patted his cheek. He removed the handkerchief from his breast pocket and tenderly wiped Johnny's mouth.

"Good . . . Very good. Now let me hear you tell me what you gonna do when we let you go."

Johnny struggled to find the words that would satisfy his tormentor—whose name he didn't know and whose face he'd never seen.

"I-I'm g-going to convince Mr. Conti that you're serious . . ."

Strozzi's pinched face expanded into a grin and he turned to Fatso.

"Throw him back inna car. He stinks of sweat and piss."

CHAPTER FIVE

TWENTY MINUTES LATER Fats parked behind the Wimbledon Suites, a seven-story luxury tower located behind the Desert Inn's main building and golf course. The penthouse floor had only three accommodations—four thousand, three thousand, and two thousand square feet—with four, three, and two bedrooms respectively. These three were controlled by the casino and comped to high rollers.

The rest of the building was made up of smaller yet equally lavish suites, with many having their own patio swimming pools.

Nick's was one of the latter on the sixth floor.

Carlo ordered Angie to haul their victim's ass up there, and soon Johnny was spewing out the story as best he could while he bled on Nick's carpet. He was barefoot, his left eye was a rainbow, and a chipped tooth winked out of leaking lips.

As soon as the hulk had thrown him through the door, he'd tossed Johnny's loafers in after him. Angie Angelino had never uttered a word; he didn't have to—the message was clear. His frame had taken up half the doorway while he glowered through his harelip.

Johnny said he'd been hauled out of his trailer after he'd wrapped for the day, taken out into the desert, and beaten up.

Nick knew why and what it was about.

It was a shakedown, and the shaker was Carlo Strozzi.

Six weeks after the show went on the air it had become a huge hit, and it was obvious that *The $trip* would be filming in Vegas for the foreseeable future. Strozzi, a known wiseguy, realized it and tried to sink in his hooks. He'd dropped into *The $trip*'s production-office complex in the basement of the Desert Inn, and Julie, Nick's secretary, ushered him in. Strozzi said he wanted five thousand dollars a week to ensure that filming would not be interrupted by any unforeseen circumstances popping up.

Extortion—pure and simple. He left a phone number in case Nick wanted to talk.

Nick told him to fuck off.

He'd figured Strozzi for a punk looking to make a score on naïve Hollywood types in a Mob-connected town. He then called and left word for Nello Marchetti in Kansas City.

In the next two days a trio of unforeseen circumstances popped up. Slashed tires on the camera and prop trucks, a bomb threat during a location shoot at a ranch house, and a small fire in the warehouse that housed the main set. The obvious messages all held up production, and that got expensive, but Nick had handled them and had not called Strozzi.

The first three incidents had been comparatively minor. But beating up Johansen was different. It was a major escalation. Nick would have to shut down production while the kid's face healed. It could take weeks—and even after production resumed, there would be further escalations that could again shut it down. That would not only cost a fortune, it would threaten contractual network-delivery dates. With no new episodes of *The $trip* to put on the air, the network would be forced to resort to repeats and preemptions. Strozzi had to be shut down or a quickly bored public would desert, the ratings would plummet, and that would be it—the show would be canceled.

Strozzi had to be stopped . . . but sheriffs or cops were not an option.

Both were on the take and their investigations would undoubtedly go nowhere. Worse, their Mob paymasters would likely tell them to leak the story to further increase the pressure. The headline would surely be: ALTMAN PRODUCTIONS DOING BUSINESS WITH THE MOB.

If Nick paid off Strozzi the story would be true, if he didn't it would be false, but either way the headline would put *The $trip* on life support.

UTB—or for that matter any network—could ill afford to be involved with even a whiff of anything associated with organized crime. Networks had licenses to protect. The last thing they wanted was to have Congress all over their ass.

And on top of it all, Sam Altman would go ballistic. It was the kind of fuck-up that supposedly couldn't happen with Nick running things in Las Vegas.

Nello Marchetti returned Nick's call and revealed three things he knew about Strozzi. He had money on the street, dealt coke, and was part of the Chicago Mob—the Outfit.

Not good.

However, out of respect for Nick's father, Nello promised to relay his call for help upstairs to Corky—Carl Civella—who was the new Kansas City capo since the recent death of his brother.

But Nello had pointed out: "KC would probably have no desire to go to war with Chicago over a fucking television show."

CHAPTER SIX

TWENTY MINUTES LATER, as Johnny fumbled to finish his story, Nick's fully clothed rompee emerged at last. She peeked around the bedroom door looking for the man she believed to be the house fuzz. By now she'd undoubtedly armed herself with a plausible story regarding her presence in the suite.

This in spite of the fact that Nick was still only wearing a towel.

When she saw the bleeding Johansen, she gasped, dashed toward the door, brushed Nick with an air kiss, and once again vanished behind a hastily slammed door on unbelievably long legs.

Johnny was still too shaken to comment and Nick too pensive to explain. He poured Johnny a tumbler of scotch, settled him into the suite's second bedroom, and told him they'd be flying to L.A. in the morning.

He then went to his bedroom and called Sam Altman's assistant. He woke her up and told her to cancel everything on Sam's morning slate—he'd be in Sam's office by 10:00 A.M.

After pouring a large scotch for himself he made a second call to Nello Marchetti.

"Nello, it's Nick."

A groggy voice sputtered, "W-what . . ."

"Nick Conti, I . . ."

"Christ! You know what time it is?"

Nick had forgotten the two-hour time difference. "Sorry, Nello, but things out here just got . . ."

"It's three o'clock in the fuckin' morning!"

"I know, Nello, but Strozzi just took this thing to the next . . ."

"At three o'clock in the fuckin' morning?"

Exasperated, Nick said, "Nello, I can tell time."

"Then why the fuck don't you?"

Nick heard a blowsy voice in the background come to life. "Uhh . . . W-who ish it baby . . ."

Nello sighed. "Go back to sleep, Cordelia."

"Cordelia?" Nick erased a mental picture of Nello's bedmate and pressed on. "This afternoon Strozzi torched my set and tonight he beat the shit out of my costar."

Nello was quiet for a moment, and then Nick heard him order Cordelia out of the room. "Go take a shower."

The reply was, "Huh?"

Nello, exhibiting extreme patience, slowly drew out the words. "Get up . . . go in the bathroom . . . and take a shower."

Cordelia yelped. "Ish three o'clock in the fuckin' morning!"

The time was becoming a mantra.

Nello exploded. "Go take a fuckin' shower!"

The last word on the subject was, "Christ! Awright awready—I'm goin' . . ."

After a rustle of sheets and a door slam, Nello sighed. "Look, Nick, I talked to Corky. It's like I figured. We got no dog in this fight. He says to pay the two dollars!"

17

"It's not that simple, Nello."

"It never is. But gettin' into a pissing contest with Joey Doves over a measly five grand to bail out a fuckin' TV show don't make no sense."

Joey Doves was Joe Aiuppa, the current Chicago capo. He'd replaced Felix "Milwaukee Phil" Alderisio in 1971, who'd replaced John "Jackie the Lackey" Cerone in 1969, who'd replaced Sam "Teets" Battaglia in 1967, who'd replaced Sam "Momo" Giancana in 1966, who'd theoretically replaced Tony "The Big Tuna" Accardo back in 1957.

The names were classic Mob monikers, but if you were in the know, you knew that Accardo had never really been replaced. Joey Doves might be the man you talked to in the Windy City, but the Big Tuna was always the power behind the Chicago throne.

"Thanks, anyway, Nello. I know you tried."

"Yeah . . . The thing is, Corky knows this guy Strozzi is a prick, but he's some kinda fercockt relative of Tuna . . . a cousin by marriage or somethin'. And nobody, not even Corky, wants to fuck with Tuna."

"I got it, Nello. I'll have to figure some other way. Tell Corky thanks."

"Ya gottit. Good luck, Nick. But I agree with Corky. Pay the two dollars."

Nick hung up and noticed a card on the nightstand. It had an embossed sketch of a *Folies* dancer, a phone number, and a name—"Brie."

So that was her name.

CHAPTER SEVEN

DAY ONE

THE NEXT MORNING Nick had fresh jeans and a shirt sent over for Johnny while he dressed in slacks, a sweater, and jacket. He then put dark glasses and a baseball cap on the kid and intentionally took him through the casino to see if he would be recognized.

It was early and there were only a few tables going, but they paused and watched the action. They were thrown a few cursory glances by the dealers and the pit boss, but even though they waved to Nick, they didn't seem to recognize Johnny.

Nick was pleased as he could be under the circumstances, and they grabbed a cab to McCarran Airport for an eight o'clock flight to LAX.

Nick led Johnny into a few crowded fast-food shops, but again didn't note a flicker of recognition from any of the customers. Convinced they were in the clear, they boarded the Southwest flight at seven thirty and took their seats in first class.

The flight was uneventful until a stewardess came by for drink orders. It was Nick's bad luck that she happened to be proud of her ability to spot disguised celebs on her Vegas run. There were many celebrities who didn't want a hassle, and she had become an expert at seeing through their fake mustaches and baseball caps.

The stewardesses made a game of it—complete with a cash prize going to the stewardess with the most busts at the end of each month.

Her eyes widened when she busted Johnny.

"Johnny Johansen!" she bellowed. "Welcome to Southwest—love your show!"

So much for Nick's trial runs in the casino and fast-food joints.

Johnny, still in pain, forced a smile, and several passengers turned for a look.

Eager to shut her down, Nick quickly ordered a drink. He made it as complicated as possible in an effort to make her leave quickly before she forgot the ingredients.

"A Bloody Mary—light on the vodka—extra Worcestershire—no Tabasco—a squeeze of lemon—dash of pepper—no celery stick."

"What about you, Johnny?" she chirped without blinking an eye.

Forget the shutdown.

"Uh . . . the same," he managed.

"What happed to your lip?" she asked—all concern.

The alerted passengers strained for a better peek.

Louder than necessary, Nick rattled off an unlikely but professional-sounding scenario designed to confuse and stultify.

"A ten-K slipped a hasp, split from the grid, and knocked the DP off a high-hat into the gaffer, who fell on Johnny and knocked him on his ass. It's all kind of embarrassing and not something my boy here is in the mood to relive. Now how about those drinks?"

The stew hit Nick with a look that could freeze lava, spun on her heels, and took off for the drinks. Johnny buried his face in *People* and Nick groaned. The disguise was a flop, and what was under it sure as hell meant facing a camera anytime soon was a nonstarter.

Shit.

CHAPTER EIGHT

T HEY WALKED INTO Sam Altman's office on the penthouse floor of the tallest building in Century City twenty minutes late.

There had been a pileup on the 405.

A school bus carrying disadvantaged kids to a more-advantaged learning environment had hit a cement truck and given the disadvantaged kids the advantage of learning about trauma centers.

Sam's outer-office receptionist was the latest in a succession of bimbos who could have been in *Playboy*. The girls at this desk didn't last long because of the line of producers, directors, and stars that streamed through the office. A few wound up with screen tests, others became "personal assistants," and some actually snagged a significant other. The word spread and a flood of applicants soon vied for the first rung of a ladder to fame in La-La Land—a town that sucked in the best and bustiest from fifty states.

The current gold medalist was Angeline, a knockout blonde with perfect legs, an angel's face, and fake tits. Her job definition required an intellectual stretch that involved answering phones, smiling greetings, and escorting visitors into the next office. A good bet would be that she was banging the boss and the only thing she could file were her nails.

Big smile. "Good morning, Mr. Conti." Bigger smile. "Hi, Johnny." Faded smile. "Oh, my!" Hand to the mouth. "What happened to your lip?"

The lip line was becoming as much a mantra as "It's three o'clock in the fuckin' morning."

"Softball. I got hit with a line drive."

Good, Nick thought. He'd have to remember that. He patted Johnny on the back and turned back to Angeline.

"Is Sam in yet?"

"Yes sir, Mr. Conti—he's expecting you."

"You don't need both, Angeline. Either a 'sir' or a 'mister' is adequate."

Confusion appeared, but she performed one third of her specialties admirably and escorted them into the next office.

There were three assistants in the second tier of insulation—all middle-aged, all impeccably dressed and coiffed, and all with bona fide assistant's credentials.

They in turn were overseen by the "gatekeeper," Rachel Feinstein, who entered from her own private office off the middle sanctum. In her mid-fifties, she was wearing a black pantsuit, no jewelry, and sensible shoes. With her white hair pulled tightly into a bun and the attitude of Cruella De Vil, Rachel was alternately known as the Bitch, the Queen, and Adolf.

She'd been with Sam twenty years. With her aquiline nose blazing the trail like an icebreaker, she led them to the inner sanctum and the man.

Sam's office was big enough for half-court basketball and housed a desk that belonged in Versailles. One corner featured a forty-foot wrap-around sofa in fawn suede situated behind burled walnut coffee tables. The opposite corner displayed an elaborately inlaid conference table for fourteen. Floor-to-ceiling windows overlooked a balcony with vistas from Alvarado to Avalon, while pile carpeting swallowed your shoes and impressionist art assaulted your eyes. The wall opposite the desk was dominated by an aquarium big enough to hold a great white—but didn't. Two doors flanked the tank, one leading to an adjoining kitchen manned by René and José, the chef and waiter, the other leading to Rachel's office—the shark that wasn't in the tank.

The office was meant to awe and intimidate—which it did. The air held the unmistakable aroma of cigars, cologne, and cash.

When Nick and Johnny entered, Sam bounced up from his desk, threw out his arms, and embraced them both, beaming with the energy of a tsunami. He was in his standard office attire: a casual suede tracksuit—Sam loved suede—and Mephisto sneakers.

He had both in six colors.

"Nick—Johnny—come in, come in . . . Coffee—tea—Perrier—anything. Sit—what's your pleasure. Rachel—send in José to take an order."

Sam was five four and weighed 130 soaking wet. His narrow face was clean shaven, sallow, and lined beyond his years. His high forehead was topped by thinning gray hair and dominated by intense, slightly bulging brown eyes. He would never be considered handsome but he could be irresistible. The vast space should have shrunk Sam's diminutive stature even more—conjuring images of midgets riding elephants.

A mistake. The image would only apply to his size. His personality was six six, 260. Sam was a human iceberg. Ninety percent of him was invisible.

He didn't immediately register Johnny's condition behind the dark glasses and ball cap, but as he became aware of it, his smile faded. He cupped Johnny's chin and tilted his head back.

"Johnny—you look like shit."

Johnny's lips parted to respond and Sam noted the chipped tooth for the first time.

"Jesus Christ!" He turned to Nick wide-eyed. "What the hell happened?"

"The shakedown."

"You said you'd handled it!"

Nick had kept Sam in the loop after the first incident, telling him that it was a minor annoyance from a punk he could handle. Sam had believed him because Nick was Nick.

"I thought I could until this. Right now we need a discreet dentist and some rehab until I make the problem go away."

Sam quickly moved behind his desk, mashed an intercom button, and rattled off orders. He was as diminutive as Napoléon and just as effective in his element.

"Rachel—get Stearman and tell him Johnny Johansen'll be in his office in fifteen minutes. Tell 'im to fix the kid and keep his mouth shut. Call Cojo and tell him to rent a cottage down south—I want the kid sequestered until this blows over. Then get Jake up here."

Stearman was Sam's dentist, Cojo his head of security, down south was the La Costa resort, and Jake his chauffeur/bodyguard.

"Can I bring my girlfriend?" It was Johnny with a timid request.

Sam's head whipped around and he slapped the phone into its cradle. He considered for a second but clearly didn't like the idea.

"Can she keep her mouth shut?"

"I-I'll tell her." The kid was obviously intimidated.

"Good, but that's all you tell her," Sam snapped. "From now on you've had a car accident. Got it?"

Johnny managed a chastised "Yessir."

Sam suddenly became aware of the kid's distress and instantly altered his tone. His gruffness vanished like it was on a toggle switch. A benevolent father suddenly appeared. Smiling warmly, he left the desk, put his arm around Johnny, and gently led him toward the door.

"Don't worry . . ." He soothed and patted the kid's shoulder. "You're with family. We'll handle everything. Eat—rest—heal. We've got a show to shoot."

Sam opened the door and walked Johnny into the next office. As it closed behind them, Nick heard him saying, "You need anything, just ask—money—anything—just ask."

You had to admire his style. The man was a pro. He had the bedside manner of Dr. Kildare, the conviction of a rabbi, and the chutzpah of a bandit.

CHAPTER NINE

T HE $TRIP'S PROBLEM in Las Vegas was doubly serious because of the timing. The feds were finally exposing the real reason the Mob wanted to own Vegas hotels and the newspapers were beginning to get wise to it.

The skim . . .

It was the illegal siphoning of millions in cash from gambling tables in Mob-owned casinos. The government couldn't convict the hoods for extortion, union control, or murder, but they could nail them for something far more benign but just as effective—tax evasion.

Wiretaps had recorded Mob bosses across the country discussing the skim and all the casinos it came from—capos in Chicago, Detroit, Kansas City, Milwaukee, New York, and elsewhere were being targeted. Indictments began to rain down in a legal Niagara.

The good news was that Nick had kept Altman Productions well off the radar. He'd made his company's deal for a base of operations with the Desert Inn. It had been owned by Howard Hughes and was completely devoid of any Mob connections.

The bad news was Nick Conti was Nicolo Condini. If the headline ALTMAN PRODUCTIONS DOING BUSINESS WITH THE MOB ever appeared, any serious investigation would target the man who ran the show in Vegas—Nick. It wouldn't matter that he'd been clean all his adult life. Once his connection to the Kansas City Mob was uncovered, the whiff of *anything* associated with organized crime would become a stench. If the original headline didn't get them canceled, the later revelation surely would.

Sam returned after escorting Johnny out, waved Nick to a seat, and sat behind his desk. Nick then revisited everything Sam didn't already know. They went over the bent law-enforcement problem, the probable press exposure, an investigation that could reveal Nick's background, and the network's certain reaction—cancellation of a cash-gushing, smash-hit television series.

Sam took a Cuban panatela out of the humidor on his desk, removed the tip with a gold cigar cutter, and expertly lit it. He took a satisfying puff without inhaling and blew a perfect ring.

"What are the chances you can turn around your people in Kansas City?"

"Less than snow in Tahiti."

"Who's Nello Marchetti?"

"My cousin."

"And he said no?"

Nick nodded. "But he took it up to the boss—Corky Civella. They won't get involved."

"They're your family, for chrissakes!"

"They're family as in relatives—not as in business associates."

"What happened to blood is thicker than water?"

"Look . . . Sam. My father and uncles were in the Mob—my cousins still are. I never was. I split. I changed my name. I told you that when you had me traced and busted me."

"Sure, but who the hell would think you wouldn't have some influence?"

Nick waved off the question."

"What now?"

"I'm gonna have to figure another way to handle Strozzi."

"What way?"

"That's what I'll have to figure."

Sam let out an exasperated sigh.

"How long can you shoot around Johansen?"

"Not long. He's the costar."

"Can you double him?"

Nick nodded. "In the long shots. But the kid's got a shitload of dialogue. We'll have to shut down in three or four days."

"Christ! His face won't heal for three or four *weeks*!"

"The left side, no. The eye's a problem. But the tooth cap is a no-brainer and the swelling should go down within a week. I figure we'll lose a total of five days, but then we'll resume filming—shoot him from the right and accelerate postproduction to make up the lost time. If we're not hit again we won't miss a delivery date. But if Strozzi's not stopped, we're toast."

CHAPTER TEN

NICK'S FLIGHT BACK to Vegas didn't leave until three, so he decided to lunch at the Polo Lounge. A valet took his rental when he arrived at the Beverly Hills Hotel and he strolled into a lobby awash in history and wallpapered in banana leaves. The legendary lodgings were a stop for everyone from Duke Wayne to the Duke of Windsor. Gable and Lombard, Burton and Taylor, Montand and Monroe had all cavorted between its storied sheets. Howard Hughes used to rent twenty-five rooms at a clip and lived in one set of bungalows for almost thirty years.

At the pool, Johnny Weissmuller supposedly got the title role in *Tarzan* after a swan dive to save a drowning girl; Joan Crawford learned to freestyle there, and Katharine Hepburn once jumped in fully clothed.

The maître d' escorted Nick through the Polo Lounge's indoor section—plush carpeting and dark-green booths with plug-in phones utilized by movers, shakers, and the beautiful people—to the back patio. It was ablaze under a sunlit canopy of flowering vines, shocking-pink archways, and an ancient knotted oak. Round tables buzzed with more deal makers, power brokers, agents, socialites, international playboys, assorted glitterati, and the occasional star.

The aromas were flora and food; the sounds light jazz and commerce.

Eyes shifted as Nick walked in and acknowledged the occasional nod before taking his seat at a table for two. No one who entered the fabled area went unnoticed. The mere fact that you could command a table meant that you had to *be* somebody even if nobody recognized you.

Nick ordered a straight-up martini, got it, and was savoring his first sip when she walked in.

The drink froze in his mouth before he swallowed.

Patrons facing the entrance once again shifted their eyes, and the buzz became a murmur. The maître d' led her to a table where three men had already gotten to their feet. The youngest was the current directorial flavor of the moment, Stavros Papadopoulos. The oldest was Irving Shelly, the legendary agent. The middle man was Sidney Black, president of Allied International Studios.

Light embraces and brush-kisses around.

Stavros's last two epics had racked up over three hundred million dollars. Irving had Tinseltown's largest stable of stars, and Sidney had recently seen his stock options double because of Stavros. They had just signed a contract for three more films.

It gave a whole new meaning to power lunch. But none of them was as powerful as the girl.

Nick saw her ice-blue eyes flicker as she noticed him. She hesitated a moment while Stavros pulled out her chair. She sat—slowly—not taking her eyes off Nick while Stavros lingered over her shoulder and admired her braless cleavage.

Erin Conroy was to the fable of Irish beauty what blarney was to the gift of gab. She had the tall, lean body of a former model, although exquisitely more rounded. Her face was an ideally sculpted array of angles—the cheeks slightly hollow, their bones slightly high—contours a camera loved. Her sensuous mouth seemed mildly amused, her eyes sparkled, and her luminescent skin was framed by a crown of fiery red hair that dropped to her shoulders.

Nick gave her an almost imperceptible nod.

She smiled.

The three men at the table assumed that she was responding to one of their witty remarks—probably about Stavros's latest project. Erin had rocketed to fame in the title role of his last blockbuster, *Granuaile, The Pirate Queen*—the historic tale of a beautiful Irishwoman who battled Henry VIII in the sixteenth century, played by Erin Conroy, a beautiful Irishwoman in the twentieth who became a star in the role.

But Nick was incorrect about the subject of the men's conversation. It wasn't about Stavros's latest project—it was about the upcoming presidential election. Irving Shelly, a Carter Democrat, was jousting with Sidney Black, a Reagan Republican, over the latest polls.

Shelly sadly shook his head in frustration.

"Can you believe it? The latest polls give Reagan a double-digit lead."

Black smiled as if the reason was obvious. "Because Carter gave us double-digit inflation, gas lines, and the Iran hostage debacle."

"That wasn't all Carter's fault!"

"Maybe not, but in the televised debate, when Regan asked, 'Are you better off now than you were four years ago?' Carter was toast."

"A line right out of the script his handlers wrote for him!" Shelly turned to Erin. "Can you believe it? An actor is about to become the leader of the free world!"

Erin smiled. "Why not? The current leader's a peanut farmer."

Black chuckled.

Shelly winced.

Nick ordered steak tartare and saw Dan Dietrich approaching—known as the "private investigator to the stars," he was also an occasional technical advisor on *The $trip*. He was a flat-faced, crew-cut. Bavarian with a bull's shoulders and limpid eyes that hid a fiercely honed cunning—the entire package masked by a constantly jovial demeanor.

Nick liked him.

He arrived at the table with his hand extended and a wide grin on his face.

"Nick! What's shakin'?"

Nick took his hand and shook it warmly. Dan was wearing a shirt and tie, slacks, and his signature corduroy jacket. The tan jacket had leather elbow patches that would make an unwary target think he was a mild mannered professor. A mistake.

Nick waved him to a seat.

"Same ole same ole, Danny. You?"

"Big saps and wiretaps. Marital stupidity is a booming business. I get hired to dig up the dirt, get paid up front, and the Caymans love the cash flow."

"Not worried about Uncle Sam?"

"Sure. But a good accountant and a better lawyer can set up a smoke screen that could cover Kansas."

Nick smiled and a thought occurred to him. The problem in Vegas might become severe enough to require the kind of "off the book" talents of a man like Dan.

"Lemme ask you a question. You happen to know any wiremen in Vegas?"

"You writing a show about taps?"

"Not necessarily."

Dan cocked a suspicious eyebrow. "Oh . . ."

"So?" Nick asked.

"The answer's affirmative—but my trust level in the guy is negative. You think you might need a little hookup?"

"I might."

"You do—I'll handle it myself. I owe you that much."

"Thanks, Danny. If it comes up, I'll call. Appreciate it."

"No problem, pal." Dan stuck out his hand. "See ya around the campus."

Nick knew the problem he'd face if he ever had to use Dan's talents. Illegal wiretaps were felonies. If caught, investigated, and exposed, throughout the trial he'd be futilely denying that, although Nicolo Condini was his real name, he was not a member of the Kansas City Mob. No one would believe it.

He'd go to jail.

CHAPTER ELEVEN

S AM HAD RACHEL call Norman Manners the minute Nick left the office. Manners was the senior partner of Manners, Clayman and Boyle, a heavyweight Los Angeles public-relations firm.

She finally got him on the phone an hour later, having pulled him off a golf course in the middle of a tournament. He was in Phoenix. Summoned by his most lucrative client, Manners changed in the clubhouse, chartered a private jet, and arrived in Century City at six that evening.

Sam was out on his balcony smoking a cigar. He was looking west and adding to the smog that stretched all the way to Santa Monica.

Rachel walked into the office and hovered at the sliding glass doors. "Norman is here . . ."

Without turning, he acknowledged Rachel with a nod and she departed. Moments later Angeline escorted Manners in and lit up the room with a smile. She announced him, twirled around, and left.

Sam took another puff on his cigar and, again without turning, announced the reason for the summons.

"We may have a problem, Norm."

Sleek, urbane, and seventy years old, Manners was a master of his art. He looked like a casting director's dream to play a chairman of the board. He was a slender, silver-haired gentleman who wore monogrammed silk shirts, thousand-dollar suits, and custom-made shoes. An eyebrow cocked, and he walked a bit closer to Sam.

"Oh?"

"The $trip . . ." Sam continued without turning. "Nick Conti flew in this morning with Johnny Johansen. We're about to be shut down."

"The reason being?"

"The kid had an accident—let's call it a car." He suddenly rethought it. "Better yet, his motorcycle—more romantic for his teenybopper fans. Put out a press release."

"What happened?" Manners was no one's fool.

"Not relevant at the moment. Maybe later, if we need damage control."

"Do you want it to go out under your name? And how long will you be shut down?"

"Yes, and a week."

"Anything else?"

"Yes—about tonight. Gwendolyn and I will hit the red carpet at seven thirty. Hire a bunch of screamers and autograph nuts for our arrival in the limo. Heart fund-raisers draw half the stars in the galaxy. Make sure our screeches and squeals are as loud or louder than anyone else's. Get the cash from Cojo."

"Thirty as usual—mixed genders and races?"

"Fifty. I've had a bad day. I want a great night."

CHAPTER TWELVE

A FTER NICK'S LUNCH arrived he spent the next half hour eating and trying to give the impression he wasn't staring at Erin. Which he was. If anything she'd grown more beautiful since he'd first seen her. She'd auditioned for a show he was producing in New York. At the time she was a model and a student at NYU. Nick gave her the part—her first. She was good and he gave her another in the same role. Then he made her character recurring. Before long, the fan mail was tremendous and the press even better.

The rest was history.

When Nick finished his coffee, the waiter brought the check. Nick handed over a credit card and noticed Erin stand, brush-kiss her lunch dates, and say good-bye.

She started toward the door but walked past it and straight over to Nick.

Nick stood and put out his hand. She took it and leaned into the customary embrace and brush-kiss—then eased away smiling.

"It's been a while, Nico."

He nodded and returned her smile. "You could say that."

"You haven't changed."

"And you've improved."

"Are you going to ask me to sit down?"

"With pleasure."

He held her chair and she sat—both aware of the piqued interest of nearby patrons.

"Your series seems to be a megahit."

"Thank you. We got lucky. Hank Donovan was perfect for the lead, the supporting cast clicked, and the time slot's a lock."

"And the Altman name and your writing had nothing to do with it." It wasn't a question.

Nick smiled. "Naturally . . . You doing another picture with Papadopoulos?"

She nodded. "The studio's been keeping it extra quiet because they're planning a big splash later . . . but Irving negotiated billing over the title for me, and we start shooting tomorrow."

Nick was taken aback and his jaw dropped a touch. Secrets were rare in a company town, and the only thing that had hit the trades was that Papadopoulos was preparing a new film with Allied International. There was no mention of the subject matter or that Erin would be starring—with her name above the title, no less.

Nick was suitably impressed.

"Mere congratulations seem feeble."

She gave Nick a teasing smile. "We're shooting in Las Vegas."

Nick's jaw slid a bit lower. Erin? In Vegas? Now? How goddamn complicated could his life get, for chrissakes?

"I'm flying up tonight."

"That's terrific." He'd struggled with the comment.

"You don't sound that pleased . . ."

"No—no. Just surprised. Where will you be staying?"

"The studio's leased a home for me but it won't be ready until next week. Until then at the Trop."

Nick knew the Tropicana very well. It was a Mob-owned hotel fronted by Joe Agosto, who was supposedly there to run *Les Folies Bergere*. What Agosto actually ran was the casino and the skim for Kansas City.

Les Folies Bergere and Kansas City again. Intimate with the former last night—rejected by the latter this morning. Curious.

"The studio has a deal there?"

"Not my area. Why do you ask?

Nick made light of it. "*My* area. My deal's with the Desert Inn."

The waiter appeared with the receipt, Nick signed it, and Erin took it as a cue to exit. She got up and Nick followed.

"Well . . . It was nice seeing you again, Nico."

Nick smiled.

"You're the only one who's ever called me that."

"You said you liked it."

"I did."

"Well . . ." She embraced and brush-kissed him again. "Until next time . . . Be well, Nico."

She glided out and every pair of eyes on the patio followed her.

CHAPTER THIRTEEN

J AKE S IEGEL DROVE Sam through the gates of his
Bel Air estate at seven. Hilltop, the eighteen-room Mediterranean
palace on eight acres overlooking the Los Angeles basin, was
meant to, and did, invoke the same awe as his office.

Sam had to pinch himself every time he passed the towering palms
lining the drive toward the mansion's massive facade. It was an eternity away from the clapboard bungalow of his youth.

Sam was the sickly son of a hard-working Jewish tailor from Odessa,
Texas. The mere fact that he survived his youth in the hardscrabble
world of oil fields and rednecks during the roaring twenties was a minor miracle.

He'd graduated at the top of his class from Permian High School
and received an academic scholarship to Rice University. In the next
four years he earned a B.A. degree—was captain of the cheerleading
squad—and became writer-director of the University Theater.

Sam was writing advertising copy for BBD&O when Japan bombed

Pearl Harbor and spent the next four years in the Signal Corps writing shows for the GIs. 1950 found him creating radio shows in New York, and by 1960 Sam was producing television shows in Hollywood.

He was a natural.

Altman Productions had its first hit in 1965, signed a seven-figure exclusive deal with UTB in 1970, and by 1980 broke its own record of six shows on the air—with eight.

A phenomenon.

Alfred, an English butler who had once worked for the royal family, met him at a side courtyard door. Alfred was wearing a black suit, winged collar, and bow tie. His perfectly manicured hands were holding a silver tray with bourbon over ice in a crystal tumbler. He inclined his head and greeted Sam in a clipped English accent.

"Good evening, sir."

Sam swept the drink off the tray and continued down the hall toward the elevator.

Alfred followed.

"Jerome has laid out your formal attire in your dressing room, sir. Mrs. Altman is wearing her ruby ensemble this evening. She would like you to wear your complementary cuff links and studs."

"Whatever . . ." He got into the elevator and hit the button for the second floor. The broad upper hallway, lit by Venetian sconces, led to a three-thousand-square-foot master suite—an imperial boudoir with a raised canopy bed and his-and-hers baths with adjoining dressing rooms and a sauna.

Sam stopped at his wife's dressing-room door and peered in. Gwendolyn was looking over her shoulder into a full-length gilded mirror, alternately twisting her body left and right to observe the back of her gown. It was a vivid yellow designed by Balenciaga that matched her blonde upswept hair. Once considered a beauty, she was now showing signs of her forty-odd years, although she could still turn heads. A brilliant ruby necklace, bracelet, and drop earrings sparkled against her unblemished skin—baubles that came from a walk-in safe containing similar ensembles of emeralds, pearls, and diamonds.

Cartier, Tiffany, and Winston loved Sam Altman.

"Do hurry, dahling," she said in her affected accent. "We've less than half an hour."

The accent was phony. She'd been raised in Yorba Linda. Gwendolyn Fein was the daughter of a Chevrolet dealer who'd gone belly-up and become a used-car salesman. Stripped of his business and working solely on commissions, money quickly became an issue. They were forced to give up their home and move into a small apartment on the wrong side of the tracks. While her high school girlfriends engaged in camaraderie and extracurricular activities, Gwen was forced to take an after-school job as a supermarket bagger.

But the worst part was the humiliation. Her former friends dumped her like tarnished goods, and she vowed that someday she would get even—no matter what it took.

Driven by a burning will to succeed, she descended on the Hollywood nightclub scene at eighteen, looking for lightning in a bottle. She found it in an unattractive, blossoming genius named Sam Altman, and nailed him like a butterfly in a display case.

Sam turned to leave, throwing away his excuse. "I got hung up at the office. *The $trip* is shut down."

Feigning mild interest, she casually adjusted an earring.

"Really . . . why?"

Sam turned back. "Johansen had a motorcycle accident. Nick Conti brought him in to clean him up."

"I never liked him."

"Johansen?"

"Conti. He's arrogant. The whole aura of mystery he allows and probably promotes—avoiding the press—hiding from paparazzi."

"Maybe he has a reason."

"Of course he does! He's jealous of the attention you get—interviews, photos, profiles. So he does the opposite to draw attention to himself—he hides!"

"You don't know what you're talking about. Attention is the last thing he wants."

"I still think you should get rid of him."

Sam's voice tightened. "Gwen—if I ever need to bury Nick Conti, I can do it in heartbeat. But that's on my nickel—not yours. You worry about Balenciaga, I'll handle Nick . . ." He started to leave but turned back. "By the way, it's a great-looking gown."

"It should be, my sweet . . ." she said proudly. "You could buy a Cadillac for what I paid for it."

Sam sighed and shook his head.

"I'll go get ready."

He knew in his heart it wasn't simply about the beauty of acquisitions for Gwen—not of jewels, furs, artwork, or mansions—it was about money and the thrill of spending it.

It was about Gwen getting even.

Getting even for the humiliation of everyone knowing she'd once been a supermarket bagger. Getting even with the friends who had dumped her in school. And getting even with anyone who talked behind her back.

Gwen finally had fame and fortune through Sam Altman—the king of television—and she was determined to throw it in the face of everyone who'd crossed her.

CHAPTER FOURTEEN

NICK WAS MET at McCarran by Mitchio Tanaka, a line producer who looked like an *Esquire* model. Tonight he was wearing a blue blazer, white shirt, gray slacks, and a matching tie.

Mitch was third-generation Japanese from a family that emigrated from Hokkaido to Hawaii in 1920—literally from one island to another. He was a tall, toned, black belt who was handsome enough to be an actor, but, after graduating from UCLA, had chosen the Directors Guild's intern program. From intern to second assistant to first assistant to unit production manager to producer in ten years—he was one of the best, and had been working for Nick most of those years. He took Nick's briefcase.

"Johnny gonna be okay?"

"Sam's got it under control. How'd it go today?"

"We shot around Johnny—Hank's car-chase sequence with the

heavies. We got the action stuff with Snuffy and the stuntmen—but there was a problem when we went for the coverage with Hank."

Nick stopped. "Shit! What now?

They were in the terminal's lobby, surrounded by slot machines creating a cacophony that rivaled departing jets and arriving guests. Vegas wanted to rip the cash out of your wallet from the moment you set foot on the tarmac.

"Somebody fucked with the brakes on the picture car."

The picture car, a 1957 classic Corvette, was the ride of the private investigator—Zack Taylor played by Hank Donovan—and was used for the glamour shots with Hank driving. A second, identical, but souped-up Corvette—the stunt car—was driven by Hank's double, Snuffy Benton, and was used for the dangerous action shots in high-speed car chases.

"Was Hank in it?"

"No. Snuffy picked it up at the warehouse, but he crashed backing out when the brakes failed. He wasn't hurt."

"Thank God for small favors." Nick resumed walking and they headed for the exit. "How was it rigged?"

"That's the zinger. It was acid. The mechs figure it had to have been done yesterday—when we were supposed to shoot the chase before we rescheduled. If we shot then, the acid would have slowly eaten through the brake lines while we were covering the chase with Hank driving."

Nick absorbed the implication.

"Even if the brakes went tits-up at only forty miles or fifty miles an hour, it could've been one helluva pileup."

Tanaka nodded. "But as it happened, the car just sat there almost two days and the acid ate the lines. When Snuffy backed out of the garage the pedal hit the floor and the car hit a Dumpster."

"Christ, Mitch—that means Hank was set up *before* they grabbed Johnny last night."

A teamster driving a Town Car was waiting at the curb. Mitch stopped Nick before he got in.

"Right, Nick . . . They went after Hank yesterday morning. And when that failed, they picked up Johnny last night."

"No more slashed tires, small fires, or bomb threats. They wanted us shut down. Period."

"There's more . . . That Corvette's been locked up in the warehouse over a week. But somebody got in yesterday morning before we were supposed to shoot the chase and rigged the brakes."

Nick's eyes narrowed.

"We made the switch because our permit to film the car chase on the Strip was pulled at the last minute."

"Right again . . . Whoever rigged the brakes couldn't have known that was going to happen—the only information he had was the call sheet with our original schedule."

Nick took a deep breath and let it out.

"It's someone on our crew."

"That's the way I read it. We've got a rat in our crib."

They got in the car and during the drive to the DI they continued talking about the rigged brakes, knowing their teamster driver could hear them. It would have been unnatural not to. But they made no mention of their suspicions regarding the perpetrator. The man at the wheel was a member of the crew, and they had no idea where the treachery started or stopped.

The driver dropped them off, Nick changed in his suite, and Mitch made an eight thirty reservation for them at Luigi's. Over the years the two bachelors had spent time together and enjoyed each other's company—occasionally hitting the night spots with a succession of lovelies. But while Mitch Tanaka was Nick's friend, he only knew what everyone else in Hollywood knew: that Nick was a successful writer-producer who avoided the spotlight and was popular with some of Tinseltown's female elite. He knew nothing of what

Sam Altman had uncovered regarding who Nick was and where he came from.

Nick walked back into the living room wearing slacks, a sport coat, and a shirt and tie. He poured a pair of three-finger Chivas Regals over ice, handed one to Mitch, and took a slip of paper out of his wallet. He held it up.

"I didn't throw it out. Call it instinct."

"It?"

"Strozzi's number. We've gotta make a move."

A bewildered look spread across Mitch's calm Asian face. "You're gonna pay him?"

"I'm going to make him think I'm gonna pay him."

"How the hell are you gonna do that?"

"Unless I'm wrong, this guy's got a short complex and a chip on his shoulder. He thinks he's a scam artist who's smarter than all his marks. For the moment, I'm going to let him think that."

Mitch smiled. "You're buying some time."

Nick nodded. "Hopefully enough to figure out who that sonofabitch bought to set us up."

CHAPTER FIFTEEN

LUIGI'S WAS A retro-classic Italian restaurant with leather booths, soft lights, and a whole lot of attitude. It gave the place a delightfully sinister atmosphere. For years the Rat Pack had dined on its marinated-calamari antipasto, linguini vongole, roasted peppers, and scallopini parmigiana, finishing off their meals with homemade spumoni and espresso-laced anisette. "The Sinatra Special."

Nick and Mitch entered past the single "21" table on their right and a long bar on their left. Both were full. The aromas were garlic and cigarette smoke—the sounds, festive diners and mandolins. At their booth a waiter took two orders for Chivas rocks and left menus.

Mitch picked one up. "You think it'll work?

Nick shook his head. "The odds are too long. But it could buy us a few days."

"What then?"

"By then we'll have figured how to stop him."

"You're sure."

"No. But there's no point being negative." Nick opened his menu.

"Holy shit . . ." Mitch was staring at the door.

Nick glanced at him and then followed his eyes.

Erin Conroy had entered the restaurant. She was stunning as usual, and the usual stunned stares greeted her. Most of the room was focused on her black sheath dress and its plunging neckline.

But Nick couldn't take his eyes off the man she was with.

Alphonso Saltieri possessed sinister good looks and bore a startling resemblance to George Raft—taller, but the resemblance was remarkable. He was a caporegime under Kansas City's Corky Civella. "Big Allie" was in charge of overseeing their Vegas operations—most importantly the Tropicana and its front man, Joe Agosto.

He had a rep as a ladies' man—was always elegantly dressed and often appeared in print with gorgeous women. His hero was Sam Giancana, whose notoriety had been magnified by his affair with Phyllis McGuire of the McGuire sisters. Like Giancana and Bugsy Siegel before him, Allie lived to see his name attached to the rich and famous. Like Bugsy, he had the money, power, and looks to impress them.

An obvious question flashed through Nick's mind. When he'd asked Erin why she was staying at the Tropicana, she'd said, *Not my area*. Was she implying that the choice had been Allie's?

Maybe not, but Nick figured that was the way to bet.

Mitch tracked her as she crossed the room.

"She sure looks great. You know she was in town?"

"Yeah, I'd heard. She's doing a picture with International."

Mitch knew the backstory of Nick and Erin. He'd witnessed it. But Nick hadn't mentioned he'd seen Erin in L.A.

"You know the slick dude with her?"

"No." It was a lie, but at the moment Nick didn't want to get into how he knew Allie.

"You figure to find out where's she's staying and call her."

"I don't know . . . Maybe."

Erin and Allie were led to a booth directly across from Nick's. While Allie fussed with the wine list, Erin spotted Nick but gave no indication she'd seen him.

Mitch picked up on it.

"I think she saw you."

"I think you're right. Let's order."

The waiter arrived, they both selected Sinatra Specials, and Nick checked his watch.

He'd made an appointment to meet Strozzi at ten thirty.

CHAPTER SIXTEEN

CARLO STROZZI, FATS Arnheim, and Angie Angelino celebrated with dinner at the Leaning Tower of Pizza—a low-end restaurant with a leaning, three-story replica of its namesake in Pisa. Strozzi loved tripe and it was the only place in Vegas he could get it. Fats and Angie were both eating fourteen-inch pizzas with the works.

They were celebrating because of the call Strozzi had gotten from Nick Conti. He'd ignored their sabotage for two days but had obviously cracked under the last assault.

"Kickin' the shit outta the kid did it." Strozzi was exuberant.

Fats nodded his agreement and answered while he continued chewing a mouthful of seven-topping pizza.

"Yeah."

Angie nodded enthusiastically, causing his ponytail to bounce off the back of his neck. Angie hardly ever said anything. He thought talking drew attention to his harelip.

"Folded like a chump with a winning hand!" Strozzi was on a roll.

Fats supplied another food-garbled "Yeah."

Angie threw in a few more nods.

Strozzi circled his fork like a baton.

"Five grand a week, and from now on we don't have to do shit to get it."

He got a grunt from Fats and a nod from Angie.

"But I been thinkin' . . ." Strozzi shoveled a forkful of tripe into his mouth and chewed while contemplating the ceiling.

Fats picked up a slab of pizza and keep tracking its journey into his mouth until he became cross-eyed. He chewed through a one-word answer.

"Yeah . . ."

"We been kickin' twenty-five percent of our take from dope, vig, and boosted swag upstairs to Chicago for years, right?"

"Right."

"Because that's what they put us into out here, right?"

"Right."

"But *I* figured out this thing. Its got nothin' to do with them. They didn't do shit on this TV deal. Nothin'!"

"Nothin'." Fats shook his head vigorously.

"So why should we cut 'em in on somethin' they never gave us, never figured out, and don't know about? It's our own private thing. It's ours! Am I right?"

Fats looked at Angie and they both stopped chewing. If brains had gears there would have been gnashing sounds. The two leviathans smiled at each other, and Fats looked back at Strozzi.

"You're right!" It came out like a revelation.

CHAPTER SEVENTEEN

S TROZZI'S DOWNTOWN OFFICE was on Fremont Street. In 1931, ten years before El Rancho Vegas became the first hotel on the Las Vegas Strip, the Apache Hotel and the Northern Club were gambling casinos on Fremont. The street soon became famous and was named Glitter Gulch because of the dazzling array of lights powered by the soon-to-be-completed Hoover Dam.

But by 1980 it was a blue-collar adjunct to the newer and more lavish hotels featuring pools, spas, and star entertainment on the nearby Strip. Nonetheless, Fremont Street was lined with casino hotels, bars, and restaurants and still did a booming business.

Poolorama was a billiard parlor and saloon a block from the Four Queens. It was Strozzi's only legitimate business and an ideal front for his illegal cash flow. His office was a small room in the rear.

Strozzi, Fats, and Angie arrived at ten fifteen.

Nick and Mitch entered twenty minutes later.

Clacking balls, loud voices, and shitkicker music accosted them as they made their way to the rear between a crowded bar and pool tables. Most of the clientele was boisterous and almost all sported jeans, cowboy boots, and Stetsons.

Nick recognized Angie Angelino leaning next to a door on the back wall, wearing his game face. He tapped Mitch's arm and they walked up to him.

"Hello again, big guy. Your keeper in there?"

Angelino's harelip twitched, but he thought better of answering the insult and readjusted his game face. He closed his fist and rapped on the door with two thick knuckles. He let a few seconds pass and opened it.

Strozzi was seated with his feet up on a gray metal desk in the cramped office. There were two mismatched chairs, a filing cabinet, a narrow table holding a coffee maker, and a threadbare couch. A door next to a small window led to an alley.

Fats Arnheim was sitting on the couch with his pudgy hands folded over a protruding belly. A .38 revolver in a shoulder holster looked smothered between his massive left arm and chest.

Strozzi's eyed wandered over Mitch.

"Who's the Chink?"

Nick glanced at Mitch. Mitch smiled and Nick gently corrected Strozzi.

"A Japanese-American, actually. Third generation. But I'm sure he'd be happy to take you into the alley and make the introduction himself."

"Oh! A tough guy!" Strozzi's normal sneer intensified. He glanced at Fats. "We love tough guys. Ain't that right?"

Fats nodded mirthlessly.

"That's right—we love 'em."

Angelino walked around Nick, stood behind Strozzi's desk, and grinned. Strozzi dropped his feet to the floor and folded his hands in his lap.

"So . . . Whaddaya got to tell me, Conti?"

"You got my attention, Carlo. Congratulations."

"Yeah. Sorry about the kid, but like you say, we hadda get your attention."

"Okay." Nick proceeded in a reasonable tone. "Let's say I come up with five grand a week. How do I know that at some point the tab won't go up?"

"You don't. That's the beauty of our positions here. I got you by the balls, and all I gotta do is squeeze to make you squeal." He looked at Fatso. "Ain't that right?"

"That's right." Fats looked at Angie. "Ain't it?"

Angie nodded slowly. The ponytail didn't bounce, but his hare-lipped grin got wider.

Strozzi spread his hands and gave Nick a sardonic smile.

"But I'm an honorable kinda guy over here. You come up with five large a week and I'll see you skate along nice and smooth."

"You? You'll see? What about the boys in the Windy City? Suppose they decide your five grand a week is too light and tell you to up the ante?"

"You let me worry about that, Conti. I'm the guy with the deal." He again looked at Fats—totally satisfied with himself. "Tell 'im."

"He's the man." Fats broke into a wide grin.

Nick heaved a theatrical sigh. "Okay, Carlo . . . It's your pot—I fold . . . But it'll take a few days for me to generate the cash. I've got to figure a way to hide it in the budget. There are audits. Company, network, and the IRS."

"That's your problem. Mine's keeping my boys from rearranging the face of another one of your pretty-boy actors."

"Won't be necessary. I'll get the cash."

"Good. Ya got two days."

CHAPTER EIGHTEEN

SAMMY DAVIS JUNIOR belted out the last notes of "The Candy Man" to a standing ovation. Sam and Gwen Altman, sitting at Lew and Edie Wasserman's stage-side table, were among the first to rise. There were over two thousand people packed into the Beverly Hilton ballroom in a sea of tuxedos, gowns, and jewels. As predicted, the heart fund-raiser drew a flood of hundred-dollar-a-plate supporters ranging from glitterati to wannabes—all choking down rubber chicken and soggy peas.

Sammy blew them kisses galore, made multiple bows, and ran off the stage. A few moments later Dean Martin walked out carrying Sammy in his arms—and Frank Sinatra appeared from the opposite wings. They met stage center. It was an old routine from their days at the Sands in the sixties.

When the laughter and applause died down, Dean held out Sammy and asked Frank, "Do you know who this belongs to?"

"Yeah," replied Frank. "The rabbi at Temple Emmanuel."

The three legends then did a ten-minute medley of standards that brought the house down.

During a second standing ovation, Cojo Kulakowsky appeared at the table and whispered something in Sam's ear. Sam excused himself and they walked out to a quiet corner in the lobby. In spite of the solitude, Cojo kept his voice low.

"I just got a call from Manners. It seems the kid was spotted checking into La Costa with a fat lip and a black eye."

"So what? He's supposed to be recuperating from a motorcycle accident."

"Right. But the problem is the guy who spotted him was a reporter from the *Times*. He's on vacation with his girlfriend, who's a big Johnny Johansen fan."

"Christ!"

"So this reporter's trying to impress his girlfriend and they go up to Johnny while he's checking in and the asshole introduces himself."

"Get to the goddamn point!"

"The point is the reporter notices Johnny's face and asks him what happened. Johnny tells him he's had a motorcycle accident like we planned, but he comes off nervous and the reporter gets suspicious. So he starts asking for details. Well, there ain't no details, so the dumb kid gets really nervous and the reporter gets really suspicious. Then Johnny clams up and takes off."

Sam stared at his head of security in disbelief—calculating the odds on the chance meeting. He groaned and pinched his nose between his fingers.

"Un-fucking believable."

"So the goddamn reporter smells a story and starts calling Vegas. Cops, sheriff, hospitals, TV, and radio. He tries to find out about reported accidents and comes up with zip. That's when he called Manners to get a statement."

"What'd Manners tell him?"

"That it happened on the set and we wanted to keep it quiet."

"Did he buy it?"

"Who the fuck knows? But I'd lay ten to one against. He smells a story. My bet is he starts calling anyone he can reach on *The $trip*'s crew to find out if it's true."

"This reporter got a name?"

"I'll check."

"Do that. And then buy him. There's no goddamn way the real story can get out!"

CHAPTER NINETEEN

NICK AND MITCH returned to the DI and stopped by the lounge for a nightcap. It had been their habit since they'd started filming in Vegas—the last stop before retiring when they were without female company. They called it "scouting targets of opportunity."

Fortunately, the lounge after midnight was always frequented by women indulging in the same pastime. Some were single, some married on a business junket, others were hookers, but all were available.

Nick found himself less interested since seeing Erin again, but was keeping his friend company until he cut a prospect out of the crowd.

It took fifteen minutes.

Mitch spotted a sinewy brunette tall enough to play basketball for the Lakers and was off and running. His suite was six floors above, in the main building, and Nick was sure the brunette would be introduced to it within the hour.

Nick returned to the Wimbledon and picked up his messages.

There was one from Sam instructing Nick to call his private number at home—no matter what time it was.

Nick dialed Sam at midnight, almost twenty-four hours to the minute from the time Angelino had thrown Johnny Johansen through his door.

Sam was wide awake.

"Nick?"

"Yeah."

"Our problem just got more complicated."

"Christ—now what?"

"A reporter saw Johnny checking into La Costa and asked him what happened to his face. He told the guy it was a motorcycle accident and the guy asked for details. Naturally there were none. Johnny got nervous. The reporter got suspicious."

Nick groaned. He knew Johnny wasn't the brightest bulb on the tree—sensed what was coming, and got it.

"The guy's name is Peter Gans—he's just a young stringer, but he smelled a rat and called Vegas to see if it checked out. When it didn't, he called Manners. Manners said it happened on the set and we wanted to keep it quiet. But we think he'll call some of your crew and see if they verify the story. Which they can't."

"Sam—there's no way I can get everybody to clam up on this. Tonight I found out we've got a rat in our crew and I don't know who it is."

"The guy who slashed the tires and set the fire?"

"Gotta be."

"Shit."

"So what the hell do you want me to do?"

"About Johnny—nothing. I'm just giving you a heads-up. I've sent Cojo and Jake to La Costa to buy the asshole off. What are you doing about Strozzi?"

"I met him tonight and told him we'd pay off."

Sam exploded. "What?"

"Relax, Sam. I told him I needed a couple of days to get the cash. I'm buying time."

"For what?"

"I don't know yet."

"Jesus Christ, Nick! You've got bubkes!"

"No—in a couple of days I'll have plan B."

"What the hell's plan B?"

"I'll let you know as soon as I come up with it."

Sam slammed down the phone.

Nick smiled even though there was nothing funny.

CHAPTER TWENTY

DAY TWO

THE FOLLOWING DAY, Nick put the Firebird's top down and drove the short distance to where they were filming. Base camp was on an empty lot next to the Hacienda, at the south end of the Strip. Pulling in past several support vehicles, he parked behind the catering truck.

The late-morning crew call was for ten o'clock, since they again had night shooting on the schedule. Their normal twelve-hour day would again end at ten that night, giving them four full hours of darkness to film the night sequences.

The director, Rodney Lang, was setting up for the first shot, which would be the car-chase coverage they couldn't get the prior day because of the sabotaged brakes on the picture car. He was discussing the shot with Snuffy Benton, who, in addition to being Hank Donovan's stunt double, was the second-unit director. He bore an essential if not uncanny resemblance to the star. Brad Tilden, the local actor who played an LVPD detective, was also in the shot and was looking on.

Nick walked over to a table containing finger food, fruit, and soft drinks, and filled a Styrofoam cup from the coffee urn. He heard footsteps approaching behind him and a chipper female voice call out.

"Good morning . . ."

Nick turned to see the show's female costar approaching. Lori Donner was wearing shorts, a halter, and heels that showed off her finely tuned figure. She was beaming a dimpled smile and Nick returned it.

"Morning, Lori. Nice outfit—wardrobe or personal?"

"Personal. I'm not scheduled to shoot until two."

Lori was beautifully and innocently aglow in the morning sunlight— a 34-24-34 blue-eyed blonde with irresistible dimples. It was a look the fawning press never failed to depict as "adorable" when describing her. Playing Hank's secretary, she was the perfect contrast to his smoldering PI.

"Why so early?"

"I wanted to see you."

"Oh? There a problem?"

"You tell me. Where were you last night?"

Oh shit . . . With everything that'd happened because of Strozzi, he'd completely spaced their date.

"Lori, I'm sorry . . . something came up. I had to fly to L.A. yesterday and I got lost in hurdles."

"Want to make it up to me tonight?"

Nick had met Lori when he'd cast her in the pilot of *The $trip.* They were both single, available, and attracted. The show was picked up, and their casual affair picked up with it. Nick liked her, but suspected the affair might be more casual for him than her.

"I'd like to, Lori, but it's a bad time. A rain check?"

"Sure. How long do you think it'll last?"

"It?"

"The rain."

"A summer shower. I'll call you."

"Don't forget your rubbers." She gave him an impish smile, twirled around, and glided off.

Lori was definitely not the girl next door.

Hank Donovan was drinking coffee with Mitch next to the Corvette. The bright sun was highlighting the high cheekbones that were echoes of his Cherokee heritage. They were in startling contrast to the green eyes he'd inherited from his Swedish mother. The package was impressive enough to have made him a candidate for the replacement role of James Bond.

Hank's stand-in was sitting in the Corvette while the director of photography set lights and camera. Nick dropped a lump of sugar into his coffee and joined them.

"Morning, Hank . . . Mitch."

The whole crew had heard about the sabotaged Corvette but Hank's macho image required him to joke about it.

"Morning, Nick . . . Up early to test hop the Vette?"

"I'm sure the mechs and Snuffy've been all over it since dawn."

Mitch nodded.

"We could run it at Daytona."

Suddenly serious. Hank asked the question that was on everyone's mind.

"Any idea who's behind this shit?"

"Probably the competition in our nine o'clock time slot. We're killing 'em."

Mitch and Hank chuckled and the second assistant director broke away from the group around the Corvette.

"First team!"

Hank touched his temple with a quick two-finger salute.

"Showtime."

He walked off and a makeup lady quickly followed, applying a last-minute swipe of powder to his face. Hank handed her his coffee cup and replaced his stand-in in the Corvette. Brad Tilden got into an un-marked LVPD sedan.

The film crew took off down the Strip for the first shot, and Nick signaled Mitch to follow him. He stopped behind the catering truck.

"We're getting a run-down on everyone in this crew in the next two days."

"Really . . . How?"

"I called Dan Dietrich. I told him to forget their résumés. I want backgrounds—where they went to school—what they studied—friends—hobbies."

"You think it'll help us nail the rat?"

"Maybe. Whoever rigged those brakes knew what he was doing. He had to learn it somewhere."

"Good point. But there's over sixty people in the crew."

"Dan's putting four of his best operatives on it. I told him to skip the mechs and special-effects people at first. It's too obvious they'd have the know how and be suspect. Initially he'll dig into everybody else—wardrobe, makeup, hair, set dress—everybody."

"Fine—but somehow I can't picture a woman shooting acid into a brake line."

"Ma Barker, Lizzy Borden, and Bonnie Parker might disagree."

Mitch allowed that anything was possible, and Nick got in the Fire-bird. It was eleven when he pulled out of the lot and called Nello Mar-chetti in Kansas City.

"Yeah?"

Nello always sounded pissed off.

"Good morning, Nello—Nick."

"What the hell is it with you and time? It's one in the afternoon."

True, thought Nick—the two-hour time change again. "Sorry, Nello, but I need another favor."

"What now? I told ya, we ain't gettin' involved."

"I don't need involved, Nello—just a little information."

"My mother's sister ever tell you you were a pain in the ass?"

"From my First Communion on."

"What is it now?"

"I saw Big Allie in town last night."

"So? He's checkin' in with Agosto. You forgettin' who's who and what's what? Besides, word is he's got a new squeeze out there."

Nick let his last comment slide and pushed on. "Nello . . . just hear me out."

"Okay, but not now. Tell me when I get there. I'm on my way and I'm late for the plane."

"You're coming here?"

"Yeah. It's a three-hour flight. But I pick up two with the time change—which you wouldn't understand since you know shit about time. I'll be in at three and meet you at the Trop at four."

Nello hung up.

Nick stared at the phone a few moments and recycled Nello's comment. *The word is he's got a new squeeze out there.*

CHAPTER TWENTY-ONE

COJO KULAKOWSKY AND Jake Siegel arrived at La Costa at noon. Like many of the hotels in Las Vegas, the plush four-hundred-acre Spanish-colonial resort had been built with Teamster pension-fund cash under the auspices of the Chicago Outfit. It immediately became a favorite destination for the cognoscenti of organized crime, sports stars, politicians, and Hollywood celebrities. Ninety miles south of Los Angeles, it featured luxury accommodations, fine dining, a world-class spa, and a championship golf course.

Cojo and Jake were well aware of La Costa's history. Cojo was an ex-LAPD detective, Jake a former pro wrestler. They had been hired by Sam Altman as security chief and bodyguard, respectively, and both were burly examples of their former professions.

But it was their additional talents that had intrigued Sam. They both had an intimate knowledge of the underbelly of Sam's world.

They learned that Peter Gans, the young *Times* reporter they were looking for, was playing golf. It required several inquiries, and as usual Jake let Cojo do all the talking. They were told Gans would return before lunch. They obviously couldn't approach him on the course, so after getting a solid description they went to see Johansen.

He was ensconced in a luxurious two-bedroom suite overlooking the golf course. Chrissie, the Playboy Bunny who was Johnny's girlfriend, answered the door in a robe that did little to obscure what he liked about her. The cleavage was canyonesque.

"Who're you?" The accent was New York and annoyed.

"Friends of Johnny. We work for Sam Altman."

"Oh!" The voice was suddenly impressed and welcoming. "Come in—Johnny's in bed."

Neither one could blame him.

They entered, and Chrissie crossed toward a closed bedroom door.

"Johhhnieee . . ."

Somewhere a glass shattered.

A few seconds later a weary voice from the bedroom answered.

"What . . . ?"

"Two men are here to see you—from Mr. Altman."

The voice was suddenly alert when it called out the second time.

"Be right there."

There was a room-service caddy with breakfast next to the patio. Chrissie indicated an open bottle in a silver ice bucket.

"Can I get you something? We've got champagne."

Cojo cocked an eyebrow, glanced at it, and back to her.

"No, thanks. It's a little early for that."

"Oh . . ." She was apologetic but suddenly brightened. "I can order Bloody Marys . . ."

Cojo held up his hand.

"We'll just wait on the patio."

They walked out and were joined by Johnny a few seconds later. His swollen face, fat lip, and black eye hadn't improved. The blond shock of hair drifting over his forehead covered the wrong eye.

They all sat at an umbrella table. Johnny squirmed nervously in his seat.

"What's up, fellas?"

Cojo shook out a cigarette, flipped open a Zippo lighter, and lit it off before answering.

"It's about this Gans guy—the reporter."

Johnny's eyes darted between the two men. If Altman had sent these two men to see him, it probably meant he'd fucked up.

"I haven't talked to him again."

"Good. See that you don't. He's trying to bust the motorcycle story . . . No matter what, you stick with it. We'll talk to Gans. I don't think he'll bother you anymore."

"Am I in trouble with Mr. Altman?"

"Nah . . . He loves you." Cojo got up and stuck out his hand. "Put some more ice on that face."

The two men walked back through the living room toward the door. Chrissie hung up the phone and stopped them.

"I ordered coffee . . ."

"Good. Drink it."

Cojo smiled and both men left.

At twelve thirty they were waiting outside the men's locker room when a sandy-haired man in his mid- to late twenties walked out. He had a narrow, preppy face and was wearing lime-green golf attire on an Ichabod Crane frame.

Cojo called out to him.

"Gans?"

"Yes?"

"We represent Johnny Johansen. We'd like to talk to you."

Gans's eyes swung to Jake and back to Cojo. If he was frightened by their obvious ability to intimidate, he didn't show it.

"This about the so-called motorcycle accident?"

"It is. Johnny's very embarrassed about what really happened because it involved another woman, and his girlfriend is very jealous."

"Bullshit."

Cojo ignored the remark and removed a thick envelope from his inside jacket pocket.

"Would you consider five thousand dollars bullshit?"

"He wants to bribe me?"

"He wants you to have a nice gift for your cooperation."

Gans shook his head derisively. He felt safe in the middle of a world-class resort.

"Look, I made a few calls to the set in Las Vegas early this morning. Nobody knew anything about a motorcycle accident. What the hell are you guys trying to cover up?"

"An indiscretion."

"More bullshit."

Cojo glanced at Jake. He had to admire the kid's spunk in the face of two men twice his size.

"I'm sorry you feel that way, Mr. Gans—but you're young and don't understand that hundreds of more important stories will come your way in the future. Take the money for this one and move on."

"No way. I smell something fishy. This could make me a rep."

"Something fishy . . ." Cojo was amused and shook his head. "You get that from reading *Police Gazette*?"

"Maybe, but it's true. And I'm going after the story."

Cojo smiled and gently touched Gans's fingers.

"What's true is that you're gonna need healthy fingers to write that story. I'd hate for you to have an accident that would cripple them."

Gans's eyes popped and he jerked away his hand.

"You're threatening me?"

"Of course not. I'm merely making an observation. But I'll tell you what I'll do. I'll let you think over my offer. Until—say—five, at which point we'll visit you again—maybe even say hi to your girl-friend . . ." Cojo patted his face. "Have a nice lunch."

Gans watched slack-jawed as the two men strolled away.

CHAPTER TWENTY-TWO

SAM ALTMAN JOYOUSLY finished off his second hot dog and dabbed his mouth with a monogrammed linen napkin. He was alone in his office and seated at the head of the conference table.

He never went out to lunch.

Sam had a chef and full kitchen at his disposal, but twice every week he ordered hot dogs with chili from a place called Pink's. He also ordered fatty corned beef from Nat 'n' Al's twice every week. That only left one day a week for René, a very expensive French chef, to cook for his boss—usually a pepperoni pizza that Sam washed down with a bottle of Coke that he'd laced with peanuts. Putting peanuts into a Coke to create a salty-sweet drink was a Texas thing.

Sam was never considered a gourmet.

René, however, did cook lunch—begrudgingly—for the office staff Monday through Friday. They ate at their desks. There was no such thing as a normal lunch break at Altman Productions.

Sam leaned back in his chair, lit a cigar, and seconds later erupted into a violent coughing fit. He frantically mashed down on an intercom button and seconds later, when Rachel came flying in, he was choking.

"M-medicine . . ."

Rachel dashed to his desk and withdrew a small bottle from a side drawer. She unscrewed the top while running back to Sam—he grabbed it and took a hefty gulp. A few seconds later, although he was red-faced and wet-eyed, the coughing subsided. The prescription cough remedy was laced with codeine.

A tear appeared in Rachel's eye and her voice overflowed with tenderness.

"Sam . . . Please. Listen to your doctor. You've got to stop smoking."

"Doctors." Sam's tone was contemptuous and he wiped his mouth with a handkerchief. "What the hell do they know?"

"Sam . . ."

Rachel was pleading. She was married but harbored an unrequited love for Sam that had spanned twenty-five years. There was never a more devoted slave. She knew more about Sam than his parents, his closest associates, and his wife.

Any attempt to continue her plea was interrupted by a buzz and Angeline on the intercom.

"Phone call for Mr. Altman . . . Mr. Kulakowsky from La Costa."

Sam wiped his mouth again, cleared his throat, and picked up the phone.

"Cojo?"

"Yeah, boss. We talked to Gans. He says he doesn't want the money."

"What the hell do you mean he doesn't want the money?"

"He wants the story . . . He's being stubborn."

"Up the offer!"

"Okay, but I don't think it's about the money. He just wants the story."

"I don't give a shit what he wants. What I want is for him to go away. Get it done."

"I will, boss. I gave him until five to think over the offer. He'll take it or we'll change his mind."

"You're goddamn right you—" Sam's tirade was interrupted by another coughing spasm. He thrust the phone into Rachel's hand and reached for the medicine bottle.

Rachel said, "Call back later," and hung up.

CHAPTER TWENTY-THREE

NICK ARRIVED AT the Tropicana at four o'clock and called Nello's suite. Nello said he'd meet him at the Havana Hideaway. Unlike most boisterous Las Vegas lounges, the Hideaway had a relaxed, intimate atmosphere with leather sofas and cushioned chairs—an ideal setting for a quiet conversation accompanied by muted jazz.

Nello arrived smoking a cigar and wearing a three-piece suit. The blue chalk stripe made him look more like a banker than a button man—were it not for his swarthy face and broken nose. They made him look like an ex–Golden Gloves middleweight—which he'd been in his youth. It also made him look pissed off—which he'd been all his life. A peptic ulcer was part of the reason. His natural demeanor did the rest. Nick rose to greet him with an outstretched hand.

"Welcome to Vegas."

Nello took the hand and shook it perfunctorily but forged ahead without missing a beat.

"Okay—what's the story?"

Nick smiled.

"And a very good day to you, too."

Nello ignored the comment and they both sat. Nello unbuttoned his vest and crossed his knees.

"I'm a busy man, Nick. What is it?"

"Like I said on the phone, I saw Allie in town."

"So?"

"So I thought I could get you to ask him to get me some information."

"I, you, him, me. Christ, it sounds like a daisy chain. What kind?"

"About Strozzi. The prick who's trying to hold me up for five grand a week . . . It's a big score for him. The point being he's a blowhard asshole who ordinarily wouldn't keep his mouth shut. It would make him a big man in his circle."

"Probably. So what?"

"I think this time he'll swallow his ego and clam up."

"You got a reason?"

"Yeah. When I talked to him, the cocky little bastard made a mistake. I asked if his bosses might push him to up the five grand a week once I was hooked. He waved it off—said he was in total control. Total control? We're talking Chicago here. Nobody controls them. I think he's flying solo. Tuna may be out of the loop."

"He's gotta be nuts to pull that kinda shit."

"I told you—he's a cocky little bastard. And if I'm right, he won't make a peep about his latest score."

"What's this got to do with Big Allie?"

"He knows the Mob guys in town including the Chicago bunch. I've seen him here before—he hangs out with them. I want him to casually ask some questions. See if anybody's heard about anything going on with *The $trip*. Allie can say he's interested because there's a movie crew in town staying at his hotel—Allied International made their production deal with the Tropicana. He can say he's an investor and wants to know if anyone's trying to scam Hollywood types."

"You figure Allie'll find out squat and that'll mean Strozzi's cuttin' out Chicago."

"That's what I'm hoping,"

"Even if it was true. How the hell're ya gonna prove it?"

"I haven't figured that out yet."

Nello nodded, grudgingly.

"Okay, Nick . . . It's no big deal. I'll talk to Allie. He'll do it because he loves to play the Hollywood big shot."

"Yeah. He gets a lot of face time in the press. You don't mind?"

"Me—no. Corky, yes. He's gettin' nervous about it."

The possibility of getting a little more information about Erin's relationship to Allie occurred to Nick.

"That mean you're here to tell him to cool it with 'his newest squeeze,' as you put it?"

Nello studied the end of his cigar. He didn't figure he was betraying a confidence by repeating information that was public knowledge.

"Corky remembers the shitstorm over Giancana and McGuire. No one was happy with that, and no one's happy with this. Between the two of us, Corky wants me to tell him he can fuck anybody he wants but keep his goddamn name out of the papers . . . Meantime I'll tell him he can make some points if he asks around for you. I'll let ya know if anything comes up."

"Thanks, Nello. I appreciate it."

"You should. But this is the last goddamn time."

Nello got up and left.

Nick said "Ciao" to his back.

CHAPTER TWENTY-FOUR

COJO HAD STATIONED himself in a quiet corner of the La Costa lobby right after he hung up with Sam. Jake had taken the parking lot.

As Cojo predicted, at four o'clock, one hour before they were to meet Gans, their quarry appeared at the checkout desk. He was joined by a mousy brunette wearing shorts and a halter. She was leading a bellhop with a luggage cart.

The brunette's name was Tina.

Gans's eyes danced around like ricocheting pinballs but didn't pick up Cojo, who was obscured by a potted palm. He was too flustered to even give his bill a cursory glance before signing his credit card. The clerk casually separated the hotel copy from the customer copy and stapled it to the bill. He was about to place the items in an envelope when Gans snatched them out of his hand and practically bounded toward the parking lot.

The bellhop and Tina dashed after him, trying to keep up. The luggage was piled into the trunk of a new Ford, the bellhop was tipped, and the fleeing pair got into the car.

A moment later Jake's Cadillac crossed behind the Ford, stopped, and pinned it into the parking space.

Cojo walked up to the driver's window, gently tapped the glass with a large signet ring, and signaled Gans to lower the window. The reporter's face twisted in fear but the window slid down.

"Going somewhere?"

Gans stammered. He'd been caught trying to escape, was petrified and struggling to control his bladder.

"I—I . . ."

"No—*I*." Cojo poked his chest with his thumb. "*I* thought we had a date at five."

"I—I . . ." More stammering.

"Get out of the car."

The passenger door suddenly jerked open, causing Gans to snap his head around. A clublike hand had reached in and pulled Tina out of the car. In the middle of her scream Gans's door flew open. He was jerked upward, and he suddenly found himself on tiptoes, staring into Cojo's eyes.

"Look—Peter . . ." Cojo's voice was eerily calm. "Let me be clear . . . Are you listening?"

Gans nodded weakly.

"Good . . . Either you accept the five thousand and keep your mouth shut, or I slam the car door on the fingers of your right hand. Do we have a deal?"

Gans nodded, slowly, reaching out to accept the money.

"And Peter? If I hear a word about this anywhere, you're gonna lose a lot more than your fingers."

CHAPTER TWENTY-FIVE

NICK WALKED OUT of the Tropicana's main entrance, handed the valet a ticket, and waited for his car. Turning his back to a stiff wind, he donned sunglasses against the blowing dust. Vegas had reverted to its normal weather pattern. Two days earlier the mercury was over one hundred, but it had now dropped into the mid-sixties.

Nick took a step back as a stretch limo pulled up and stopped next to him. The driver bounced out of his seat and then literally ran around the back of the car to open the passenger door.

Erin Conroy stepped out and paused.

She was standing less than six feet away from Nick. They locked eyes and then she smiled. She seemed pleased.

"Well . . . good afternoon, Nico."

"Erin . . ." Nick dipped his head noncommittally and then glanced at the limo. "Quite a chariot."

"Stavros demands the best for his minions."

"Stavros or Big Allie . . ."

"Ah . . ." She obviously understood the comment. "Luigi's. I saw you."

"I know." Nick just as obviously wanted her to understand he hadn't missed her furtive glances.

She was wearing a puff-sleeved white blouse with padded shoulders, tight-fitting black slacks, and patent-leather spikes. It was a look made popular by England's Diana and TV's *Dynasty*—the royalty of both.

Nick thought she looked like a spectacular female pirate. Why not? She'd played one in the film that made her a star.

The limo driver stepped forward, cleared his throat, and removed his cap.

"Excuse me, Ms. Conroy—will you need the car again this afternoon?"

"No, Bob. I'll call when I need you again."

The driver touched his forehead in a two fingered salute and Erin rewarded him with a dazzling smile. He reentered the limo and she checked her watch. She read the result with a tantalizing tilt of her head.

"Cocktail time . . . Care to join me for a drink?"

Nick's Firebird had pulled up and the valet was holding the door open. Nick handed him a five.

"Put it back."

Erin smiled, hooked her arm into Nick's, and led him back into the hotel.

CHAPTER TWENTY-SIX

J OE AGOSTO WAS smiling broadly as he proudly took Allie and Nello on a quick inspection of the Tropicana casino—the viewing ports and cameras above the ceiling, the tables on the floor below—and finally the Tropicana's counting room, where the skim took place.

Nello looked over both sets of books—official and actual—and, when satisfied that all was in order, dismissed Joe and ushered Allie into Joe's office for a private conversation.

Allie had held his temper but he remained miffed about Nello's sudden request for an inspection tour of the casino. He considered it an intrusion into his designated domain and addressed Nello testily the moment he closed the door.

"Okay, Nello, what's the beef? Suddenly Corky doesn't trust me to oversee this operation?"

Nello lit a cigar and studied it—letting the question hang in the air a few seconds before forcing himself to sound reasonable. For Nello it took considerable effort because being and sounding pissed off was his natural state.

"The walk around was for Joe's benefit."

"The hell are you talkin' about?"

"A smoke screen—has nothing to do with why I'm here."

"Then why the hell *are* you here?"

"Sit down, Allie."

Allie hesitated, shrugged, and reluctantly sat.

Technically, Allie was on the same level as Nello. Both were caporegimes under Corky Civella, but Nello was older, more senior, and much closer to the boss. Allie knew that any failure to respect that fact was at his own peril.

Nello took a long drag on his cigar and slowly let it out.

"It's about your lifestyle. Corky's got a problem with it. A lot of us do."

"What the hell're you talking about?"

"Your name in the papers. Pictures with celebrities. Especially Hollywood types."

"That's my private life. It's got nothing to do with you guys."

"Wrong. It may be your life. But it's not so private."

"And Corky sent you all the way out here to tell me that? Why all of a sudden now?"

"He heard about Erin Conroy."

"What about her?"

"Come on, Al, fer chrissakes, she's a star. And the press has long since connected you to Kansas City and our thing here. Your antics've been bringin' down a lot of heat on us and we think it's about to get worse. You're fucking around with Erin Conroy. You got her shacked up in this hotel. When it hits the gossip columns the civilians are gonna get pissed and the feds are gonna get pushed. You might as well be shinin' a goddamn spotlight on yourself—and us."

Clearly angry, Allie got up and poured himself a hefty vodka from

Joe's bar. He slammed it down in one gulp and turned back to the messenger.

"No disrespect, Nello, but you guys are askin' for something that's none of your goddamn business."

"All we askin' is for you to use your head. Fuck her all you want, but keep it quiet and keep it out of the goddamn papers!"

"And this comes straight from Corky?"

"Him and everybody else. Includin' me."

"And if I don't agree?"

"You don't want to go there, Al."

Allie took a deep breath and struggled to hold his temper. He didn't answer until he was sure it was fully under control.

"Okay, Nello. I got the message. I'll think about it."

"Good, Allie. I know you'll come up with the right answer . . . In the meantime there's a little something you can do to earn some points."

"What's that?"

"I'd like you to ask some of the Chicago guys if they heard anything about Carlo Strozzi and a scam goin' down on a TV show that's filmin' here."

Allie knew who Strozzi was—an Accardo guy with multiple rackets—but he was taken aback at the mention of a TV show. His thoughts quickly turned to Nick Conti. His eyes narrowed suspiciously.

"*The $trip?*"

Nello was a little surprised he knew of the show and answered with a cocked eyebrow.

"Yeah . . ."

"What's that got to do with you?"

"Nothin'. I'm doin a favor for a friend of a friend."

Allie thought about Nello's answer a few seconds and then decided to test the waters.

"This friend of a friend wouldn't happen to be Nick Conti, would it?"

Nello was even more surprised, but saw no reason to deny it.

"Yeah . . . You know him?"

"No. He was in Luigi's last night. I was there with Erin and I caught her staring at him a couple of times. I asked who he was—she told me his name and said she worked for him once."

Nello figured that was all Allie knew about Nick. He was sure Allie didn't know Nick was a Condini and his cousin. Nick had walked away from the Kansas City family over twenty years ago. Allie had been involved with it less than fifteen. He dismissed the comment with a wave of his hand.

"Ah . . . Well, whatever. It's no big deal. Find out what you can and let me know."

"I'll ask around. How long are you gonna be in town?"

"A day or two. See some shows. Relax around the pool. Jump a few broads . . . Like that."

"Okay, Nello. Catch you later."

Allie left feeling extremely suspicious and didn't think he was being paranoid. *What the hell was going on?* Suddenly Nello shows up in Vegas and tells him he has to cool it with Erin—"*on orders from Corky.*" But Corky's never said anything about his lifestyle before.

So it couldn't be about his lifestyle. It had to be about Erin.

Last night at Luigi's he'd caught her staring at Nick Conti on several occasions and asked who he was. Her answer was, "*I worked with him once.*"

At the time he suspected that there was a lot more to it than that, but he'd let it pass.

And today Nello asks him to do *a favor for a friend of a friend*. Who's the *friend of a friend?*

Nick Conti.

Allie strung the events together . . . Suddenly Nello shows up in Las Vegas and tells him to lay off Erin—Erin has a connection to Nick Conti—Conti has a connection to Nello—Nello wants to do Conti a favor—and he says it's about Strozzi and a possible scam with *The $trip*. Is it?

Or is it about scamming him out of his affair with Erin.

Allie let out a derisive snort. It was all coming out of nowhere and too goddamn coincidental. But the one thing that connected it all was a guy called Nick Conti.

He'd have to find out more about that asshole.

CHAPTER TWENTY-SEVEN

ERIN STIRRED TWO perfect Rob Roys in a crystal carafe filled with ice. Four parts Chivas Regal and one part each of sweet and dry vermouth. She was behind a mirrored bar in her four-bedroom suite—one of an extravagant pair on the penthouse floor that had been designed to accommodate very high rollers and their entourages.

Nick was at the window looking at a wide-angle view of the strip. Erin selected two stem glasses and placed them on the bar.

"Still straight up?"

"Still . . ." He crossed to the bar and sat.

"You remember the first time I made you one of these?"

"I do. You made it half and half. It was terrible."

She filled the stem glasses.

"I wasn't a bartender, I was a model—and I was only nineteen."

"You were twenty in two weeks and we were in New York. You were legal."

"And you were a cradle robber."

"Point taken." He raised his glass. "Salut . . ."

They sipped. Nick savored the drink, swallowed, and smiled.

"Perfect."

"I had an exceptional teacher."

"You were an outstanding student."

"Until you, anyway. A's, a 4.0 average, top of the honor roll. I was a model citizen."

It was true. When they met she was a junior at NYU, an English-lit major. Her father was head of the department. On their first date they'd argued whether Christopher Marlowe or Francis Bacon was the real Shakespeare. Nick speculated it could be either, and she maintained it was neither.

She won.

Nick cocked an eyebrow. "Until me?"

She nodded. "When I met you, I failed Caution."

"You regret dropping out and becoming a star?"

"No . . . It was my choice. I haven't regretted it. But my father still hasn't forgiven me . . . or you."

She smiled, came around the bar, and sat facing him.

Nick indicated the suite.

"Do you have any idea what you might be costing the hotel if a whale shows up and can't have this playpen?"

"Allie explained it to me. I was impressed."

"With him or the explanation?

"Both, actually."

"Where'd you meet him?"

"At a premiere. He was with Stavros."

"You're aware of who he is?"

"Of course."

"And it doesn't bother you?"

"Should it?"

"If you're concerned with your reputation—yes."

"It's been a long time since you've been concerned about my reputation, Nico."

"Old habits die hard."

"Why are we fencing?" She shrugged evasively. "Al is a friend of mine. I have a lot of friends. Some in the business, some in politics, others in sports. This one happens to be in the Kansas City Mob."

"Okay . . . Let's drop it. It's none of my business."

Erin paused and studied his face. She seemed to be considering her next comment carefully. Finally she sipped her drink and decided on the truth.

"Actually, I wish it were."

"Oh . . . ?"

"I still think about you every now and then." She said it with a reluctant shrug, but the shrug looked forced.

Nick's heart did a quick twist. He'd had dozens of affairs in the past two years but there'd only been one Erin—before or since. All his instincts told him to avoid what he was thinking but he couldn't follow them.

Nick echoed her shrug—it looked just as forced.

"Then there are two of us."

"Ah . . ." She smiled approvingly. "Can I take that to mean you might like to see me again?"

How the hell to answer that. This time the truth was not in the cards.

"Describe 'see.' "

"Describe 'coy.' "

"We're fencing again."

"Sometimes people fence over things they're afraid might hurt them."

"Most times people are right."

"A lot's happened since we were together, Nico. I'm not that young girl anymore."

"Older and wiser?"

"Both."

"Erin . . ." Nick shook his head sadly. "The cliché is, 'You were the best thing that ever happened to me.' And things become clichés because they reflect truths. We had three unforgettable years. Do you really think we can go back and relive the past?"

"Maybe not . . . but it doesn't stop me from being curious about the future."

"It killed the cat."

"I know." She smiled.

"It's a bad time, Erin."

"Another woman?"

"No."

"Allie?"

"Maybe. I'm not sure."

"I should be flattered."

"Yes . . . you should." Nick finished his drink and got up.

"You'll call me?"

"If I can."

He left without kissing her. If he had it wouldn't have ended there. It never had and probably never would.

CHAPTER TWENTY-EIGHT

ALLIE CALLED ERIN and told her that something had come up and he had to cancel their dinner. Erin lied, saying it was just as well because she had a splitting headache and would turn in early.

Neither was true.

Since she'd seen Nick again, her old feelings had flared up and Allie no longer intrigued her. She'd been a chance taker most of her life, and Allie was just one more adventure in a line of escapades that had started after Nick.

She wondered if he really didn't want to revive their affair, or if he was afraid of revisiting the pain.

Their breakup had been stormy—awash in ridiculous accusations. She was young, academically brilliant, but a bit naïve, and Nick was her first real love affair. Nick was mature, successful, and sophisticated, with a string of affairs in his wake.

Erin knew the breakup was her fault—caused by her uncontrolled jealousy. She couldn't handle watching women hurl themselves in Nick's path. Many wanted a role in whatever television series he was producing, and others just wanted to go to bed with the man of mystery.

Hell, no one understood that better than she.

But now she was older, much wiser, and infinitely more polished. Somehow she'd have to prove it to Nick—because in the last twenty-four hours she realized she was probably still in love with him.

Twenty-two floors below, Allie was meeting with Stavros Papadopoulos in the hotel's Seafood Grill. He'd met Stavros socially on several occasions and cultivated the friendship—Allie loved celebrities. One of Allie's ploys was to call Stavros with hot tips on sporting events that he knew were sure winners. Stavros made money and Allie made a friend.

Stavros was a slightly built man who looked nothing like his Greek film hero, Zorba—but he did have his boisterous personality. Only twenty-eight but with a full black beard that made him look ten years older, he was an exotic wunderkind sans accent because he was born in Boston.

After dinner, out of deference to Stavros, Allie ordered ouzo and got to the point of the meeting. He sipped his drink and opened the conversation without preamble.

"Tell me about Erin."

Stavros knew Allie was dating her so he was a bit surprised by the question.

"Anything in particular?"

"What do you know about her relationship with Nick Conti?"

"Not much . . ." He shrugged. "I know she got her first break in a TV show he was producing. It's on her résumé. She was a model in New York."

"That's it?"

"As far as I know. But if I had to guess, I'd suspect the usual."

"The usual . . ." It was a statement, not a question.

"Nick's been in the business a long time and has a rep as a ladies' man. She was young—he gave her a break—she probably appreciated it and fucked him. Pretty standard stuff."

"But she hasn't seen him since you've worked with her?"

"Not that I know of—although I saw her say hello to him yesterday at the Polo Lounge."

"Oh?"

"Yeah—we had a business lunch and then she stopped by his table."

"What'd it look like? Just casual—friendly—or something more?"

"I couldn't tell. I was across the patio. But it was quick and they didn't leave together."

"Stavros . . . Would you do me a favor?"

Stavros spread his hands and grinned as if the answer went without saying.

"Could you find out what there was between them back then, and if anything's been going on since?"

"No problem, Al. Tomorrow I'll call some people who worked with her early on and let you know."

"Thanks, Stavros . . . I appreciate it. And by the way, Danny Boy tomorrow . . . the third at Aqueduct."

Allie signed the check, said good night to Stavros, and left for Maxi's—a strip club frequented by members and associates of the Chicago Outfit.

CHAPTER TWENTY-NINE

SNUFFY BENTON ORDERED another vodka tonic and checked his watch. It was after ten, Strozzi hadn't showed up yet, and Poolorama's clacking balls and shit-kicking music were giving him a headache. He'd been waiting at the bar over an hour and had gone out to his car twice to tell his two friends to sit tight. It'd only be a short time longer and they'd be out of there.

A buxom blonde with a boozy voice was sitting between him and her boyfriend. The boyfriend was apparently ignoring her and she was miffed. He was a bull-rider type wearing boots and a Stetson and was having a chummy conversation with a female bartender with big hair who was as buxom as his girlfriend. They were practically face-to-face.

Fed up, the blonde finally retaliated. She leaned into Snuffy and pressed her breast against his arm.

"Hi, handsome."

Snuffy had been monitoring the scenario in the back-bar mirror since he'd sat down. He ignored the advance since the last thing he wanted was a brawl with a jealous boyfriend. He merely nodded mechanically and stared at his drink.

The blonde wasn't about to be ignored twice.

"Di'ja hear me? I said, Hello, handsome."

Snuffy sighed and decided to take the path of least resistance. He turned to her and smiled weakly.

"Hi."

"You look like somebody I seen somewhere. You somebody I could've seen somewhere?"

This happened a lot to Snuffy. He obviously looked like Hank Donovan or he wouldn't be the star's stunt double. When it happened, he turned full face to the inquirer to make it apparent that he wasn't the real Donovan and it usually worked. He decided that was the best course and turned to face the blonde.

"I'm nobody. I just look like I might be somebody."

Snuffy turned back and again stared into his drink. It didn't slow down the blonde.

"You may be nobody, but you're a handsome nobody."

"Thank you."

"Wanna dance?"

"No, thank you."

"Why?"

"I don't dance."

"Everybody dances."

"Not nobody."

The blonde thought about that a few seconds, thought she was being put on, and scrunched her face up.

"Are you makin' fun-a-me? I think you're makin' fun-a-me."

She turned to her boyfriend, sharply poked his arm, and jerked her thumb at Snuffy.

"Randy—this nobody's makin' fun-a-me."

Randy's head popped back from the bartender's face and he turned to his girlfriend as if he'd suddenly become aware that she'd been sitting there.

"Huh?"

"Him." She threw a thumb over her shoulder. "He's makin' fun-a-me."

Randy leaned forward over the bar and the blonde leaned back to give him a clear view of Snuffy.

"Are you makin' fun of Amanda?"

"Absolutely not."

"You sure?"

"I'm sure."

Satisfied, Randy leaned back and faced Amanda.

"He's sure."

Randy turned back to the bartender and Amanda went ballistic. She started whacking him on the shoulder and letting out a stream of X-rated abuse that would've embarrassed a stevedore.

At that point Snuffy spotted Strozzi, Fats, and Angie making their way toward Strozzi's office. He quickly slipped away while Randy and Amanda erupted into verbal warfare. He got to the trio as they were entering the office. Strozzi motioned him in and closed the door.

"What can I do for ya, m'man?"

"I need some of the good stuff."

"How much?"

"An ounce is good."

"Four C's."

"Done."

The phone rang and Strozzi picked it up. Snuffy took out a roll of cash and peeled off four one-hundred-dollar bills. Strozzi punched a button under the desk and a four-by-four-foot section of the side wall popped open. The shoulder-high opening revealed a wall safe. Strozzi cupped the phone and motioned Fats.

"Give 'im an ounce of the uncut stuff."

He went back to his phone conversation. Fats spun the combination and opened the safe. He removed a clear plastic bag containing an ounce of uncut cocaine and handed it to Snuffy.

Fats smiled.

"Pure as it gets before we step on it for the amateurs. Enjoy."

Snuffy nodded, waved to Strozzi, who was obviously engaged in a heated phone call, and left.

The altercation at the bar had apparently subsided but Snuffy walked down the opposite side of the room and into the street. He got into the car and proudly brandished the plastic bag.

"Voilà! Let's party!"

Lori Donner and Brad Tilden, the actor who played a Las Vegas detective in *The $trip,* both let out a whoop of delight and Snuffy pulled away.

CHAPTER THIRTY

S AM AND G WEN returned home at eleven after a dinner party at Edie Goetz's followed by a screening of *Ordinary People,* Robert Redford's Academy Award–winning directorial debut. The film was not Sam's cup of tea, but not taking advantage of a coveted invitation by one of Hollywood's doyennes was out of the question.

Edie was the educated and urbane daughter of Louis B. Mayer and widow of William Goetz. Billy Goetz had been president of 20th Century Fox and Universal International Pictures, produced *Sayonara*, and owned one of the largest collections of impressionist art in Tinseltown. The Goetzes were Hollywood royalty.

Edie was everything Gwen wanted to be and wasn't.

"I hate going there." Jake was holding the door as she got out of their limo at the side-patio entrance.

Sam got out behind her.

"Live with it."

"And I hated the picture."

"Call Redford and let him know. I'm sure it'll mean a lot to him."

Alfred was waiting at the door, having been called by Jake, who gave him the Altmans' arrival time.

"Why are you defending her?"

"Because offending Edie is worse than pissing in shul."

"Good evening sir—ma'am . . ." Alfred held out a message slip. "There was a call for you from Mr. Manners. He would like you to call him at home as soon as possible. He said it was about your Vegas problem."

"Christ! What now? At eleven o'clock it can't be good."

"It never is when it's about Vegas and the brilliant Nick Conti!" Gwen's tone dripped with sarcasm.

"Leave it alone, Gwen."

"Why? You put him there to solve problems. But you're the one who's always called when one comes up!"

"I said, leave it alone!"

Sam headed for his den. Alfred followed Sam, and Gwen took the elevator to their bedroom.

Gwen fumed as the elevator rose to the second floor. Sam was dependent on Conti. But Gwen feared him.

Shortly after *The $trip* began filming, Gwen had come to Vegas with two of her lady friends, but without Sam. They'd played baccarat until two in the morning, drank too much, decided to have some fun, and hired two male strippers.

Nick had used the buff young men as extras while shooting a pool scene and saw them enter Gwen's suite. Before Gwen left the next day, Nick quietly advised her she'd left herself open to blackmail . . . but he'd spoken to the young men and convinced them it would be a very unwise course of action.

Gwen was furious because she believed it was *Nick* who was holding the threat of blackmail over her. Since then, she'd been determined to get Conti out of their lives.

Alfred stopped in the doorway of Sam's den.

"Would you like anything, sir?"

"Yes. Arsenic—but I'll take cognac."

Sam's den was a posh mini-library. Floor-to-ceiling bookcases accessed by a rolling ladder, empire furniture, and oriental rugs. One wall of books was completely dedicated to bound, leather-jacketed scripts from every one of Sam's productions, spanning thirty years.

Alfred went to the den's bar and retrieved a decanter of Courvoisier. Sam dialed Manners.

"Okay, Norman, what the hell is it?"

"I'm afraid we've had another little glitch."

"Goddamm it, Norman, with you the plague was a little glitch."

"It seems our cover story regarding Johnny Johansen is in jeopardy again."

"How, for chrissakes? Cojo told me Gans took the money!"

"He did. But it seems that while having dinner this evening his girlfriend—the petrified Tina—she let slip that Gans was on to a big story but had wisely abandoned it."

"So what's the glitch?"

"Their dinner companion was Benjamin Hall. He wanted to know why."

"Who's he?"

"Gans's mentor. A *Times* staff writer."

"Oh, shit . . ."

"Exactly. He cajoled Cojo's bribery attempt out of Tina, and I got a call two hours ago."

"What's he want?"

"The real Johansen story, obviously."

"I know that, goddamnit. What'll he take?"

"He's not Gans. He's a seasoned reporter. I don't think he'll take a bribe."

"Then stall him. Tell him we need a couple of days to complete our own investigation . . . Tell him there's much more to the story . . . Promise him an exclusive . . . Anything. But I've got to give Nick a little time to get us off the hook."

"All right, Sam, I'll do my best."

"I pay you for better than your best."

He slammed down the phone, followed by his cognac.

CHAPTER THIRTY-ONE

BENJAMIN HALL WAITED patiently in La Costa's bar and sipped his third ginger ale. Hall didn't drink but he was a chain smoker, and there was always a cigarette dangling from the side of his mouth.

Following his very intriguing dinner with Peter Gans and Tina, he'd smelled a big story and had immediately driven down from Los Angeles. Tina had been petrified of the two thugs who had said they represented Johnny Johansen. She was still petrified when he'd persuaded her to tell the story, over the objections of her boyfriend.

Peter Gans had remained silent through her entire description of the event—probably because if he was ever confronted he could swear that *he'd* never said a word about the bribe. He could ask for a lie-detector test and pass it.

Tina had said they'd been violently jerked out of their blocked car in the parking lot, and then one of the thugs had threatened to smash

Peter's hands in the car door if he didn't accept the bribe and keep his mouth shut.

Her hands were shaking when she told him the story. So were Peter's. He couldn't blame them. He assured them that it was a fascinating story but that he would do nothing.

That, of course, was a lie.

Hall felt he could thwart any attack on Peter if he could ferret out and print the real story because of the high-profile players involved. What he wanted was a simple confirmation of what Gans had said about his encounter with Johansen—that his face was injured and that he was very nervous about what had happened to him.

Based on Tina's description of the thugs, they weren't representing Johnny Johansen; they were representing Sam Altman. Cojo Kulakowsky and Jake Siegel were well known in Hollywood as Sam's security chief and his chauffeur. They'd been with him for years.

If Sam had gone so far as to threaten and bribe the kid, there had to be one helluva story behind it. And if he wrote the story in the *Times* with his Benjamin Hall byline, Sam wouldn't dare take action against Peter Gans.

Hall was shaken out of his reverie by a tap on the shoulder. It was the concierge. After finding that Johansen wasn't in his room, he'd taken a chance that the concierge might have spoken with the young star. He had—and, after accepting a twenty-dollar gratuity, he informed Hall that he'd gotten Johnny tickets to a rock concert at the Del Mar Fairgrounds. Hall said he'd be in the bar and to please inform him when Johnny returned.

He had.

Johnny and his girlfriend had just come in and were sitting on the outer patio having a nightcap. Hall thanked the concierge and walked outside. There were a few couples scattered about the softly lit patio and Hall spotted the couple at the far end, isolated from the other guests. He walked up to them, noted the exceptional physical attributes of the blonde, and saw the swelling and discoloration on Johnny's face.

He extended his card.

"Benjamin Hall, *Los Angeles Times.* I'm a great admirer . . . And the lady is?"

Johnny was surprised by the sudden intrusion but automatically took the card. The man was middle-aged and well dressed in a shirt, coat, and tie, and there was a cigarette dangling out of the corner of his mouth. But what Johnny was staring at was his completely bald head. It was almost shining, for chrissakes!

He seemed to be struggling with an answer when Chrissie leaned forward and proudly jumped in.

"I'm Chrissie Christian—Johnny's girlfriend. You really write for the *Los Angeles Times?*"

"Yes . . ." He smiled, turned back to Johnny, and spoke with apparent concern. "A colleague of mine saw you yesterday and said you'd had a motorcycle accident."

Johnny recovered from the shock of yet another intrusive reporter and gave Chrissie an admonishing look that was unmistakably meant to shut her up.

He looked back at Hall.

"I—uh, yes."

Hall hadn't missed Johnny's visual warning to Chrissie nor his sudden anxiety. He feigned an even deeper concern.

"That's terrible. Will it keep you from shooting?"

"For a while. Yes."

"I'm sorry . . . What happened?"

"I had a motorcycle accident."

"Oh, my . . . Where was it?"

Johnny suddenly got up and snapped his fingers as if he'd just remembered something. He grabbed Chrissie's hand and pulled her up with him—his response pouring out in a single rapid sentence.

"On the set—well it was nice meeting you—we're late—I'll look for your name—have a nice night."

Hall watched Johnny tow his girlfriend away without giving her a chance to say good-bye. He smiled. No question about it. There was a story here.

CHAPTER THIRTY-TWO

ALLIE WATCHED A tall brunette with bubble tits slither around a pole to the Jackson Five's "I'll Be There." He had ingratiated himself to two wiseguys from Chicago and was casually chatting them up. The booming disco and a raucous crowd were making his conversation with Skeets Travalino and Leo Carlin difficult even though patrons were packed shoulder to shoulder at ringside tables. Above them, on Maxi's narrow stage, a kaleidoscope of multicolored lights was raking the gyrating dancer's formidable figure.

Allie leaned to his right, placed a cupped hand over his mouth, and raised his voice above the din.

"That broad should be on that TV show shootin' here."

Skeets laughed and mirrored Allie's cupped hand without taking his eyes off the dancer.

"You got that right—a solid ten."

Allie dropped his hand but leaned in closer. They were head to head, but their eyes never left the dancer.

"You watch that show?"

"Nah, but Leo does. He likes the Doris Day–type secretary. Lori somethin'. The guy's a pervert."

"Yeah . . ." Allie nodded. "But some guys'd like to jump that look . . . Leo been bird-doggin' her?"

"Nah—he's just a lookie-loo."

"How about any of our other friends? You hear anything about any of them sniffing around the show for some action?"

"Nah . . . Who needs hard ta get—" he indicated the dancer— "with all the ready-and-willin' waitin' to be had?"

Allie was about to ask Skeets if he'd heard about any action *other* than broads when Bubble Tits ended her routine. The next girl slinked onstage bathed in blue lights and started moving languorously to "Blue Moon." She began her act fully clothed, and bored patrons looked around for waitresses. They could give a shit less for preliminary artistry—they only got interested when the tits came out.

Skeets was such a customer.

He was straining his neck looking for a waitress when he noticed a passing trio, raised his arm, and called out.

"Hey Carlo! Buy you guys a drink?"

Carlo Strozzi, with Fats and Angie in tow, smiled and walked over. Allie suppressed a lucky-break grin. He did a quick study of the man he'd been asked to bait regarding *The $trip* and hoped for a second lucky break that would let him broach the subject.

Strozzi looked at Allie, trying to place him, while he shook Skeets's hand.

"Thanks, pal. We're just leavin'."

Skeets indicated Allie.

"You know Allie from Kansas City?"

Strozzi studied Allie a few seconds in the dim light and then snapped his fingers.

"The Trop, right? Yeah, I seen you around."

Allie extended his hand and Strozzi took it.

"Right. We ran into each other at Joe Agosto's birthday party."

"Joe—right. So . . . How's business in KC?"

Allie again suppressed a grin. He'd caught his second lucky break.

"A little here, a little there. Lately I been throwin' a few bucks at show business."

Strozzi was impressed. In a very different way he figured he was also involved in show business. He nodded appreciatively.

"No shit? What shows?"

"At the moment *Seven-Eleven*—shootin' out of the Trop."

"Yeah, I heard about that one. You get to meet a lotta those movie broads?"

"Sure—the movie broads, even the TV broads. *The $trip*'s in town."

Strozzi glanced at Fats at the mention of *The $trip*, but Fats gave away nothing. Angie was silent as usual, but Strozzi thought he saw his harelip twitch.

He looked back at Allie and smiled.

"Yeah, I heard about that one."

Allie recognized a flicker of interest in Strozzi's voice. Now that *The $trip* had entered the banter—if Strozzi was trying to rip them off and wanted to blow a Chicago horn at a Kansas City Jericho—this was his chance.

Allie blithely attempted to set the bait.

"Those Hollywood types—you know, the producers, directors, stars, everybody—*Seven-Eleven, The $trip*—they all hang out together. I know a lot of 'em."

"Must be a real kick in the ass."

"It's a blast . . . Like to meet some of 'em?"

For a brief second Strozzi was tempted. It might be interesting to mix socially with the very people he was ripping off illegally.

"Me? Nah—I get all the action I need."

Allie smiled and took a final shot.

"So I take it business is good . . ."

"Yeah . . . But it's same ole, same ole. Sometimes I think the rackets are gettin' boring."

"Yeah . . ." Allie nodded. "Other than my thing with show business, there's been nothin' exciting in years."

"Ain't it the truth . . ."

Strozzi shook Allie's hand, said good-bye to all, and left with Fats and Angie in tow.

Allie returned his attention to the stage. He was sure Strozzi wasn't involved in a scam. Strozzi hadn't taken the bait and he'd given him every opportunity. Nonetheless, he figured he'd hang around a while longer to see whether he'd learn anything more.

"Blue Moon" had segued into "St. Louis Blues," and clothes began flying.

CHAPTER THIRTY-THREE

THE NIGHT WATCHMAN heard the freight train's whistle and checked his watch. Eleven forty-five. Right on time. The tracks were fifty feet behind the large warehouse that contained *The $trip*'s permanent sets, and their flimsy walls shook as the train rumbled by. Whenever the show was filming, irritated directors were forced to call "Cut!" and impatiently wait for it to pass.

Irritating and expensive, but unavoidable.

The watchman filled the metal cap of a large thermos with coffee and resumed reading the *Las Vegas Sun* at his small desk. It took four minutes for the train to pass before the building returned to complete silence—and then he heard what sounded like scuffling. It seemed to be coming from the loading dock behind the warehouse.

Probably a stray dog. But he rose to check it out.

He mentally chastised himself for being jumpy since the arson blaze four nights earlier, but he put down his coffee and picked up his flashlight.

Andy Anders was a retired Boston fireman who had moved west because he was sick of snow. That was ten years ago. Now at age sixty he was basically a rent-a-cop—but a conscientious one.

Walking out the back door, he carefully let his flashlight quiz the loading dock from stem to stern, but it revealed nothing. Satisfied, he locked the door, slid the dead bolt home, and returned to his desk on the opposite side of the warehouse.

A solitary figure hidden behind a forklift had watched Andy disappear into the building. He was dressed in black and his face was masked by indigo grease paint. He'd depended on the train to cover his attempted break-in but had discovered that a second lock had been installed after the fire—a dead bolt.

He only had the key to the original lock. The dead bolt had to be sawed through with a thin hacksaw blade inserted between the door and the frame. He'd been within a millimeter of success when the train's last car had passed behind him. He'd heard Andy coming— apparently reacting to the sound of the hacksaw blade—and dashed behind the forklift.

Picking up a five-gallon jerry can filled with gasoline, he returned to the door. It took only two very quiet strokes with the hacksaw blade to finally cut through the dead bolt. He then removed a key from his pocket, carefully opened the door, and entered. Twenty feet in, he opened the jerry can and started walking backward toward the door, spilling the contents as he went. When he arrived at the door, he opened it, lit a match, and threw it into the fuel.

On the other side of the building Andy heard a whoosh, saw the flickering light of flames against the ceiling, and leapt out of his chair.

"Oh, shit!" He ripped the fire extinguisher off the wall behind the desk, pulled the alarm, and charged toward the blaze.

The fire had already ignited the walls of Hank's PI office set and was crawling up toward the building's exposed rafters. Andy knew if it reached them, the building was toast. He scrambled up a tall ladder the gaffers used to trim the ten-K's and attacked the blaze from above.

His small extinguisher was no match for the gasoline-fed inferno, and it soon expired. Andy scrambled back down the ladder as flames scorched his trousers. He screamed when the flames touched his calf, misstepped, and crashed to the floor. Stunned, he crawled away choking on the smoke. The set's flimsy side wall toppled over in an explosion of sparks and showered his face with burning embers. Somehow he made it to his feet, ran out the front entrance, and collapsed as he heard the wail of sirens.

CHAPTER THIRTY-FOUR

NICK AND MITCH heard the same sirens from a half mile away. They'd finally finished the night shooting in Red Rock Canyon and were heading back into town. Lang, their director, had gotten behind, and they'd been forced to shoot until midnight to finish the day's work.

Mitch pointed at a glow in the eastern sky and frowned. The glow was in a direct line between them and the Sahara—and they both knew it was the approximate location of their warehouse.

"It looks like it's on Industrial Road."

Nick's car phone buzzed. It was Julie from his office. Since they were working late, she was still holding the fort.

"Nick—it's our warehouse again! I just got a call from the fire department. They got the alarm and they're on the way!"

Nick mashed the Firebird's accelerator, roared around a pickup with his horn blaring, and yelled into the phone.

"Stay put. I'm two minutes away!"

The fire trucks had arrived and a dozen men were frantically unloading hoses and running them to nearby hydrants when Nick and Mitch skidded up to the front of the building. They saw that the front of the warehouse was uninvolved, but flames were licking the night sky behind it.

Two paramedics were carrying a body on a stretcher toward a van and Nick rushed over to intercept them. Andy was the casualty. His face was black with soot and it was apparent there were burns on his right cheek. The paramedics set down the stretcher to open the van's rear doors and Nick knelt next to Andy.

"Andy . . . What happened?"

"G-gasoline . . ."Andy was sputtering. "Somebody with gasoline . . . I tried . . . I couldn't stop it."

"Okay, Andy, I got it. You just relax and let these guys take care of you."

Andy reached out and gripped Nick's arm. There were tears in his eyes and he choked up.

"I'm s-sorry, Nick . . . I really tried to . . ."

"I know you did everything you could, Andy." Nick patted his shoulder. "Don't give it another thought . . ."

"My wife . . . She'll be . . ."

"I'll call her—tell her you'll be fine and see that she gets to the hospital."

"Th-thanks Nick . . ."

The paramedics loaded Andy into the back of the van. When the doors were closed Nick grabbed one by the arm.

"I'm Nick Conti and this is my warehouse. Get him the best. I'll take care of everything. Desert Springs Hospital?"

"Yessir."

Nick ran back to his car, picked up his phone, and called Julie.

"The night watchman—Andy Anders—is on his way to Desert Springs. Call his wife, tell her he'll be fine, and make sure she can get there. Then call the security company and have them send another man out here to cover the building after the fire department leaves."

Nick hung up, ran over a maze of hoses, and joined Mitch behind the building. He immediately saw that the firemen might be able to save the front of the thirty-thousand-square-foot warehouse, but he knew the rear, which was the location of their primary set, was history. Mitch had come to the same conclusion and was infuriated.

"That son of a bitch!"

Nick had made up his mind about what he was going to do the moment he'd seen the warehouse again in flames. He nodded slowly.

"Yeah . . ."

"But why? He said he'd give us two days!"

"Let's ask him?"

They reentered Nick's car and he released a hidden compartment under the glove box. A nine-millimeter Beretta slid out and he handed it to Mitch.

Mitch smiled, stuck it in his waistband, and they headed downtown.

CHAPTER THIRTY-FIVE

NICK DROVE DOWN Fremont Street, passed Poolorama, and turned right on North Third. He then took another right into the alley behind the buildings and parked next to the fourth building from the end—Poolorama. He'd noted the location when they passed in front of it on Fremont.

There were two doors in back of the building. One had a Dumpster next to it and was obviously the bar's rear door. Mitch pointed to a second door with a small window next to it.

"The office?"

"Probably."

They left the car and Nick took a quick peek through grimy glass.

"Carlo's at the desk. I don't see Fats and Angie."

Mitch indicated the door, smiled evilly, and looked to Nick for confirmation.

"Shall we?"

"By all means."

Mitch raised his foot and lashed out at the knob with a pulverizing martial arts kick. The frame shattered and the door flew into the room. Nick followed it in, pulled the dumbfounded Strozzi out of his chair, and pinned him to the wall.

Before he could cry out, Nick slapped a hand over his mouth.

"Where're the flunkies, Carlo?"

Strozzi's terrified eyes darted toward the door leading to the bar and pool room. Nick signaled Mitch with his head.

He went to the door and opened it a crack.

"They're shooting pool."

Mitch closed the door, locked it, and took out the Beretta. He walked up beside Strozzi and jammed the snout in his ear.

"Now, you wouldn't be thinking of calling out to the tons-of-fun twins when Nick takes his hand away, would you?"

Strozzi frantically shook his head and Nick uncovered his mouth. He tightened his grip on Strozzi's jacket and increased the pressure against the wall.

"Why?"

Carlo's face scrunched in confusion. He clearly had no idea what Nick was talking about.

"Why . . . ?"

Nick pulled him onto his toes.

"The fire tonight, asshole! Why'd you do it?"

"Th-the fire tonight?" His eyes danced between Nick and Mitch. "What fire?"

Nick slapped his face—twice—backhand and forehand.

"Talk, you prick!"

"Wait! Hold it! I'm tellin' ya! I don't know nothin' about no fire!"

Carlo was so shaken that Nick was tempted to believe him. Tempted but not convinced.

"Are you telling me you didn't torch my warehouse tonight?"

"Yes! I mean, no, I didn't—I don't know what you're talkin' about! I didn't torch nothin'!"

"Who did?"

"Who did? I got no idea who did! Why the hell would I? We made a deal. I want the cash—I got no reason to set another fire."

Nick thought about it. It made sense. Strozzi would have no interest in screwing up what he saw as easy cash in a slam-dunk deal.

He looked at Mitch, who shrugged.

Nick took a breath and looked back at Strozzi.

"Who did it the first time?"

"A guy I brought in from Chicago." It was a lie but he had no intention of revealing his inside man. "I sent 'im back when we made our deal."

Nick was sure it was bullshit and that the arsonist, as well as the tire slasher, brake saboteur, and whoever called in the bomb threat, was a member of his crew. But he knew Dan Dietrich would come up with that rat. For the moment he was more concerned about the second arsonist whom Strozzi apparently knew nothing about.

"Okay, Carlo, but if I find out you're bullshitting me, I'll be back. And it won't be with the money."

Nick wheeled around and stalked through the vacant doorway, followed by Mitch. The moment they disappeared, Strozzi lunged for the interior door and opened it—his brain reeling.

"Fats—Angie . . ." He was screaming. "Get in here!"

The two hulks rushed in and Fats looked at the shattered door, wide-eyed.

"W-what happened to the door?"

"Forget the fucking door and get the car. That stupid sonofabitch torched Conti's warehouse again! We gotta find out why!"

CHAPTER THIRTY-SIX

NICK AND MITCH drove back to the warehouse lis
tening to reports of the fire on local radio that revealed there
were also TV reporters on the scene. It was a big fire, and *The
$trip* was a big deal.

They realized they'd have to rewrite all the scenes that were to take
place in the set that was Hank's PI office. It had been destroyed and
the scenes that had been written for it would have to be put in other
locations. That meant they'd have to find excuses for Lori Donner,
Hank's on-screen office secretary, to be with him in scenes where she
would otherwise be out of place. Either that or they would have to
write out the very popular female costar.

This was not an option. They were already forced to maximize their
other costar's screen time until Johansen's face healed.

Mitch knew Lori had been seeing a variety of men, including Nick,
since they'd started shooting, but he hadn't seen Nick with her for a
while.

"You still seeing her?"

"Lori . . . ? Off and on."

"I hear she's quite a player."

"Verily . . . Why? You interested?"

Mitch held up his hands and laughed.

"Not if I have to compete with the legendary Conti."

Nick chuckled and gave Mitch a playful backhand on the arm.

"Not a problem Tanaka-san . . . If you'd like to make a pass, by all means go for it. I'm sure she'll enjoy it."

Mitch steepled his fingers in front of his lips and bowed his head.

"*Arigato*, Conti-san."

They arrived at the warehouse and saw that the fire had been extinguished. The front half of the building had been saved but the damage to the rear was extensive. They were told an arson investigator was already on the scene, and they walked behind the building to talk to him.

Nick hadn't reported the first fire since it was small, put out quickly, and was only meant as intimidation in attempted extortion. At the time Nick didn't feel the need for—or want—a hassle.

But there was no way to cover up this blaze. They'd have to deal with an investigation and hope the real reason behind the arson didn't come out.

Nick saw a stocky man wearing coveralls poking around the charred area. He walked up to him and extended his hand.

"Nick Conti—executive producer, and Mitch Tanaka, our line producer."

"Gene Naspo . . ." The man took Nick's hand and shook it. "Clark County Arson."

Nick waved his hand at the charred area.

"You find anything?"

"Definitely arson . . . The first firemen on the scene reported yellow-and-white flames with black smoke—gasoline. They could smell it, too."

"My night watchman said it was started inside the building."

"It was . . ." Naspo led them to the charred loading-dock door, which he'd leaned against a forklift. "Whoever set it off came through this door. The dead bolt's been sawn through but the main lock is undamaged. Unless you leave this door unlocked, the perp must have had a key."

"Someone on our crew . . ."

"If they're the only ones with keys—yes."

"We'll start looking at it from our end. If we come up with anything, we'll let you know what we find."

CHAPTER THIRTY-SEVEN

NICK AND MITCH returned to the Desert Inn and went straight to the production offices in the basement. The complex contained a dozen offices off a large central area with desks for secretaries and assistants. Julie was the only person remaining, since the rest of the staff had wrapped for the night.

Julie Zimmerman was a middle-aged mother happily married to a baccarat croupier in the DI's casino. She'd been secretary to Paramount's production chief in Los Angeles and had jumped at the chance to be with her husband in Vegas.

When Nick hired her, she got her husband and Nick got a jewel. A win-win.

When the two men entered she shot up from behind her desk.

"How bad?"

Mitch followed Nick toward his office and answered without stopping.

"Bad . . . Arson again—and someone on the crew again."

Julie followed them into the simple but cozy office—one couch, end tables with lamps, two captain's chairs, and a coffee table. There was a small built-in bar and framed photos of *The $trip*'s cast on the walls, but no windows since they were below ground level.

Julie frowned at Mitch's answer.

"Will we have to shut down?"

"Not yet—but soon. We've still got a few days' work without Johnny."

Nick sat at his desk and lit a cigarette.

"Get me Dan Dietrich, Julie—at home in L.A."

Julie disappeared into her office. Mitch sat down on the couch and started thinking out loud.

"Strozzi says it wasn't him and I believe the prick. But then who? And who's *he* working for?"

"I've got no idea. We can rebuild the warehouse, rewrite Lori's scenes, and shoot around Johnny. But our main problem's still Strozzi and the extortion threat. If we don't solve that and keep it quiet, all the rest is academic."

Julie came back into the office and pointed at the phone.

"Dan's on one."

Nick picked it up.

"Wake you?"

"Are you kidding? Half my action is after midnight."

"We had another torch job on the warehouse tonight."

"Holy shit! Bad?"

"Bad."

"Christ . . . But we got through background checks on about half your crew today. So far nothing."

"Keep going, Dan, but I don't think the same perp who did the brakes on the picture car did the fire tonight."

Nick told him why, and also that it wasn't the reason he'd called. He wanted Strozzi's office wiretapped. Tonight if possible.

Dan said he'd lease a plane and be in Vegas in three hours. Nick gave him the address of Poolorama and hung up the phone. Mitch got up and stretched.

"Anything else we can do tonight?"

"No . . . Let's log some sack time. I've a feeling we're going to need it."

Nick told Julie to lock up, said good night, and left. He walked past the pool toward the Wimbledon and caught a whiff of freshly cut grass from the golf course. Clear skies with the temperature in the high sixties and zero humidity should have made an idyllic desert night— were it not for the past forty-eight hours. And at this point he was no closer to solving his problem.

He went straight to the built-in bar when he entered his suite and poured himself a Chivas. He drank deeply and checked for messages. There were over a dozen ranging from Bert Cohen, the president of the DI, to Hank Donovan to local vendors to crew department heads. It was after one o'clock so he figured he'd return them all in the morning and got into a steaming shower. Ten minutes later he was about to get into bed when the chimes sounded. He put on a hotel robe and answered the door.

Lori Donner was standing there with her arms folded and was wearing a robe identical to Nick's.

Lori, along with the rest of the major cast and guest stars, all had suites in the Wimbledon. Mitch—the lone exception—had elected a suite in the main tower. It was part of the production package Nick had negotiated with the Desert Inn. In return the DI had their hotel and casino featured in twenty-five million homes for one hour every week on the UTB network.

The production package was costly but the publicity was priceless.

"I heard about the fire." Lori looked adorable in the robe, but then Lori always looked adorable. It was the dimples.

Nick didn't step aside to let her into the suite. He just nodded.

"Yeah . . . It got our office set."

She frowned and was obviously very disturbed.

"I know. It was on the news . . . Almost all my scenes are in that set."

If Nick had thought that her late-night visit was carnally motivated, he quickly saw otherwise. First, last, and always, Lori was an ambitious actress, and although they might love sex, ambitious actresses counted lines and screen time—and that's what this was about.

"I know, Lori . . ." Having recognized the problem, Nick attempted to placate her. "I'll handle it. I'll rewrite them."

"You're sure?" It was a plea delivered with a pout.

"I'm sure."

"Even the ones for the show we're shooting right now?" The plea had turned persistent.

"Yes."

"Why are we having this conversation in the hallway, Nick?"

"It's late, Lori."

"I know it's late, Nick. I've been waiting up to see you—worried sick." She had gone from pout to persistence to vulnerability.

Seeing her standing there wide-eyed, full of innocence and concern, Nick couldn't help feeling like a shit even though he knew she was playing him. After all, she was his female costar, she was worried about her role, and he had been fucking her brains out.

"Sorry, Lori. Come on in. I'll buy you a nightcap."

Nick stepped aside, Lori entered, and he closed the door.

At the far end of the hall, a man had been angrily watching the exchange even though he couldn't hear it.

He saw Lori enter the suite, muttered a curse, and clenched his fists.

CHAPTER THIRTY-EIGHT

DAY THREE

SAM ALTMAN WAS normally an early riser. By six thirty he was taking his morning constitutional around the estate, by seven his masseuse was giving him a rubdown, by seven thirty he was in his shower, by eight he was dressed, and by eight thirty he was having coffee, a bagel, and his first cigar of the day.

The coffee was black, the bagel buttered, and the cigar Cuban. All three were enjoyed while reading *Variety* and the *Hollywood Reporter.*

But not so this morning.

The previous day had been a nightmare. The dinner party was a chore and Gwen a pain in the ass. And Manners's late news flash had created a migraine. After tossing and turning for an hour he'd taken a pair of sleeping pills and didn't wake up until nine fifteen. He never wanted to be in the office later than ten so he showered, dressed, and went directly to coffee, bagel, and cigar.

The kitchen intercom squawked at nine fifty and Gwen's voice grumbled, "Is he gone?"

She was obviously thinking Sam would have left by now and that she would be addressing Alfred.

"No, he's not gone," Sam shot back. "He was enjoying coffee and a bagel until a moment ago."

"With a cigar . . ."

"With a cigar."

"Sam, you know I can't stand the smell of cigars in the morning."

"So stay out of the kitchen. Have breakfast in bed. Or get creative and have Alfred spritz air freshener."

Gwen clicked off and Alfred arrived with *Variety* and the *Reporter.*

"Sir—I don't know if you've heard, but there was a fire in your Las Vegas warehouse last evening. It's been on the morning news."

Sam almost choked on his coffee.

"What?" He slammed down the cup. "For chrissakes what next . . . Get me Nick Conti!"

Alfred dialed the DI and waited while the hotel operator rang Nick's room.

Nick had just let Dan Dietrich into his suite when the phone rang. He was anxious to hear the private eye's report, so he decided to let the operator take a message and poured Dan a cup of room-service coffee.

As promised, Dan had flown in at four that morning and gone straight to Poolorama. He'd been in and out in an hour, grabbed a few hours' sleep, and was reporting to Nick before returning to L.A.

"Any problems?" Nick handed him the coffee.

"Piece a cake. They'd temporarily hung a plywood door in the smashed frame and I jimmied it back out. The racket from the pool hall could've drowned out D-Day. I planted bugs in the office and phone, reset the door, and was out."

"How do we get the product?"

"I taped the receiver behind a drainpipe in the alley. It's on the building next door—the unit's waist-high. The bugs are voice activated. You can pull the cassette and check it whenever you want. Bring spare tape to put it back." He handed Nick another cassette. "Replace the old cassette with this. The batteries should last a week."

"Thanks, Dan. What do I owe you for the plane and all?"

Dan chuckled and held up his hands.

"I'll add it to your consulting fee and you can send me a Christmas card." Dan headed for the door. "I'm outta here. We should have the rest of your background checks by this afternoon."

Dan left and Nick picked up the phone. He got Sam's message and called. When Sam answered he was growling.

"Another goddamn fire?"

"Last night. This one was serious."

"When the hell were you going to tell me that?"

"After I had my coffee . . . Too late last night and too early this morning. And neither one of us could do anything about it either time."

"I thought you told this guy you'd pay him off."

"I did. It wasn't the same guy."

"Tell me I'm not hearing this. There are two *different* guys after our ass?"

"I think so."

"What the hell are you doing about it?"

Nick told him.

Sam wasn't happy.

CHAPTER THIRTY-NINE

STROZZI AND ANGIE drank bad coffee that Fats had made by putting grounds into a pot of boiling water and then filtering it through a dish rag. They'd broken into the apartment and had been waiting for its occupant all night—but no one had found a coffee pot.

Strozzi was pissed, sleep deprived, and pacing. He threw his cup into the sink and it shattered.

"What kinda asshole buys coffee when he don't own a coffee pot?"

Fats was going through the refrigerator again even though he'd already consumed almost everything in it. He slammed the door.

"The same kind that's got nothin' in the pantry and next ta nothin' in the refrigerator. I'm starvin' over here. How long we gonna wait for him, boss?"

"Long as it takes! He's probably shacked up with some broad. He's gotta get back soon. The cops told me they worked till eleven last night, which means they start again in an hour."

All film crews used local police for security when filming on location. Strozzi had several on the payroll and knew not only when they'd wrapped the prior night but where they'd be shooting this morning.

Fats was so hungry he looked for any excuse that would get them out of there. He spread his hands.

"Suppose he goes straight to work?"

"Then we figure a way to pick him up there like we did with the kid. I know where they'll be. Meantime we wait."

That wasn't necessary. The front door opened and Hank Donovan's stunt double walked into the apartment. Snuffy was wearing jeans and a Stuntmen's Association T-shirt and looked enough like Hank to easily be mistaken for the star.

"What . . ." he muttered when he saw them. "What's going on?"

"That's what we'd like to know, Snuffy."

Snuffy warily moved into the room—his eyes darting between the three intruders.

"What're you talking about?"

"The fire you set at Conti's warehouse last night."

"What?" Snuffy was stunned. His eyes again darted between the three men and Strozzi stepped closer.

"You heard me. Who paid you this time?"

"Nobody! I tell you I don't know what you're talking about. I was nowhere near the place."

"You left us with an ounce of coke a little after ten. Where'd you go?"

"Sunset Arms. Brad Tilden's place." His voice pitched higher as he tried to convince them he wasn't lying. "With him and Lori Donner—two people from the show. We did some blow and I left."

"Then what?"

"I drove to Henderson and spent the night with a broad I know."

"Yeah? From what time?"

"I picked her up when she got off. Around midnight. She's a waitress."

"The fire was set around eleven. You could've done it and then picked her up."

"I'm telling you you're nuts! Why the hell would I do that? You paid me for the first one and the other stuff—not for whatever the hell happened last night."

"You're right. I paid you for the first one. What I wanna know is who paid you for last night?"

"Nobody, goddammit!"

"So you figured to go into business for yourself?"

"No!"

"You ain't respondin' to my questions." Carlo looked at Fats. "Fats— you ask 'im."

Angie grabbed Snuffy and Fats threw a vicious left hook into his kidneys. Snuffy's jaw dropped and his face twisted in agony. He was about to let out an ear-piercing scream when Angie stuffed a handker-chief into his mouth.

Their actions were choreographed and deceptively fast for big men. They'd executed the routine before. Strozzi stepped forward and got into the stuntman's face.

"Okay, Snuffy—let's play nice. You're the only one who could've done it. No one else knows nothin' about what we're into here. What I wanna know is who paid you and why?"

Angie removed the handkerchief and Snuffy gagged. He would have collapsed if Angie hadn't been holding him up.

"I-I d-didn't do . . ."

Strozzi nodded at Fats, who unleashed another kidney punch. But before Angie could gag him, Snuffy slumped and passed out. Strozzi spit in disgust.

"Get some water."

Angie let Snuffy drop to the floor and went into the kitchen. Fats lit a cigarette and threw a questioning look at Strozzi.

"You think he could be tellin' the truth?"

"How? Like I said, nobody else knows what we're doin' on this thing. It's gotta be him. What we gotta know is who's payin' him."

Angie returned with a pot of water and threw it into Snuffy's face. He sputtered awake and Angie sat him up. He then got behind the stuntman and hauled him up by his armpits. Strozzi again got into Snuffy's face.

"One more time. Who hired you?"

"N-nobody . . . I'm tell . . ."

Fats threw another kidney punch. It was the third. Snuffy passed out and Angie let him fall to the floor. Completely frustrated, Strozzi screamed at Fats.

"More water!"

Fats went to get it.

What none of the three assailants realized was that the vicious punches had damaged Snuffy's kidneys, and he had started to bleed internally.

CHAPTER FORTY

TWO DOZEN BIKINI-CLAD girls had been strategically placed around the crowded Tropicana pool by direction of Stavros Papadopoulos. It was the first shot on the first day of shooting *Seven-Eleven*. The day was sunny and the pool was heated, but the temperature was in the high sixties and the girls were chilly.

Seven-Eleven was the story of the world's premier female gambler—played by Erin Conroy. The pool scene called for her to be lounging on a chaise wearing a bikini and sipping a Bloody Mary.

The girls were exquisite—many of them being showgirls from *Les Folies Bergere*—but Erin's body rivaled their best, and none matched the magic of her face.

The camera, with Stavros glued to its eyepiece, was mounted on the boom of a huge crane positioned at the far end of the pool.

Three voices boomed out in rapid succession. The first was the soundman; the second, the cameraman; the third, the assistant director.

"Speed!"

"Camera!"

"Background!"

Suddenly the pool erupted with activity. Swimmers splashed about, water-polo balls sailed through the air, a diver with an Adonis body began moving to the end of the high board, and laughter punctuated by shrieks filled the air.

Stavros's voice roared over the din.

"Action!"

The diver sailed off the board in a perfect swan dive. The camera followed him, and then the boom lowered and began moving across the pool toward a close-up of Erin until her face completely filled the frame.

Stavros rose up from his seat and raised his hand.

"Cut!" He then called out to the assistant director and added, "One more!"

"Reset! Number one!" was the instant response.

During the next hour they repeated the action eight times before Stavros was satisfied he had exactly what he wanted for a mere ten seconds of film.

While the camera and lighting were set for the next shot, Stavros waited in his surprisingly extravagant motor home parked behind the hotel. Five minutes later he answered a knock on his door and grinned at his visitor.

"Allie . . . come in!"

"I watched the first shot. Impressive."

"Thank you . . . and for the tip on Danny Boy. I had a thousand on his nose."

"No problem. Glad to be helpful."

"Have a seat. Drink?"

"I'm good."

Allie sat and crossed his legs. Stavros knew why Allie had come to see him and opened a can of cranberry juice while he answered the unasked question.

"I talked to a few folks who knew Erin in the early days."

"Ah . . ." Allie sounded pleased. "What'd you find?"

"That she and Conti were more than a wham-bam-thank-you-ma'am. They were together, off and on, over three years."

"They lived together?"

"Not that formal. In New York she had a place, he had a place. Maybe they wanted to avoid a scandal. She comes from a good family. Her old man was a professor at NYU. She was a student there—from what I've been told, an honors type."

"What's that got to do with Conti?"

"Nothing—like I said, she was a model when he met her and gave her her first part. She was good and he gave her another in the same role. Then he made her character recurring."

"Nice way to worm your way into a chick's pants."

"True, but from all I've heard Conti's a pro. If she were no good he'd have lost her."

"But he didn't."

"No. They started seeing each other on the sly. And I'm told they were very discreet."

"Why? He was married?"

Stavros shook his head.

"Confirmed bachelor."

The notion was completely foreign to Allie, and he frowned.

"I would've thought they'd enjoy the publicity."

Stavros shrugged, waving away the thought as irrelevant.

"To each his own, et cetera . . . But they were in love, and even though a few people suspected an affair, they hid it for a long time. She'd stay at his place, he at hers, but they never showed up together in the morning. It was working out beautifully and would have continued if she weren't the jealous type."

"Erin?" Allie was shocked. From what he knew of her it was inconceivable.

"Erin . . . She got tired of all the wannabe actresses on the set constantly throwing themselves at Nick. He was reluctant to tell them to knock it off because he had a rep and thought he was protecting his relationship with Erin."

"Probably afraid of coming off a fag." Allie was happy with the concept of an insecure Conti.

"Conti? Couldn't happen. Anyway, at first there were just a few minor scenes, until one day there was a major blowup with a guest star. Conti, being a consummate pro, sided with the nonplussed guest star and ordered Erin off the set."

"I can't believe she'd take that shit."

"She didn't. She quit—but she had a contract. Conti forced her back—she apologized and they got back together. This time in the open. Everyone figured they might even get married."

"Why didn't they?"

"According to my source, part Nick, part her. Nick's always been kind of a mystery type. He'd always avoided relationships of any kind until Erin. And suddenly she was being talked about as the next break-out star. But the kicker was Erin couldn't control her jealous outbursts. Now that she and Nick weren't hiding the affair, she not only blew up on the set but when they attended non–show business functions. Charity dinners, publicity gigs, cocktail parties and the like. That did it. Nick called it off."

"That's it?" Allie still couldn't quite believe the picture Stavros had painted of Erin.

"That's it."

"Until now . . ." Allie face clouded. She'd been lying to him.

"Look—Al, I don't know what you're into with his girl, but I know her. I spent eight months with her makin' *Granuaile*. All she cares about is her career. She's a star. I can't see how she could give a shit about some goddamn TV producer."

"Maybe. I hope you're right, Stavros. I don't like guys sniffin' around in my backyard."

A second assistant director knocked on the door. A few seconds later he opened it and stuck his head in.

"Ready, boss."

Allie got up and stuck out his hand.

"Thanks."

Stavros got up and took it.

"Any time, Al."

CHAPTER FORTY-ONE

FATS THREW ANOTHER pot of water into Snuffy's face and frantically slapped it. They'd been working on him for twenty minutes and hadn't even gotten a moan. Worse, the stunt man's face was ashen and his skin was feeling clammy.

Fats was getting panicky.

"Christ—what's wrong with 'im?"

Strozzi waved his arms and kept pacing like a caged animal.

"How the fuck should I know . . . You're the one who hit 'im."

"You told me to!"

"I didn't say put 'im in a fucking coma."

"The guy's a stunt man. You'd think he could take a punch."

"Three punches—in the kidneys."

Angie watched the exchange from the sofa, where he was eating a bag of Doritos he'd found in a drawer. They were making annoying crunching sounds as he chewed. Strozzi ripped the bag out of his hands.

"Will you stop with the goddamn chomping? I can't hear myself think."

Chastised, Angie stopped chewing and pouted—which looked doubly ridiculous because of his harelip. He shrugged and spread his hands apologetically.

The phone rang and Strozzi stared at it through three rings before he announced the obvious.

"He didn't show up for work. They're probably tryin' to find 'im." He turned to Angie. "Pick 'im up."

Angie reached down to pick up Snuffy but the order didn't make sense to Fats.

"Why?"

"We're takin' 'im with us. They'll come here lookin' for him, and we still gotta find out who he's workin' for."

"Where we gonna take 'im?"

"The office. Sooner or later he's gotta wake up." He threw a dirty look at Fats. "And hopefully we'll get the answers we want without you puttin' him in another fuckin' coma."

The phone stopped ringing as they carried the unconscious stuntman to their car. Angie threw him in the backseat and Strozzi suddenly had another thought. He rushed back into the apartment and took the phone off the hook. He figured that whoever was calling would think Snuffy had returned home and was on the line.

A few minutes later Mitch again dialed Snuffy's number.

His face registered surprise as he listened to the busy signal. It was the second time he'd dialed Snuffy's apartment—first getting no answer, and now getting a busy signal. He thought it might be Snuffy calling in to say he'd gotten hung up somewhere, so he called the office.

Julie said she hadn't heard from him.

Mitch was calling from the empty lot next to the Hacienda, where they'd been the prior day. He was with a ten-man second unit and two stunt drivers. The car-chase sequence hadn't been completed and the small second unit was getting the shots needed to finish it. The first unit—with Hank, the cast, and Rodney Lang, the director—was filming downtown at the courthouse.

When Mitch hung up with Julie he saw Nick pulling the Firebird into the lot and walked toward him. There was a look of confusion on Nick's face when he got out of the car and noticed the lack of activity. The crew and drivers were lounging around the Corvette, drinking coffee.

Nick had driven directly to the second unit after hanging up with Sam. His plan was to check in with both units before returning to his office to rewrite Lori's scenes with Hank in whatever new locations he could come up with.

Mitch walked up and greeted him, and Nick indicated the idle crew.

"What's the problem?"

"Snuffy . . . Have you heard from him?"

"No, why?"

"Julie hasn't heard from him either. He didn't show up this morning. I called his apartment and got no answer—called again and got a busy signal. I just sent one of the guys over there."

Snuffy was not only Hank's stunt double, he was also the stunt co-coordinator and as such was the second-unit director. Without him they couldn't get the shots they needed and would fall further behind. Nick shook his head.

"Christ—for the past few days it feels like someone's put a curse on this show."

"Any black cats crossed your path?"

Nick again shook his head. But he *had* recently crossed paths with Erin and Lori.

"No felines—just women."

"I don't like it, Nick. It's not like Snuffy. If he had a problem he would've called in."

Nick thought about it a few seconds, looked off into the middle distance and then back at Mitch.

"You think it's got something to do with Strozzi?"

Mitch ticked off the points with his fingers. "He wants us shut down. We're scrambling to create work without Johnny. Suddenly Snuffy disappears. Taking him out of the picture sure as hell could make us come up snake eyes a lot faster."

Nick nodded. "It's possible. Hold the thought and hope you're being paranoid." He got into the Firebird. "In the meantime keep trying to track him down. I'm headed downtown to check in with Lang. Call me on the car phone if you hear anything."

CHAPTER FORTY-TWO

SAM'S OFFICE HAD taken on the look of a film set, with lights, camera, and a boom mike hovering over his massive desk. At the conference table across the room, makeup and hair artists, along with assistants and PR people, were waiting to be summoned.

A crew from *Entertainment Weekly* was about to interview Sam for another puff piece arranged by the ever-resourceful Norman Manners. Sam demanded at least one on-screen interview per month, and Norman had to figure out a way to provide it.

That was his job, and failure meant *fini*.

In addition to TV exposure, Manners was required to set up a constant string of print and radio interviews with domestic as well as foreign outlets. Actually, it wasn't really that tough. There were always stories generated by eight hit television series. And in addition to new projects, there was Sam's very active social calendar.

The inescapable fact was, Sam loved to see his face on screen and his name in print. In spite of his phenomenal success, without adulation and publicity he would have shriveled up like dried fruit.

Demi Diamond, a leggy blonde with cascading hair and a gorgeous face, was off camera at the moment, and Sam was seated behind his massive desk. He was wearing his signature suede track suit—this one a chocolate brown—and carefully puffing on one of his smuggled Cuban cigars. Puffing, not inhaling. Whenever he was in public he made a determined effort not to inhale and erupt into an embarrassing coughing fit.

Demi checked her notes and began the interview in a voice that literally cooed.

"Mr. Altman . . . Those who know you best say the secret of your success is casting. Is that true?"

Sam removed the cigar from his mouth and regarded it as if he were contemplating an answer before looking back at Demi. He wasn't. He had a stock answer for all the obvious questions he'd been asked for years.

"Casting may very well be one of my strong suits, and the stars are certainly the face of any TV show, but at the end of the day TV is about stories—short stories."

Demi countered with a twinkle in her voice. "So then—is that your *real* secret? Short storytelling?"

Sam smiled.

"Let's just say that my heroes have always been the masters of the art form—Poe, Hawthorne, and Hemingway being my personal artistic muses."

And so it went, with Sam charming Demi and Demi trying to impress Sam with her list of questions—which he knew had been made by her producer.

Rachel looked on as always with an adoring smile etched on her face in spite of the fact that she'd heard the obvious questions and stock answers a hundred times.

The interview ended after an hour and Sam flattered Demi and the film crew for their consummate expertise—hinting that he might elevate them to prime-time careers in the near future. This, of course, was his standard line of bullshit. But it worked: a reminder to everyone that Sam cared about the little people.

When it was finally over, Norman Manners took him aside.

"I just got off the phone with Benjamin Hall."

Sam impatiently rotated his hand, asking for more. "And . . . ?"

"I told him if he'd give us a couple of days before he pursued the story we'd give him an exclusive. He said we could have one day or he'd be on his way to Vegas with a very good PI."

"Shit!"

"Unless . . ."

Sam grasped at the straw. "What? Unless what?"

"He wants to see your house."

Sam exploded. "What?"

Norman, as well as everyone in town, knew that Hilltop was the fiercely guarded domain of Sam's wife. Gwendolyn Altman was a demon when Sam wanted to use their home for purely business reasons. She had never allowed photos of the mansion's interior, and getting into Hilltop was considered a coup. No one beyond the Altmans' inner circle had ever seen its hallowed halls. Close friends who were *in* the business were fine, but not wannabes, hangers-on, and all those Gwen considered below her self-crafted social station.

A newspaper reporter would certainly be barred.

Manners ignored Sam's exclamation and continued.

"And he wants to bring his wife and two kids."

"Are you nuts? Gwen'll go batshit!"

"Don't shoot the messenger. I'm only relaying his terms."

"It's impossible."

"You'd rather have him break the story—whatever the real story is—than face down your wife?"

"Don't get smart with me, Norman. Getting into Hilltop is something she knows everyone in this town wants, and she can deny to them. She knows what they say behind her back about her past and marrying me. She's getting even, and I can't say I blame her."

Manners held up his hands in surrender.

"Okay, Sam. It's your decision."

"It's not my decision, it's her decision!"

"Fine. But if you change your mind about talking to her by tomorrow, let me know."

Manners left and Sam, completely frustrated by the potentially disastrous turn of events, screamed at Rachel.

"Get me Nick Conti!"

CHAPTER FORTY-THREE

ALLIE STROLLED INTO the Desert Inn casino and let a practiced eye roam over the afternoon action. Several black-jack tables were going; players surrounded one roulette and one craps table. About half the slots were manned but the baccarat table was closed.

Not bad. He stopped a scantily clad waitress in net stockings and spikes carrying a tray of drinks.

"Where can I find *The $trip*'s offices?"

The waitress eyed the elegantly dressed man and immediately took him for a high roller. High rollers usually tipped lavishly and at every opportunity. Win or lose, they had a reputation to maintain.

She flashed Allie a radiant smile.

"They're down below . . . Take the elevator and hit LL. They'll be on your right."

The girl was right about Allie. He returned her smile, dropped a twenty on her tray, and winked.

"Thanks, baby."

The waitress beamed and Allie took the elevators to LL.

Julie hung up her phone when she saw a dapper man whom she thought resembled George Raft walking through the outer-office glass doors. An assistant pointed in Julie's direction and the man walked to her desk.

She smiled at him.

"Can I help you?"

"I'm here to see Nick Conti." His eyes glanced toward the inner office.

"Is he expecting you?"

"No. Tell him it's Al Saltieri from Kansas City."

Allie figured that the mention of KC would get results. Nick must have known Nello had asked him to check out Strozzi.

"Just a moment." Julie got up and went into Nick's office. "Mitch called. He's on his way in and still hasn't been able to locate Snuffy."

Nick looked up from his typewriter and frowned.

"Dammit! Where the hell is he?"

"Vanished. They've checked the hospitals but so far no luck . . . And there's an Al Saltieri here to see you—from Kansas City."

Nick frowned. *What the hell was he doing here?* If Nello had asked him to bird-dog Strozzi and he'd agreed, he should be reporting back to Nello.

"Send him in, Julie."

Julie left and Allie entered. Nick got up and extended a friendly hand. He saw no reason to appear adversarial.

"Nick Conti . . ."

Allie took the extended hand and shook it—squeezing firmly.

"Al Saltieri—friend of Nello's."

"Have a seat, Al. What can I do for you?"

"Later. First I can tell you that Strozzi ain't shootin' his mouth off about anything going on with your show. But why you think there would be is somethin' I'd like to know."

"It's an internal thing, Al. Production stuff. Union rumblings, supplier problems. Strozzi gets around—I thought he might be behind rumors."

Al scrutinized Nick's face a few moments. Although the answer might be plausible, he still thought the odds were that Nello's agenda was Erin. He pressed on.

"Are you aware that Nello told me to stop seeing your old girlfriend?"

"Excuse me?" Nick knew, but feigned surprise.

Allie smiled.

"Erin Conroy—your old squeeze."

Nick felt a surge of anger at the derogatory reference but held it in check to see where Allie was taking all this.

"What's Nello's business with you have to do with me?"

Allie dropped his smile. "That's what I'm trying to find out, Nicky." It was a very pointed statement.

The sudden switch in attitude was obvious to Nick.

"Does Nello know you're here?"

"No—and if you tell him, I'll make what's left of your life more miserable than you can imagine."

Nick's eyes narrowed and his voice turned cold.

"I take it that's a threat."

"You take it right, Conti . . . You see, I know all about you and Erin. What was it with you two—almost three years of hide-the-salami?"

Nick tensed.

"Watch yourself, Al . . . You're dangerously close to crossing the line."

"Really . . . That mean you're still seeing her?"

By now Nick couldn't conceal his anger and he answered in barely controlled rage.

"With what little respect you're due, my friend, that's none of your business."

"But I'm making it my business, *my friend.*" He pointed a finger at Nick and his voice started rising. "As far as you're concerned, she's off-limits. To put it another way—stay the fuck away from her!"

"Are you serious or just sick?" Nick found himself snarling. "If I want to see Erin Conroy, not you or ten like you have a gnat's hair's chance of stopping me."

Allie got up and his voice became menacingly low.

"Don't make me prove you wrong, Conti. Because I can make whatever problem you think you might be having with Strozzi seem like a walk in the park."

Wheeling around, Allie strode out the office—confident he'd left the Tinseltown patsy shaking in his boots. He passed Mitch Tanaka in the outer office and brushed past him before slamming through the glass doors.

Mitch continued into Nick's office.

"What was that all about?"

"Allie dropped by to tell me, quote: 'Stay the fuck away from Erin,' unquote."

Mitch knew nothing of Nick's family history, but in all the years they'd been together he'd never seen him back down. The few times when confrontations had become physical and they'd taken on all comers, Nick was formidable.

"Is he nuts?"

"Probably. But don't underestimate him. He holds high cards."

Mitch was clearly confused by Nick's inaction.

"So . . . what now?"

"With him? For the moment, nothing. We still have to stop Strozzi. What're you doing tonight?"

"I made an early dinner date with Lori."

"Can you be available after dark? Say eight or nine?"

"I'll make it work. Why?"

"Two things. One—I want to confront Strozzi about Snuffy. And two—he gave us two days to pay him off. They end tonight. But before we make another move I want to check Dan's bug to see if we've got anything."

"And if we don't?"

"We see him anyway. We shook him up pretty good last night. I don't think he set the second fire, and he's gotta be trying to figure out who did. We'll say we have a lead on the perp but need another day or two. As soon as we figure it out, our deal stands and we'll pay him."

Mitch thought about it for a few seconds and nodded.

"He may buy it. He can't ask questions about the fire on his own or somebody's gonna want to know why he's asking. That could expose his scam, and word could get back to Chicago. If they find out Strozzi is cutting them out, he's history."

"Meet me here at eight and we'll see what we've got on tape."

"Got it."

"In the meantime maybe we'll hear from Snuffy?"

Mitch shook his head. "Maybe . . . but I'm beginning to get some very bad vibes."

CHAPTER FORTY-FOUR

JASON PEARL PARKED his car in the alley behind Poolorama and reached for a small black bag on the seat behind him. He had no idea why he'd been called away from his late-afternoon martini, and he resented the intrusion.

He'd met Carlo Strozzi through a mutual acquaintance while taking in the splendors of Maxi's strip club. When Strozzi was informed of his profession, the short wiseguy had asked Pearl for his card, which read:

JASON PEARL
HOMEOPATHIC REMEDIES
ALOE TO SULPHUR
702-555-2828

The card, of course, was nonsense. Pearl no more sold aloe than he sold used cars. No matter what remedy you called for, he was always fresh out.

He got out of his car and knocked on Strozzi's plywood rear door. A harelipped hulk he didn't know opened it.

He greeted the hulk nervously.

"Jason Pearl . . ."

Angie nodded and silently motioned him in.

Pearl was a fifty-year-old doctor from Miami who'd lost his license in an ugly malpractice suit six years earlier. The patient's lawyers proved Pearl was badly hungover when he left a sponge in a woman's abdomen after a cesarean section. Testimony also revealed that he'd spent the prior night in the apartment of his young nurse.

His wife divorced him and was awarded most of his money, after which his three grown kids disowned him. One month later he moved to Las Vegas, where he continued drinking and made a living by illegally removing the occasional bullet from nameless patients and performing no-paperwork abortions on showgirls and UNLV students.

Pearl shook Strozzi's hand.

"Hi, Carlo, what's the problem?"

Strozzi indicated Snuffy.

"It's on the couch."

Snuffy was stretched out on his back, looking very pale. Pearl walked over, kneeled, and opened the bag he'd brought.

"What happened to him?"

"That's what I want you to tell us."

The three nervous men moved in closer and looked over Pearl's shoulder. He removed a stethoscope from his black bag and noticed the logo on Snuffy's T-shirt.

"He's a stuntman?"

"Yeah," answered Carlo.

The doctor raised Snuffy's eyelid and peered in. He then quickly donned the stethoscope's earpieces and listened to Snuffy's chest. He moved the instrument to several areas and then removed the earpieces.

"This man's dead."

"What?" Strozzi was wide-eyed. It was the last thing he suspected or wanted.

Fats was aghast. His pudgy eyes were bulging in their sockets.

"I only hit 'im a few times!"

"Where?"

"Inna k-kidney. We was tryin' to get some information."

Pearl rolled Snuffy onto his side and lifted the T-shirt. The skin in his kidney area was badly bruised.

"I can't say for certain without an autopsy, but my guess is you ruptured his kidney . . . The man bled to death internally."

"Christ!" Carlo threw up his hands in disgust and turned away. A moment later he turned back and removed a fat bankroll from his pocket. He peeled off a pair of hundreds and slapped them into Pearl's hand. "Okay, Doc, forget you were ever here."

Pearl took the money, picked up his bag, and left.

"What do we do with the body?" Fats was still in shock.

"We bury it, you dumbshit!"

Fats was truly contrite—not because he'd killed the man, but because he killed him before making him talk. He bowed his head sheepishly.

"I'm sorry, boss."

"Forget it. The guy's dead and there's nothin' we can do about it. I'm more worried about who paid him to set the second fire. And if for some reason he didn't set it—who did?"

CHAPTER FORTY-FIVE

A FULL-DRESS REHEARSAL of the *Folies* had Joe Agosto's undivided attention when Allie walked into the Tropicana's showroom. The finale was an extravaganza of long legs, towering headgear, and bare tits. In any other circumstances Allie would have lingered and admired the spectacle, but not in his present mood. He walked to the booth where Joe was seated with Donn Arden, the choreographer, and slid in beside him.

Allie looked at Arden and jerked his head away from the table in an unmistakable command to get lost. Arden left immediately. He knew who Allie was.

Sensing Allie's mood, Joe faced him, showing concern.

"Problem?"

"Maybe. I want a pair of eyes put on Erin Conroy."

Agosto was taken aback by the order. He knew Allie had been seeing her—had demanded she be housed in one of their high-roller suites, and as far as he knew there hadn't been a problem.

"A tail?"

"No. I already know where she is and who she sees when she's on the set. I've got eyes over there. But I want to know who comes and goes in her suite, and when."

Allie got up, threw a last look at the stage, and left. He walked through the casino to the pool and arrived in time to witness the last shot of the day for *Seven-Eleven*.

"Cut and print!" Stavros grinned and nodded to his first assistant.

The assistant raised a megaphone to his lips.

"That's a wrap!"

A hundred extras left their positions around Tropicana's pool and headed home at the end of the day. Erin was on her chaise. Allie watched Stavros walk over to her and then turned and walked back into the casino.

Stavros bent over and kissed Erin on the cheek.

"Fabulous take, Erin. We got it all."

"Thanks, Stavros. The casino tomorrow?"

"Seven o'clock call. But for you—ten in makeup and hair should be fine. I'm starting with establishing shots."

"Glad the first day's in the can?"

"Always." He kissed her cheek again and scampered off to set up the next day's work.

Erin's assistant, a young girl named Trudy, hurried through the departing extras carrying a clipboard and looking frazzled. Trudy always looked frazzled, even when she wasn't. She wore a head of crazily askew hair, as if she'd stuck her finger in a light socket.

She lurched to a stop, panting.

"Will you be stopping at your motor home or going directly to your suite?"

There were three luxurious motor homes assigned to the picture. One for Stavros, one for Erin, and one for Brandon Butler, her male costar. The rest of the cast, depending on their status, were in single or double trailers.

"To the suite, Trudy. I'll just stop to pick up a robe and my purse."

Trudy nodded and they headed for the parking lot behind the hotel.

Nick pulled the Firebird next to Erin's motor home, cut the ignition, and waited. After Allie left his office he'd called to find out when *Seven-Eleven* would wrap. He'd been trying to rewrite Lori's scenes for an hour but couldn't concentrate. He finally angrily flipped his pencil across the room and left.

Stay the fuck away from her! Nick couldn't get the threat out of his mind. Until Allie's visit, he'd been debating whether or not he should begin seeing Erin again. The hood's visit had shut down the debate. It wasn't a question of whether or not he still loved her—that was laid to rest the moment she walked into the Polo Lounge.

All the memories had flooded back—from the beginning when she'd initially refused to date him. She didn't want to become the cliché: "an actress sleeping with the producer." Her integrity only made her more fascinating. When she finally agreed to see him, Nick was surprised that they actually had intelligent conversations. It was obvious that there was a mature, inquiring, and many-faceted mind in her twenty-year-old body.

Even better, she loved New York sports—the Yankees, the Knicks, and the Giants. So did he. Disguised in dark glasses and hats, with her in a wig and him wearing a mustache, they went to home games and cheered themselves hoarse. On Sundays they walked in Central Park, ate hot pretzels, and rented rowboats on the lake.

He met her parents. Her father was wary, her mother wonderful. Nick loved them both. And when they finally made love—they were *in* love. Nick had never met anyone like her.

The question was whether or not he could handle a rewind of what had happened before.

Nick had ended their affair after a very public blowup at a dinner party given by Alan Jay Lerner to announce a revival of *Camelot.* It was a star-studded event attended by, among others, Richard Burton, Ethel Merman, and Ava Gardner.

Everyone had had a few drinks and Ava flirtatiously attached herself to Nick and Erin. Nick was gracious but Erin was affronted. Ava was fifty-six at the time, but remained a sultry beauty of legendary fame.

Erin finally lost it and called Ava an obnoxious drunk.

Ava had been drinking, but she wasn't drunk, and she was a star—a very big one. There was no way a comparatively unknown TV actress was going to get away with insulting her.

She threw her drink in Erin's face.

Erin hauled back her arm to slap Ava, but Nick grabbed her wrist in midflight and called her a jealous idiot.

Erin burst into tears and fled the room.

Nick helplessly began to apologize but was shocked to see a wry smile appear on Ava's sensuous lips. Unable to grasp what could possibly be funny, a questioning look crossed his face. She noted it and answered his silent query.

"Darling . . . What's amusing is that I wasn't interested in you, I was interested in her."

Rumors of Ava's bisexuality had abounded for years. She had many liaisons with high-profile stars, and it was said that Frank Sinatra had once found her in bed with Lana Turner.

The next day Erin's agent informed Nick that she was leaving his series—mental fatigue being the legal excuse for the breach of contract. This time Nick let her go. He simultaneously wrote her out of the show and his life.

She'd been out of sight, but not mind, for two years.

Then she'd walked into the Polo Lounge. She looked like a goddess and his mouth had gone dry with a sip of martini still in it. All the good times had flashed by—and none of the bad.

Nick's car phone rang and he picked it up. It was Julie.

"I just heard from Rodney Lang on the set. He thought you should know that Benjamin Hall was at our location at the courthouse this afternoon. He was asking some of the crew questions about Johnny's motorcycle accident. Obviously they'd read the press release, but knew nothing about the accident."

"Obviously . . ."

"It gets worse. He's checked into the hotel—left messages here and at the main desk."

"What do the messages say?"

"He wants to see you. What do you want me to do?"

Nick knew he had to see Hall or risk having him do a story about what he'd uncovered: that no one knew anything about Johnny Johansen's supposed motorcycle accident. He'd report there was a major cover-up taking place, and there was no telling where that kind of speculation could lead with Strozzi still out there.

Julie thought she'd lost the connection.

"Nick?"

"Don't answer the messages. I'll talk to him tomorrow . . . But call La Costa. Tell Johnny I want him to hire a limo and get his ass back here tonight. I'll see him first thing in the morning."

Nick saw Erin approaching with Trudy and hung up. Erin was still in the bikini she'd worn for the pool scene and Nick felt his pulse jump. A light breeze was causing her red hair to fan out behind her, and even though she was wearing spiked heels, she moved with the sinewy grace of a leopard.

He got out of his car and Erin saw him. She hesitated—surprised—and smiled.

"Well . . . to what do I owe the pleasure?"

Nick waited for Trudy to go into the motor home, and Erin noticed his hesitation. He looked—and sounded—tense.

"I'd like to talk to you."

She frowned.

"That sounds serious . . ."

"It is. Something's come up."

"Now it sounds ominous."

Trudy reappeared with a robe and Erin put it on.

"You always seem to appear at cocktail hour. Care to join me for a drink again while we talk?"

"Your suite?"

She smiled and opened the robe.

"I'm hardly dressed for the cocktail lounge, Nico."

Trudy watched them walk into the hotel and then went straight to a nearby pay phone. The extra money she was earning would allow a solid down payment on a very nice condo—and perhaps even some furniture. She punched in a number she'd very recently memorized and waited to make her report to a man she'd just met.

Between Trudy and Stavros, Big Allie Saltieri had Erin's days very well covered.

CHAPTER FORTY-SIX

S AM ALTMAN'S DOCTOR removed the tongue depressor from Sam's mouth and shook his head.

"You've got to quit smoking, Sam."

Doctor Manuel Kline was an eminent Beverly Hills ear, nose, and throat specialist who was chief of ENT at Cedars-Sinai. He'd been warning Sam for years that cigars could kill him, but Sam refused to listen. Cigars were as indispensable as adulation and publicity—not worth living without.

"You're a broken record, Manny."

"I'm *on* record."

They were in Kline's office, which could be conveniently reached from an underground garage in his Camden Drive building. As was the case with any high-profile figure, a visit to a specialist was grist for the tabloids, and that was the kind of negative rumor Sam didn't want. What he wanted was to be perceived as invincible, and so far no one had given him reason to think otherwise.

"What do you see?"

"Your throat's as raw as ground beef. It never recovers."

"It's because I cough a lot."

"Because you smoke a lot."

"Not a lot—in moderation."

"Describe moderation."

"I smoke when the spirit moves me."

"And that is when?"

"For chrissakes, Manny. What? You're writing a book?"

"No—I'm trying to make you realize that your throat's raw meat!"

"My throat's been raw meat for years! I've been coughing for years. You've been taking biopsies for years."

"And I'm taking another one."

"So take. You see anything different?"

"No. Not yet. But I'm warning you, Sam—you can't stay lucky forever."

"So one day I'll die of cancer instead of a heart attack or stroke because I'm so stressed out. Why? Because I can't relax smoking cigars."

"That's illogical."

"Why? Everybody has to die of something."

"I can't talk to you anymore."

"Good. Don't talk to me. Talk to your nurse. Tell her to call Jake. I'm ready to go home and face another pain in the ass."

CHAPTER FORTY-SEVEN

TWENTY MINUTES LATER Sam was met at his estate's side entrance by Alfred. His butler was holding a silver tray with a crystal tumbler containing bourbon over ice.

Some things never changed.

Sam nodded to Alfred and steeled himself with a long pull of the bourbon. He knew what he had to do and was determined that this time he would have his way, come hell or high water. In this case he knew it would be both.

"Where is she?"

"In the solarium, sir."

Sam finished the bourbon and handed the glass to Alfred.

"Get me another."

The solarium was at the rear of the house. It was semicircular, its thirty-two-foot diameter enclosed by glass on three sides plus the ceiling. Sunlight streamed down on a dazzling array of flora surrounding a central fountain spewing water from the mouths of cherubs. The generous seating area featured rattan sofas and lounge chairs around a large glass coffee table.

It smelled like a funeral parlor.

Gwen was sprawled on a sofa sipping a manhattan and reading *Architectural Digest* when Sam entered.

She looked up and smiled.

"Good evening, *dah*-ling," she crooned in her ersatz accent. "Did you have a pleasant day?"

"No."

Gwen recognized his attitude from long experience and immediately put herself on guard.

"Oh?"

Sam proceeded gruffly, sans preamble.

"I need to give a reporter a tour of the house."

Gwen's eyes popped. Her mouth moved but nothing came out. Alfred entered with Sam's bourbon, which Sam took and downed.

Gwen used the momentary delay to recover and replied icily.

"Did I hear you say you want to show my home to a *reporter*?"

"*Our* home—and yes—with his wife and two kids."

"Impossible! I won't have it!"

"Possible! And you *will* have it!"

Gwen was aghast. Sam had never insisted when this subject came up. He'd occasionally asked if he could bring home a star he was courting, but she'd never had any trouble squashing the request.

She threw the magazine aside and leapt to her feet.

"What's gotten into you?"

"It's *who's* gotten into me. This guy could blow *The $trip* out of the water if he uncovers what's going on in Vegas."

"Showing him the house is a bribe?" She was even more horrified.

"Yes, goddammit!"

"*No*, goddammit."

"Gwen, be reasonable . . ."

"Was this solution Conti's idea?"

"No!"

"Then let your resident genius come up with one. You've told me a hundred times that that's what he's there for."

Completely exasperated, Sam slammed his glass on the coffee table and an explosion of ice cubes filled the air.

"This isn't about Conti!"

Gwen's hate for Nick had been an agonizing thorn in her side. Now her perception that he was the root cause of this invasion of her ferociously guarded private domain made her completely irrational.

She blew up—shrieking.

"If it's about *The $trip*, it's about Conti—it's his show! But this is my house. You're not going to use it to save him."

"Not him! *Me!*"

Gwen paused—studying her husband—the wheels of negotiation spinning in her head. She calmed herself, took a deep breath, and exhaled.

"Fine! If you want to bow to extortion with a disgusting violation of my home, I'll let you. You can bring this reporter and his brats in here but on one condition. Get rid of Nick Conti! Fire him! Make a choice—him or your disgusting tour."

"That's not a choice! It's two impossible options!"

"They're my terms! You can have the house or Conti. Either, or. Not both."

Gwen stormed out of the room and Sam slumped into a chair. Alfred came in a few seconds later, having heard the argument and seen Gwen tear past him—her face a mask of fury.

"Can I get you anything else, sir?"

"Yes. Another bourbon, Cojo, and Jake."

Sam had made a decision.

CHAPTER FORTY-EIGHT

T H E S E C O N D O F the two suites on the penthouse floor had been recently occupied and a cocktail party was in progress when Nick and Erin got off the elevator. Nick noted a uniformed guard sitting outside the door and assumed there was a high-profile whale inside.

There was—which was the excuse Agosto had used to position his spy.

Erin went straight to the bar when they entered the suite, selecting Chivas, Drambuie, and a cocktail shaker. She filled it with ice.

"The usual, I assume?"

Nick remained standing and nodded. Her robe had parted slightly, revealing her bikini.

"But I'll make them if you'd like to change?"

She gave him a teasing smile and cocked her head alluringly. "The wardrobe disturbs you?"

"It would disturb a statue."

She expertly mixed the drinks and set out a pair of tumblers.

"You've seen me wearing less on innumerable occasions."

"There are some things you never get used to."

"Thank you . . . I accept the compliment."

She poured the Rob Roys and came around to sit facing him as she had the day before. Her robe fell away as she crossed her long legs. Pink nails winked out of open-toed, sling-back heels, and above them a perfectly turned ankle made the image irresistibly erotic. Nick let his eyes drift back up to hers.

She smiled, toasted, and sipped.

"Now you can tell me what's so serious."

"Allie came to see me this afternoon."

Shock slowly crossed her face as the implication of his statement sunk in. Nick knew she had to realize the reason for his visit but laid it out anyway.

"He found out about our past and assumed we either wanted to—or were—seeing each other again. He ordered me to stay away from you."

Erin's shock turned to anger. She put down her drink and her eyes flashed.

"How dare he!"

"Agreed. But for whatever reason, he thinks he owns you."

"I've never—*ever*—given him a reason to think that."

"Allie lives in a world removed from anything you've ever known, Erin. Reality is what he perceives it to be. He is used to getting what he wants when he wants it. And right now he wants you."

Infuriated, Erin exploded off the stool and went for a phone next to the couch.

"Mr. Saltieri is about to experience a colossal shock!"

Nick rushed after her and grabbed her wrist as she lifted the receiver.

"I wouldn't confront him. Not yet."

"Why not? For God's sake. I'm not afraid of him just because he's some sort of gangster."

Nick realized that in spite of Erin's intelligence, and even a few years later, she was still a bit naïve if she thought "some sort of gangster" was an accurate evaluation of Allie Saltieri.

"It's complicated, Erin. And in a day or two we'll be able to deal with it. But in the meantime I want you to trust me and do nothing."

"If you want me to do nothing, then why did you tell me?"

"Because I want you to understand that whether you believe it or not, Allie Saltieri is a very dangerous man."

Nick released her wrist and she lowered the phone into the cradle without taking her eyes off him.

"You want me to do nothing . . ." It was statement, not a question.

"Yes."

"Does that mean that when he wants to see me I should agree as if nothing's happened?"

Nick assumed she was fucking Allie as Nello had suggested, but he wasn't going to go there because he didn't want to know. With no other choice, he sidestepped.

"Use your own judgment, Erin. But please . . . be careful."

"It sounds like you still care."

"I do."

"Yesterday you said you still thought about me every now and then. What was it you were thinking?"

If ever there was a point of no return in their future, Nick knew that he'd reached it. Looking sensual and vulnerable at the same time, she was irresistible. Another sidestep was impossible.

"That I never stopped loving you."

She stared at him for several seconds and Nick saw her eyes get moist, although she wasn't crying. She leaned into his arms and buried her head against his neck. They hugged each other and then hungrily kissed as Nick lowered them to the couch and settled on top of her.

Erin cradled his face in her hands.

"My God, I've missed you."

Nick slowly lowered his head and gave her a feathery kiss on the lips.

"It's been too long for both of us."

"Tell me again."

"It was never over. I love you. I realized it the second you walked into the Polo Lounge."

They were motionless for a few seconds and then, as if on some unknown signal, their hands suddenly began moving in a blur. Neither gave any thought to removing their clothes. Erin fumbled with his zipper—Nick pulled down her bikini top. She grasped his erection and he pulled aside her bikini bottom.

She gasped when he entered her and cried when she climaxed. They remained very still for a full minute in a familiar afterglow, and the pain, anger, and regret of two years vanished.

CHAPTER FORTY-NINE

OJO JUMPED OUT of the black limo, opened the
rear door for Sam, and followed him into the Bistro—the legendary Beverly Hills restaurant frequented by the rich and famous
of show business, politics, industry, and sports. And, as Sam knew, the
unique office of the man he had come to see.

Sidney Korshak.

Among other things, Korshak was a lawyer whose dominance in the
field of labor consulting and negotiations was uncontested. Although
he was largely unknown to the public, his client list included Hilton
Hotels, Hyatt Hotels, MGM, Playboy, MCA/Universal, Diner's Club,
and literally hundreds of others. His close friends were industry giants
Kirk Kerkorian and Charles Bluhdorn, political powerhouses including Ronald Reagan and Pat Brown, and stars like Frank Sinatra, Dinah
Shore, Warren Beatty: everybody who was anybody in show business.

But it was his reputation as the Fixer that had made him rich, powerful, and feared. His extremely close ties with the Teamsters, the

Hollywood guilds, the hotel workers' union, and other suspect unions had allowed him to settle rafts of labor disputes between striking employees and their employers for years—invariably in favor of the companies.

Sidney was originally from Chicago, and the source of his power was reputed to be his close association with Anthony "The Big Tuna" Accardo, boss of the Chicago Outfit. He was not only Accardo's attorney but also represented many of Accardo's underworld associates in Kansas City, Detroit, Las Vegas, and Los Angeles.

Korshak was never indicted or convicted of anything in his fifty-year career, but according to FBI files he was the most powerful lawyer in the country and the puppet master behind innumerable power mergers, political deals, and organized-crime operations.

But the reason Sam Altman had come to the Bistro was that Korshak was known to insiders as the Mob's man in Las Vegas.

Korshak was seated at his permanently reserved corner table to the left of the entrance when Sam walked in with Cojo. The table was his office—literally. He had no other.

He was speaking on the phone—the only one at a Bistro table—and Sam waved Cojo to the opposite corner. Korshak always held lunch meetings at this "office" but seldom dined at the restaurant. He'd only agreed to the late-afternoon exception after a frantic call from Sam.

Korshak hung up the phone, recognized Sam's presence, and waved him over. As usual, his greeting was friendly, expansive, and smiling.

"Hello, Sam, good to see you. Sit. How's the family?"

Sam Altman was never deferential. In his world he never had to be. He was the reigning mogul of television. But this was not his world—it was something much more involved, wrapped in mystique.

Sam knew it, and adopted his most respectful attitude.

"Fine, Sidney, fine. Gwen sends her regards . . . and how's Bee?"

"Fine as well . . . A drink?"

"Bourbon . . . And I can't thank you enough for seeing me on short notice, Sidney—I appreciate it . . ."

"No problem . . . How can I be of service?"

"I'm in a bit of a box and I thought you might be able to help."

Korshak nodded, signaled a hovering waiter, and ordered Sam a bourbon. When the waiter departed he turned back to Sam.

"You mentioned Vegas when you called."

"I did . . . As you know, I've got a hit show shooting up there."

"I know. You made your production deal with the DI."

Sam immediately became defensive. Nick had told him the reasons he hadn't wanted to be in business with some of Korshak's Mob clients in Vegas, and now he was about to ask for a favor from the man who was the attorney for the very clients they'd snubbed.

Sam's face dissolved into remorse.

"Sidney, I . . ."

Korshak held up his hand, shook his head, and smiled benevolently.

"Forget it, Sam. I was well aware of why you made your deal with Hughes. It was smart business. I admire that. Now . . . what can I do for you?"

In the next five minutes Sam explained the events of the past few days. Korshak nodded, asked a few questions, and told Sam he'd see what could be done. Sam said he would be eternally grateful and would return whatever favor Korshak asked—whenever—knowing there was little he could do for the man that he could not do for himself.

Sam left feeling a bit more comfortable, and for a brief moment considered calling Nick to tell him of his conversation with Korshak. The problem was that Nick was a very proud man who believed he could handle any problem that came along. In fact, Sam told him that was the very reason he'd sent Nick to Vegas.

There was no question that Nick would fiercely object to interference in his domain until he was absolutely sure he couldn't resolve the problem himself. And there was always the chance that Korshak would come up with nothing—in which case Nick would never know Sam had panicked and interfered.

Sam made his second decision of the evening.

He didn't call Nick.

CHAPTER FIFTY

"**B**LACKJACK"

Lori Donner flipped her down card—an ace—atop her queen and let out another shriek.

Brad Tilden whooped and applauded the win from his seat next to Lori, and three other cast members—plus a pair of guest stars who filled out the table—all boisterously congratulated her. The group had run into each other in the DI casino after the wrap and decided to hang out and try their luck at an empty blackjack table.

There was a smattering of applause from a small group of spectators ogling the celebrities and commenting. *There's Lori Donner . . . Isn't she lovely . . . She's in that show that's shooting here . . . That's Brad Tilden . . . He plays Hank's Las Vegas detective buddy . . .* Players at nearby tables turned to see what was causing the excitement.

Lori turned, acknowledged the applause, and shyly covered her mouth with her fingers. Her feigned embarrassment was accompanied by a girlish giggle.

The spectators loved it. They were being treated to the beguilingly innocent girl next door gambling. Brad noted their reaction and whispered to Lori.

"You give a whole new meaning to 'You have them eating out of your hand.'"

"Image is everything, my sweet," she responded, sotto voce. "And my public can't get enough of mine."

"Not worried about them doing without you while Nick rebuilds your burned-down set?"

"Won't happen. Nick's rewriting my scenes in other locations."

"Same comment regarding people eating out of your hand."

The dealer dealt another round of cards with both Lori and Brad showing aces. They flipped their down cards—a jack and a king for a pair of blackjacks, and Brad let out a whoop.

"The name of the game!"

Brad and Lori high-fived each other, and there was another round of applause. He raised his drink, toasted her, and then indicated the group at the table.

"I made a dinner reservation for the group of us at the Shanghai. Care to come along?"

Lori smiled apologetically. "Love to, Brad, but I've made other plans."

Mitch Tanaka appeared as if on cue. He was wearing a tan suit, shirt, and tie that emphasized his striking Asian features. He was handsome enough to be an actor, and a murmur came from the spectators as they unsuccessfully tried to place him.

He greeted the group and stood behind Lori's chair.

"Any luck?"

"Two blackjacks in a row, Mitch . . ." She turned to face him and smiled. "But I know how to quit when I'm ahead."

"Smart girl. We have an eight o'clock reservation at Luigi's."

"Perfect. I just have to drop by my suite to change out of these jeans and we'll be off."

Lori swept up her winnings, tipped the dealer, and said good-bye to the table with a conspiratorial wink.

As they left the casino she took Mitch's arm.

"Does Nick know we're having dinner?"

"As a matter of fact, he does."

"And he had no problem with that?"

"Should he have?"

"Probably not."

Lori's suite in the Wimbledon had an outdoor patio and pool like Nick's but was a smaller, one-bedroom version. Mitch followed her in—Lori closed the door behind them and leaned against it coquettishly.

"I've an idea."

"Oh?"

She stepped forward, put her arms around his neck, and looked up into his eyes with her signature smile. Mitch thought her eyes looked a bit dilated, but the thought was banished when her dimples appeared and she pressed her body into his.

"What would you say to dinner in the suite as opposed to the long . . . long . . . trip to Luigi's?"

They both knew Luigi's was only five minutes away, but her smile made it seem like it was on another planet.

The dimples again.

"My people have always been renowned for being polite, sensitive, and agreeable . . . Dinner in the suite it will be. Consider me at your service."

"Excellent." She kissed him deeply. "You can start by carrying me into the bedroom for hors d'oeuvres."

Mitch swept her up and carried her into the bedroom, where they quickly undressed and tumbled into a king-size bed. Although the walls were comparatively solid, anyone listening would testify that the adorable girl next door was a screamer.

Outside, a man was lurking in the hallway.

His fists once again balled and he felt his anger and dismay redouble.

CHAPTER FIFTY-ONE

A ROOSTER TAIL of dust spun up behind Strozzi's sedan in what was left of daylight. The car was silhouetted against a glowing western sky and very near the place where Strozzi, Fats, and Angie had driven Johnny Johansen three nights earlier. It was one of several times Strozzi had come to the area since his arrival in Las Vegas. Accessible by a barely visible trail off a dirt road, the low dunes were an isolated stretch of soft sand perfectly suited to his purpose.

Strozzi's head was spinning with the consequences of Snuffy's death. His brilliant scam was in jeopardy, he was no closer to finding out who had started the second fire, and now he had to dispose of a body. The three men had remained silent during the four-mile drive—not out of respect for the dead, but contemplating what might be the next move in their dilemma.

Strozzi finally broke the silence.

"Pull over here."

Fats did as instructed and the men were met by a blowing tumbleweed as they got out of their car. The lights of Vegas were again visible to the north, but the temperature had cooled and the air no longer smelled of dust.

Carlo popped the trunk and turned to Angie.

"Get 'im out."

Angie hauled up Snuffy's body and threw it over his shoulder. Fats removed a pair of shovels from the trunk. Strozzi grabbed a pair of pliers and beckoned them to follow.

Fifty yards off the trail, he pointed to a depression between two small dunes.

"Here."

Angie flipped the body off his shoulder and took one of the shovels from Fats. They quickly dug to a depth of four feet and then climbed out of the shallow grave. Angie was about to push the body into it when Strozzi stopped him.

"Hold it . . ." He slapped Fats on the arm. "Strip 'im."

"Huh?" Fats thought he hadn't heard right.

"You heard me—strip 'im."

"Why?" He was bewildered.

"Because if he ever turns up, I don't want anything that could identify 'im."

"But he's prob'ly got dental records."

"Which is why you're gonna pull his teeth out."

"You gotta be kiddin' . . ." Fats was now aghast.

Strozzi handed him the pliers.

Fats's eyes nervously darted from the pliers to Snuffy, and then he took one last shot at what he thought was a logical objection.

"Carlo—he's got fingerprints!"

"Which is why you're gonna cut 'em off."

Strozzi smiled, snapped open his switchblade, and held it out.

Even though Fats had committed a wide range of brutal acts in his life, he'd never mutilated a corpse, and he was horrified. He looked longingly at Angie in a silent plea for support. But Angie, who was at the bottom of Carlo's food chain and resented always being given the dirtiest tasks, was delighted to see the shit finally fall on Fats's head. He responded with a harelipped grin.

Fats turned back to Carlo.

"Why me?"

"Because you killed 'im."

"Angie held 'im."

"True—but you killed 'im, and you're the one that's gotta give 'im his send-off. So get your ass in gear—I'm gettin' hungry an' I feel like tripe."

Fats knew that any further objections would fall on deaf ears and began his grisly work. Twenty minutes later he and Angie shoveled sand over Snuffy's mutilated body and the three killers left for the Tower of Pizza.

CHAPTER FIFTY-TWO

NICK AND ERIN had not left the couch for over two hours. They'd fallen asleep entwined after exhausting each other in connubial bliss. In more colloquial terms, they'd fucked each other's brains out.

Nick opened his eyes and found the suite totally dark. On the table next to the couch the phone's message light was furiously blinking in what seemed an ominous admonition. He checked his watch and the movement woke up Erin.

She purred like a contented kitten and kissed his neck.

"What time is it?"

"A little after eight."

"You were supposed to be gone by now."

"So I said."

"Change your mind?"

"No . . . I still think it's wise for us to fly under the radar a few more days."

She sighed, shook her head in disappointment, and nuzzled against his body.

"All right, Nico, I'll be a good girl and try not to ask questions."

Nick kissed the tip of her nose and pulled up his rumpled trousers. Erin did the same with her bikini top—both garments had remained where they were when they'd been pulled down in the heat of the moment.

Nick got up, cinched his belt, and pointed to the phone.

"You probably should get that."

Erin nodded and picked it up. Nick turned on the lamp and watched her face while she retrieved her messages. After several seconds she thanked the operator and put down the phone.

"My set call—which I already knew . . . and Allie. He wants to have dinner. He assumed I'd say yes and said he'd pick me up at eight thirty."

"He's in the hotel?"

"Yes. Room 2110 on the next floor."

There was a sinking feeling in the pit of Nick's stomach. Of course Allie was in the hotel. He'd arranged this suite for her and checked in one floor down for quick access—right? Nick still didn't want to go there. What you didn't know couldn't hurt you, he thought.

He sidestepped once again.

"As I said, use your own judgment—but you should probably have dinner with him."

There was nothing she wanted less. But in light of Allie's visit to Nick, she thought that an excuse would not be accepted and could even be dangerous.

She nodded sadly.

"All right . . . But right now you'd better be going."

Nick gave her a last, lingering kiss and cradled her face.

"I love you."

She smiled and he left.

The party in the second penthouse suite seemed to have ended, but Nick saw that the security guard was still in a chair beside the door. He considered taking the staircase to avoid the chance of encountering Allie in the elevator but thought it would look suspicious to the guard.

He decided to take his chances and the elevator.

CHAPTER FIFTY-THREE

ITCH'S EVENING WITH Lori was even more erotically spectacular than expected. The girl was a tigress in kitten's clothing. But Mitch was a light drinker and Lori was not. The proposed dinner never arrived—it was never ordered. And after two bottles of champagne and three rounds of acrobatic sex, she was exhausted. She dropped off into a deep sleep and Mitch slipped quietly out of bed without waking her.

He was as he'd said earlier: polite and sensitive.

As he dressed, he debated weather he should leave a note thanking her for a wonderful time and an apology for leaving without saying good-bye. He'd seen the Victorian hero of a black-and-white film do that and thought it was both charming and gallant. But Victoria and Vegas were an unnatural pairing, so he pulled a sheet up over Lori's naked body and left.

He took the elevator and leisurely strolled out of the Wimbledon, heading for the production office for his meeting with Nick. He hadn't taken more than a dozen steps when his keenly honed instincts sounded a warning bell. He slowed his pace, scanned the shadows beyond the landscape lighting, and stopped.

Nothing.

He resumed walking at a normal pace and then suddenly spun around. A black-clad figure darted behind some bushes about twenty yards behind him.

Mitch immediately took off after it.

He reached the bushes in seconds, but the speeding shape had made it back to the Wimbledon and disappeared around the corner of the building.

Mitch dashed after him.

He was flat-out wide-open as he turned the same corner and ran flush into a gloved fist. It caught him high on the forehead and nearly flipped him. As finely tuned as his body was, it couldn't withstand that violent an impact.

He was out before he hit the ground.

Mitch's black-clad assailant paused only a moment to rub the fist that had cold-cocked his victim and then took off toward the parking lot.

A few minutes later, Mitch groaned and got to his knees. He swore at himself for being stupid enough to run into a sucker punch and rose unsteadily. Rubbing his brow on the way to the DI's main tower, he felt the beginning of a lump.

Mitch walked into the production offices a little before eight. The company had wrapped for the day and he walked through the deserted space to Nick's office. He removed a tray of ice from Nick's refrigerator, put the contents in a towel, and held it to his forehead while using Nick's phone to again check for any sign of Snuffy. This time he added the police and the sheriff to his hospital calls.

Nothing.

Nick arrived at eight thirty wearing dark slacks, a black turtleneck, and a windbreaker.

"Sorry I'm late—I stopped by the suite for some fresh clothes . . ." Then he noticed Mitch's red forehead. "What happened?"

"I got waylaid coming from Lori's."

"By who?"

"No idea."

"A robbery?"

"I've still got my wallet."

"Then why?"

"You tell me."

Nick shook his head. There was no point trying to figure out who and why at the moment. They had work to do.

Nick indicated the bruise on Mitch's forehead.

"You okay for tonight?"

"Good to go . . . but I checked again on Snuffy. No news."

"Shit . . . I'm beginning to feel your bad vibes . . . You bring a change of clothes?"

His tan suit, shirt, and tie wouldn't do for the second part of the evening.

"In my trunk."

They stopped by Mitch's car and he changed into dark slacks, shirt, and sweater.

CHAPTER FIFTY-FOUR

NICK TURNED THE Firebird off Fremont at Third Street and parked at the mouth of the alley behind Poolorama. It was a dimly lit void and the multicolored glow from Fremont's neon lights made it all the more eerie.

Mitch scanned it.

"You want us to be holding?"

Nick nodded and got out of the car.

"Couldn't hurt. I've got a hard-earned respect for dark alleys."

Mitch slipped the Beretta out of the compartment below the glove box and followed Nick into the alley. It reeked of rotting garbage—the detritus piled high in a succession of Dumpsters behind the restaurants and bars that fronted on Fremont. A cacophony of clashing country-western music coming from the same establishments made their ears ring and muffled their footsteps as they quickly made their way toward the opposite end of the alley.

Nick spotted Poolorama's plywood door and continued to the next building. He pointed at a drainpipe that ran up the far side.

"That's it . . . waist-high, Dan said."

Nick gingerly ran his hand behind the drainpipe and removed a thin six-by-four-inch cassette recorder taped to the wall. He quickly opened it, removed the old cassette, and replaced it with the spare. Mitch handed him a roll of duct tape and he reattached the unit in place.

Nick kissed the cassette and looked at it.

"Luck be a lady tonight."

They returned to the Firebird and Nick slipped the cassette into the tape deck. For a few minutes they heard nothing but a bunch of meaningless babble from Carlo, Fats, and Angie. Then there was the sound of knocking, a door being answered, and a new voice.

The voice said, "Jason Pearl."

Silence, and then the same voice said, "Hi, Carlo, what's the problem?"

Carlo's voice. "It's on the couch."

Pearl's voice. "What happened to him?"

Carlo: "That's what I want you to tell us."

More shuffling and then Pearl's voice: "He's a stuntman?"

Carlo. "Yeah."

Nick and Mitch reacted and automatically leaned closer to the cassette deck. There was more shuffling, and then Pearl's voice.

"This man's dead."

Carlo: "What?"

Fats: "I only hit 'im a few times!"

Pearl: "Where?"

Fats: "Kidney. We was tryin' to get some information."

More shuffling and then Pearl: "I can't say for certain without an autopsy, but my guess is you ruptured his kidney . . . The man bled to death internally."

Carlo: "Christ! Okay, Doc, forget you were ever here."

Footsteps and a door opening and closing.

Fats: "What do we do with the body?"

Carlo: "We bury it, you dumbshit!"

Fats: "I'm sorry, boss."

Carlo: "Forget it. The guy's dead and there's nothin' we can do about it. I'm more worried about who paid him to set the second fire. And if for some reason he didn't set it—who did?"

More footsteps, a door opening and closing and silence.

Nick punched off the cassette, let out a deep breath and shook his head.

"They killed him . . . trying to get information."

"Are you thinking what I'm thinking? About what?"

It was obvious to both of them. Nick nodded.

"The fire. They didn't order the second fire and had to find out who did . . . So they went after the guy who set the first one . . . Snuffy."

Mitch addressed no one and swore in his native tongue.

"*Shimatta!* Why?"

"Who knows? Money? Anger? He always wanted to be an actor—looked enough like Hank Donovan to be his double but got a fraction of his paycheck. He never had the talent. Maybe, like Strozzi, he saw a shot at a big score and took it."

"I would've made it a million to one against . . . What now?"

"I don't think Strozzi'll want to explain what happened to the dead man Pearl examined in his office. We let him listen to the tape, threaten to give it to the cops, and get him off our back."

"How? It's an illegal wiretap. He's smart enough to know it won't stand up in court."

"True. But Pearl—whoever he is—was in the office and is on the tape. He'd have to explain what he was doing there in the first place. My bet is he's dirty, can be squeezed, and will cut a deal to save his ass."

"But we still have to find Pearl. And if we do, we got his name with an illegal tap. That's a felony. We'll buy ourselves a tour in Club Fed."

"We'll know, and Carlo will know, about the tap. To anyone else we'll deny it exists. Our word against his. And we'll say our information about the dead body came from Pearl."

It seemed logical. Mitch nodded.

"So first we find Pearl."

"Exactly."

Mitch still had the Beretta in his hand. He looked at it and seemed to weigh the dual repercussions of carrying a concealed weapon and approving an illegal wiretap. He pondered a few moments, shrugged in resignation, and then meaningfully stuffed the gun into his waistband.

"Okay, I'm in. But even if we find Pearl and nail down Strozzi, we still won't know who set the second fire."

"One thing at a time, Tanaka-san. First we find Pearl."

CHAPTER FIFTY-FIVE

ALLIE SALTIERI FINISHED dressing for his date with Erin and made a drink. He was still furious about the warning Nello had delivered from Corky Civella, but was determined not to let it interfere with his private life.

Who the hell did they think they were dealing with? He was a caporegime—a big earner—and in charge of the family's Vegas operations! Things were running as well as could be expected in spite of the feds, and no one could do a better job.

Fuck 'em. He'd lay low but he wouldn't lay out. His private life was his own.

The door chimes rang and he let in Joe Agosto. Joe was with a uniformed hotel security guard and didn't look happy. Allie closed the door but didn't offer them a drink or a seat.

He addressed the guard.

"What've you got?"

"The guy Joe described to me went into Miss Conroy's suite with her at five-oh-seven."

Allie looked to Agosto for conformation,

"You're sure it was Conti?"

Agosto nodded.

"It was him. His Firebird was parked out back next to her motor home, and he was seen coming through the parking-lot entrance with her."

Allie flushed.

"When did he leave?

"Eight sixteen."

Allie's face grew even redder and the veins in his forehead pulsed. *Three hours! That sonofabitch was in her suite three hours! And after he warned him! Was he crazy? Didn't he realize who he was fucking with?* With enormous effort, Allie prevented himself from erupting in front of Agosto and settled down.

"Okay, Joe. That's it. Thanks."

Agosto waved the guard out of the suite and the man left.

"You want to keep up the watch?"

"Won't be necessary. I found out what I wanted to know."

"What's going on, Al? I thought you two were an item."

"So did I, Joe . . . and we still will be, as soon as I make certain people understand who's holding the cards."

Agosto nodded, having no doubt that Allie was capable of carrying out his threat.

"Anything else I can do?"

Allie put his arm around Agosto and led him to the door.

"No . . . thanks, Joe. I can handle it from here."

Agosto left and Allie seethed . . . but he picked up the phone and ordered three dozen roses for Erin.

CHAPTER FIFTY-SIX

ERIN CHANGED INTO a pantsuit, high-necked blouse, and flats—determined to look as unsexy as possible for her date with Allie. The fact that she was forced see him at all had left her feeling angry and impotent.

Ten minutes later, when the enormous bouquet arrived, she was tempted to throw it away, but decided not to take out her frustration on the roses and put them in water.

She wondered if he'd sent them because he felt guilty about confronting Nick. She thought not. Allie wasn't the type of man who felt guilty about anything. When she'd met him three months earlier she had been told he was a member of the Kansas City Mob and had dated a lot of celebrities. At the time she remembered thinking he had a handsome, albeit sinister, look that made him resemble his hero, George Raft.

She had been intrigued.

Allie had been just one of several men Erin was seeing at the time, and when she finally went to bed with him it was more out of curiosity than sexual attraction. To her he was just one of many casual flings she'd had since she'd broken up with Nick.

In retrospect, she realized that in the past month Allie'd become more and more possessive. He'd gotten close to Stavros, made the production-company deal with the Tropicana—"his" hotel—and then followed them to Las Vegas.

She had been too preoccupied preparing for the film to recognize the warning signs. Now he thought he had exclusive rights to her and had confronted Nick.

Dammit! she thought. It had happened just when she and Nick had gotten back together? Fine . . . she'd respect Nick's wishes and avoid a confrontation with Allie. But there was no way she was letting him anywhere near her.

The chimes rang and she opened the door. Allie was dressed in an impeccable double-breasted blue suit, pale blue shirt, and white tie. He looked every inch the mobster, and was beaming as if he hadn't a care in the world.

"Good evenin', beautiful. You get the posies?"

She stepped aside to let him in and matched his jovial attitude, but was determined to get them out of the suite as soon as possible. She beamed, swiped up her purse, and blithely gushed a fountain of words.

"The flowers are gorgeous, Allie, I love them—and I'd love to offer you a drink but I'm famished. Could we have one at the restaurant? Luigi's? Or did you have something else in mind?"

"Actually I did. I'm in the mood for some Beaner food. I heard about a great Mexican joint in Boulder City."

Allie no more liked Mexican food than he liked sushi, but he'd determined that it was better to stay out of the mainstream until he could get back to Kansas City and talk to Corky Civella. Face-to-face, he knew he could straighten out the beef. Big Allie Saltieri was too valuable to lose.

Erin tried to absorb the concept of Mexican food in Boulder City and cocked an eyebrow.

"Boulder City?"

"Yeah. I was told the food will knock your socks off. You up for it?"

Erin couldn't think of a logical objection, so she laughed and shrugged.

"Why not?"

CHAPTER FIFTY-SEVEN

THE DRIVE TO Boulder City took a half hour, during which they made small talk about Stavros, the film, and the first day's shooting. When they arrived at Papagayo it was anything but impressive. Allie commented that looks could be deceiving, and they walked into the crowded restaurant.

It was obvious they were overdressed. There appeared to be a mixture of locals and tourists, probably there to visit the Boulder Dam, but there were definitely no men's double-breasted or women's pantsuits in evidence.

There was also no maître d'.

There was a cashier—a plump, pink-faced blonde dressed like a Mexican peasant. She was middle-aged, blue-eyed, and was obviously wearing the costume to enhance the restaurant's ambience.

It didn't.

She stared at them curiously and then recognized Erin. Her face flushed and she broke into a wide smile and dashed out from behind her register. Her name tag read BERNICE.

"Ohmigod . . . It's you!"

Erin smiled graciously and offered her hand. "Good evening, Bernice." Bernice took the hand and might have kissed it if Erin hadn't pulled it back—but she kept smiling. "Do you have a table for us?"

"Oh, yes—yes we do. Please—this way."

Bernice proudly led them toward a table as if she were heading up the Rose Bowl parade. Erin was greeted with the usual stares and murmuring, and several times along the way heard hushed observations: *Erin Conroy . . . That's her . . . The Pirate Queen.* Several of the tourists had cameras and snapped pictures.

They sat opposite each other at a small table against the rear wall and Allie picked up a menu.

"Is there a house special?"

"The fajitas," Bernice gushed without looking at him. She was still staring at Erin. "But Carmen—she's our chef—makes everything very special—may I have your autograph?"

She handed Erin a take-out order slip. Erin smiled and signed it while Bernice continued gushing and a waitress appeared. They ordered two martinis, the fajitas, and a bottle of Napa cabernet.

Allie made a production out of lighting a thin cigar and examining the glowing tip. Without looking at her, he spoke conversationally.

"So . . . How was Nick Conti?"

Taken completely off guard, Erin's head jerked back a few inches and she stared wide-eyed before managing a reply.

"I beg your pardon?"

It was exactly the reaction Allie had anticipated—shocked and defensive. He puffed his cigar and remained impassive

"You should—and I accept."

Erin recovered and her eyes narrowed.

"Accept what?"

"Your apology."

Erin leaned forward and her voice became more forceful.

"I didn't apologize—I misunderstood."

"What? About seeing Conti? You denying you saw him?"

Erin felt the blood rush to her face and she struggled not to raise her voice and lash out at him.

"That's none of your business."

"But it is. I'm making it my business."

Allie had remained calm, but Erin was starting to lose it.

"What in God's name makes you think you can?"

Several people at nearby tables heard her raised voice and turned to them.

Allie noticed them.

"Keep your voice down!" He leaned toward her. "You told me Conti was an old friend—not an old lover who you're seeing again."

"Who my old friends and lovers are—or were—remains none of your business!"

"What were you doing for three hours in the suite *I got for you* with your old boyfriend?"

Erin was stunned and her voice went up another notch.

"You had me watched?"

Allie's overblown ego had convinced him that Erin was falling for him and that he had her under control. Why not? All the other broads in his life had. He didn't have a clue that she'd resist him and was stung by what he considered a lack of respect.

He lurched forward and angrily grabbed her wrist.

"You didn't answer my question. Were you fucking him?"

Erin lost it. She jerked her wrist free and leapt out of her chair. The chair flew back into the next table, toppling several glasses. The patrons jumped up to avoid the spill.

Erin dashed toward the door with Allie in her wake. He blindly ran by a table where a mother was feeding a baby in a high chair and knocked it over. The baby crashed to the floor and the mother screamed.

In his anger, Allie either didn't register what he'd done or ignored it. He kept running after Erin and the child's father jumped up and ran after him. The father caught Allie at the door and grabbed him. Allie saw Erin dashing down the street and violently threw the child's father into the cash-register counter.

The man crashed to the floor, Allie ran after Erin, and Bernice dialed the police.

CHAPTER FIFTY-EIGHT

NICK REASONED THAT Pearl must have had some association with the medical profession for Strozzi to have sent for him. Pearl had examined Snuffy and come up with a conclusion as to the cause of death, so he either was or had been a doctor, a nurse, or maybe a paramedic. If he was any of the three and doing business in Las Vegas, it seemed reasonable that he might want to advertise his presence. Nick and Mitch started looking in the most obvious place.

The phone book.

They were back in Nick's office, where Nick carefully made a copy of the cassette and placed the original in his safe. Mitch was looking up names in the Vegas directory.

"Bingo. This might be him."

Nick spun the dial of his wall safe, replaced Hank Donovan's picture over it, and looked over Mitch's shoulder.

"What've you got?"

"Five spelled P-e-a-r-l, two P-e-a-r-l-e, and one P-e-r-l-e. No doctors, nurses, or paramedics, but there's a Pearl in the Yellow Pages who's hawking homeopathic remedies."

Nick scanned the ad.

"There's a phone number but no address."

"Probably working out of his house."

"I'll call Dan."

Nick reached Dietrich with a number he left on his answering service. When Dan got to the phone the background noise suggested he was in a club or a very noisy restaurant. There was a heavy dose of disco booming in the background.

"Dan? Nick . . ."

Dietrich raised his voice above the din.

"Hey pal, what's shakin'?"

"Where the hell are you?"

"At a party in Malibu—checkin' out a wayward wife whose husband's shootin' a picture in Boise . . ."

Nick chuckled. Dietrich's star clientele put him in places that made normal shamuses green.

"You're the man . . . FYI—your bug turned up aces . . . We got what we needed."

"I live to serve. What's your pleasure?"

"An address to go with a phone number."

"Shoot."

"Jason Pearl—Las Vegas. 702-555-2828."

"Got it . . . Stay by your phone."

Nick hung up and poured a pair of Chivas Regals into tumblers while they waited. Fifteen minutes later Dan called back with the results of his reverse phone search.

"The guy you want—Jason Pearl—lives at 111 Crawford Street in North Las Vegas."

"Thanks, Dan. As always—appreciate it."

"No problem. Anything else?"

"At the moment—no. Have a good one."

"I always do, pal . . . Good luck."

CHAPTER FIFTY-NINE

NICK AND MITCH put up the Firebird's top before they drove off. The night air had turned chilly and the wind was up. Vegas was signaling the onset of winter, and although it seldom snowed in the high desert it occasionally got cold enough to freeze your ass off.

They took Las Vegas Boulevard for the short drive to the house on Crawford Street—a one-story bungalow in a quiet neighborhood. There were lights in the first-floor windows but no car in the driveway. Nick parked in front of the house and they rang the doorbell.

A minute later they heard someone coming to the door and a muffled female voice called out.

"Who is it . . . ?"

She sounded wary. Nick and Mitch exchanged glances and Mitch tapped his nose. There was the unmistakable aroma of marijuana in the air.

Nick leaned toward the door.

"Friends of Jason's . . ."

"He's not here . . ."

"Do you know where we can find him?"

"No."

"Listen . . . we've got the herb delivery for Jason. He said he was running low so we rushed right over. Can we leave it with you?"

There was silence on the other side of the door for a few seconds and then a short giggle.

"The herbs?"

"Right. The herbs."

The click of a lock release was followed by the door opening. A beautiful young girl wearing shorts and a halter moved unsteadily forward. She was zaftig, probably in her late teens, and her eyes were a bit unfocused. The sweet smell of marijuana drifted out from behind her.

She was stoned out of her mind.

"Hi . . . I'm Mandy. Where are they?"

Nick smiled.

"You're stoned."

"Sure. Isn't everybody?"

She put her hand over her mouth and giggled again. She made an oblivious effort to recover, succeeded, and held out her hand for the delivery.

Nick ignored the hand.

"You live here with Jason?"

"No. He's my doctor. Where's the—" another giggle—"*herbs.*"

"Do you have the money?"

"What money?" She was suddenly confused.

"For the herbs."

"I haven't got any money." The confusion had become consternation.

"Then we can't leave the stuff. We get paid on delivery. And Jason wants it tonight. If he doesn't get it he'll be angry. Where is he?"

Mandy's stoned face screwed into indecision for several seconds and then she finally made her choice.

"Prob'bly at Maxi's. He goes there to drink."

"The strip joint?"

She was suddenly indignant and her face flushed.

"The gentleman's club! I used to work there . . . until I got knocked up."

"Thanks, Mandy. We'll tell Jason how helpful you've been."

"Is it Maui Wowie?"

"You bet. Only the best."

Her hands shot up and she twirled her fingers. "Wowieee!"

CHAPTER SIXTY

THE SECOND ALLIE dashed out the door, the diners in Papagayo poured out behind him to witness the unfolding drama. They gathered in front of the restaurant and watched, spellbound, as Allie caught up with the beautiful film star and started pulling her back to his car.

It was obvious she was resisting, and the diners shouted demands that Allie let her go. Several rushed forward and stopped him before he could open the car door. The father of the baby Allie had knocked out of its high chair shook his fist and swore he would sue Allie for all he was worth.

The diners seemed to be turning into a lynch mob.

With no other choice, Allie gritted his teeth and released Erin. She hurried back into the restaurant, accompanied by yells of encouragement and the wail of police sirens. Allie groaned.

It was a disaster.

It took an amazed Sergeant Janerone and his partner five minutes to sort out what had led up to the call from Bernice. A man identified as Alphonse Saltieri had brought the film star Erin Conroy to the restaurant, chased her out before they ate, knocked over a baby chair, and attacked the baby's father, a tourist from Des Moines named Arthur Dinsby.

Janerone turned to Dinsby and asked the obvious question.

"Do you want to press charges?"

Dinsby was fired up and snarling.

"You're damned right I do."

Allie's mind had been whirling from the moment he realized how badly he'd fucked up. He'd come all the way out here to avoid attention and then had ignited a fireball. He decided on one of the three ways he knew to deal with a problem. Violence, intimidation, or persuasion. He mustered all of his considerable charm and took a shot at the latter.

"Sergeant . . . Do you mind if I have a private word with Mr. Dinsby?"

Janerone was smart enough to suspect the reason for the request but could find no fault with it. The baby in the high chair apparently hadn't been hurt, there wasn't a mark on Dinsby, a movie star was involved, and he didn't want to spend the rest of the night in a blizzard of paperwork.

He turned to Dinsby.

"Mr. Dinsby?"

Dinsby looked at Allie suspiciously, appeared to mull over the request, and then made a decision.

"Okay . . . but I know my rights. I'm not backing down."

Allie nodded.

"I understand."

Gently taking Dinsby by the arm, Allie moved him away from the crowd until they were behind a parked pickup. When they seemed to be out of sight Allie removed a roll of hundreds from his pocket and casually began peeling them away.

He smiled amiably.

"Mr. Dinsby . . . where're you from?"

Dinsby didn't answer. He seemed mesmerized by Allie's slow, deliberate action with the cash. It was probably more money than he'd ever seen in one place.

Allie stopped counting.

"Mr. Dinsby?"

"Huh?"

"Where're you from?"

"Oh . . . Des Moines."

Allie resumed counting.

"Iowa?"

By now Allie had peeled off fifteen one-hundred-dollar bills. Dinsby's eyes kept getting wider and Allie could see his lips moving. He was counting.

Dinsby nodded absently.

"Uh-huh." His eyes never left the cash.

"A beautiful place, Iowa. What do you do there?"

"I sell shoes."

"Ah . . . Ladies' or men's?"

"Both."

Allie was now up to twenty-one bills. He stepped a little closer to Dinsby and continued counting.

"How many vacations can you take with the money you make selling both?"

"Not many."

Allie refolded the roll and held it out.

"A shame . . . But maybe I can help. There's over three thousand dollars here. Take it with my apologies and forget about tonight."

Thoughts of a lawsuit began to dissolve from Dinsby's mind. It would take time. He lived in Iowa. They were in Nevada. He knew no one here, least of all a good attorney. The man facing him was dating a

movie star. The guy was undoubtedly a big shot. He was a shoe salesman. A bird in the hand . . .

The choice was obvious. He nodded rapidly and took the money.

They returned to Sergeant Janerone and told him that they'd settled
the dispute amicably. Janerone was pleased and said he'd need to take
them to the station and have them make a quick statement to that effect. It'd take ten minutes—no more. Dinsby agreed, and, since there
was no choice, so did Allie.

Everyone walked back into the restaurant.

Erin was sitting in a chair behind the register when they entered.
Janerone smiled at her and touched the brim of his hat. She smiled
back weakly. He wanted to ask for an autograph but figured it would
look unprofessional.

The patrons resumed their dinner. Janerone, followed by Allie,
went over to Bernice. Janerone reached up and tilted his hat up higher
on his forehead.

"It's all settled, Bea. And I don't see as you've got any damage in
here, so why don't we chalk all this up to an interesting night."

Bernice hesitated and turned to Erin.

"It's all right with me if it's all right with Ms. Conroy . . ." She
glared at Allie. "But she doesn't want to go home with him. I called
her a cab."

Allie fumed, but there was little he could do. He couldn't force her
to go with him with two goddamn cops standing there, so he nodded
and walked out.

Allie and Dinsby went with the cops. Erin went with the cab driver.

CHAPTER SIXTY-ONE

MAXI'S WAS LESS than half full when Nick and Mitch arrived. And the bored girl gyrating around the pole looked like she was less than half there. "Y.M.C.A." was blaring out of the speaker system, but the thundering beat did little to motivate her desultory moves. These were the midevening warm-up dancers—neophytes performing for locals and early boozers. The first team wouldn't hit the stage for another couple of hours.

Mandy had said Pearl came here to drink. With a bombshell like Mandy at home it didn't seem logical that he came to ogle the girls—especially the early girls. Mitch and Nick figured they were looking for a man alone who was paying more attention to his drink than the stage.

They scanned the tables. Most of them had parties of two or more, and the few with solo occupants were staring at the stage. The long bar had over two dozen stools but only three pairs of drinkers in the middle and two solos at either end. The one at the near end looked to be in his early twenties and was chatting with the bartender. The other, at the far end, was in his late forties or early fifties and was hunched over his drink in the classic posture of a longtime lush.

Bingo.

They walked up to the older man and sat on either side of him. The man's head popped up—reacting to the sudden intrusion.

Nick put a small cassette recorder on the bar and turned to him.

"Jason Pearl?"

Immediately wary, he quickly glanced left and right and realized he'd been sandwiched. He had the raspy voice of a smoker but his speech wasn't slurred.

"Who wants to know?"

"Two associates of Carlo Strozzi."

Pearl again glanced left and right—alarmed this time—probably trying to determine if the two intruders were cops.

Nick answered the unasked question.

"We're not cops."

"What do you want?"

Nick slid the recorder over to a point directly below Pearl's chin and mashed the play button.

Pearl: "Jason Pearl . . . Hi, Carlo, what's the problem?"

Carlo: "It's on the couch."

Pearl stared at the cassette as if it were an alien reaching for his throat. When he heard himself say, "He's dead," he punched the off button. "You said you weren't cops." He pointed at the tape. "How'd you get that?"

"Not important. We have it and we're not cops."

"What do you want?"

"To do a little business . . . If and when it becomes necessary—and we don't think it will—we want you to tell the cops that the reason we know that Snuffy wound up dead in Strozzi's office was not this tape—that the information came from you."

The bartender came over and addressed the new arrivals.

"What're you havin'?"

"Two Chivas and another for our friend."

The bartender nodded and went to fill the order. Pearl waited until he was out of earshot and came up with an obvious objection.

"I didn't report it! I'll get busted!"

"No . . . The tape will disappear. And we'll swear that you were with us when Fats and Angie came and took you to Strozzi's office at gunpoint. They tied you up and you weren't able to escape until tomorrow."

"They'll deny it."

"Our word against theirs."

Pearl took a slug of his drink and rubbed his chin with his knuckles, trying to untangle the angles.

"What makes you think I won't have to tell the cops about the body?"

"Strozzi has more to lose than you. If any of this gets out, he'll have a murder rap hanging over him."

Pearl digested the scenario and slugged down the last of his drink. The bartender arrived with the fresh order and Mitch threw a twenty on the bar.

Pearl guzzled half his drink and turned to Nick.

"What do I get?"

Nick smiled.

"You get to *not* explain why you were called to examine a man who'd been beaten to death, and why a stoned dancer who used to work here claims you're her doctor."

At the last revelation Pearl's blood drained from his face. He was speechless. But he had enough left of his wits to nod his head.

He was theirs.

CHAPTER SIXTY-TWO

NO ONE HAD said a word all through dinner. The atmosphere was as morbid as a death watch—not because they had just buried a body—but because they didn't know how to solve their dilemma and get back on track for their five-thousand-a-week rip-off of *The $trip*.

Strozzi had finished his tripe and was thoughtfully smoking a cigar, but Angie was still devouring a large seven-topping pizza. Fats couldn't eat. His stomach was still queasy from the ghoulish work he'd done on Snuffy's body.

Strozzi's morose face suddenly brightened. He snapped his fingers and turned to Fats.

"What was that guy's name?"

"Huh? What guy?"

"The guy Snuffy said he was partying with before he went to Henderson to see the waitress."

"The actor?"

"Him."

"Brad somethin' . . . He plays the Vegas cop."

Strozzi reached over and yanked a weekly planner out of Angie's inside jacket pocket. Angie jerked his head back in surprise, and four of the pizza's seven toppings wound up in his lap.

Strozzi flipped to the addresses and phone numbers, grinned, and got up. He went to the phone next to the register and, without asking permission, or even looking at the aged, overly made-up cashier, he punched in a number and waited.

"Skeets? Carlo . . . I'm good . . . You're a fan of the TV show *The $trip*, right . . . Yeah. What's the name of the guy who plays the Vegas cop? Right! Yeah! That's it! Thanks, Skeets."

Strozzi hung up, returned to the table, and joyfully plunged the planner back into Angie's inside coat pocket. This time Angie saw it coming and jerked his pizza out of harm's way.

Strozzi sat and spread his arms. He was triumphant.

"Tilden! Brad Tilden!"

Angie didn't react, but Fats nodded.

"Right . . . I read somewhere that he's a local actor . . ."

"Also—right! And now that I remember—he said he went with Snuffy and that Lori whatshername to the Sunset Arms . . ."

"So?"

"So that means if Snuffy was with him, Tilden knows for how long and when he left."

"You think he could've set fire to the warehouse after he left Tilden and the Lori broad?"

"I do. Let's go."

Strozzi jumped up and started out, followed a second later by Fats. Angie was about to object that he hadn't finished his pizza, but thought better of it—he stuffed the last slice in his mouth and dashed after them.

CHAPTER SIXTY-THREE

THE SUNSET ARMS was an apartment complex on the east side of Vegas off Tropicana—multiple four-story buildings with terraces around a large center patio and pool shaded by palms. The pool and patio were visible between the buildings and warmly lit by landscape lighting.

Nice.

Brad Tilden's name was on the registry in the second building Fats checked. He rang the buzzer, waited a minute, and then lumbered back to Strozzi and Angie in the car.

"He's in one-oh-two but there's no answer. Maybe he's still out to dinner."

"Okay, we wait."

Angie was behind the wheel and he suddenly leaned forward. He slapped Fats on the arm and pointed.

Fats leaned forward and squinted at a dimly lit figure climbing out of the pool. It was Brad Tilden.

He turned to Strozzi.

"That's him, boss."

Strozzi opened the rear door and got out. Tilden was toweling off and there was no one else in or around the pool. Strozzi shut the door and started toward the pool.

"Let's go."

Fats and Angie followed as he walked up behind Tilden, who didn't register their presence until they were nearly on top of him. When he did, he turned and Strozzi pointed a finger at him.

"Tilden?"

Tilden's eyes quickly swept over the three men. The talker was short—no more than five six, ferret-faced, and obviously the boss. The other two were behemoths. The smaller one was probably six three, three hundred, and had a harelip and a ponytail. The larger one was at least an inch taller and thirty pounds heavier. Tilden thought he looked a little like Fatso Judson in *From Here to Eternity*. It didn't take a genius to figure out that whoever they were and whatever they wanted, it couldn't be good.

Tilden fought to remain impassive.

"I'm Tilden . . . What can I do for you?"

"A few questions. Have a seat."

Strozzi lowered his finger and pointed to a chaise. Tilden never considered objecting. The Speedo he was wearing made him feel nearly naked and even more vulnerable. He wrapped the towel around his waist and sat.

Strozzi pulled up a lawn chair and slowly lowered himself into it.

"You're a friend of Snuffy Benton . . ."

"Yes. He's our stunt co-coordinator and Hank Donovan's double."

"Right. When'd you last see him?"

"Yesterday. He didn't show up for work today."

"When yesterday?"

"Last night . . . What's this about?"

"Not important. What time last night didja last see him—say maybe after ten—when you, him, and the broad were sniffin' coke here at your place?"

Tilden knew these men were dangerous—and they knew too much. He feared what might happen if he tried to bluff them.

"Snuffy, Lori, and I got here a little after ten. He stayed about an hour and left."

Strozzi rubbed his chin and processed the time frame. It was still possible for Snuffy to have gone directly to the warehouse and set the second fire.

He decided to push Tilden a bit further.

"You guys get pretty ripped last night?"

Tilden's eyes nervously darted around. "I . . . Maybe . . . I guess so . . . It was prime stuff."

"He say anything about the warehouse?"

Again Tilden was taken aback. Where the hell was this all going? He answered the question with a question.

"What warehouse?"

"The only one in your life, junkie. The one you work in. The one that got torched—twice. The last time—last night!"

"I don't know what you're talking about. Snuffy never said a word about the warehouse. He said he was going to Henderson to see a waitress."

Again Strozzi processed the information. Snuffy and Tilden's stories matched—the time frame was possible but improbable—and Snuffy had no reason to torch the warehouse a second time. So who the hell did it? He still didn't know.

Disgusted, he got up, started to leave, and turned back.

"You like the blow you were sniffin', come see me . . . Strozzi—Poolorama. Four hundred an ounce."

They left and Tilden put his brain in gear. He knew about the series of incidents leading up to the first fire—the slashed tires, the sabotaged brakes—and Johnny Johansen's sudden "accident." It was obvious to everyone in the crew that an extortion attempt was in progress. They were in a Mob town and the Mob was almost certainly behind what was happening.

Now three guys who reek of Mob had shown up and started asking questions. Snuffy knows Strozzi because Strozzi's his supplier. But their main interest wasn't in coke—it was in Snuffy's whereabouts last night, and it obviously had something to do with the fires.

Again—why?

The only logical reason was that Strozzi and Snuffy were both involved with the extortion.

He smiled. Now that he had that interesting piece of speculation in his pocket, he'd have to figure out what to do with it.

CHAPTER SIXTY-FOUR

NICK IGNORED THE alley and parked on Fremont about a block away from Poolorama. Pedestrian traffic was mid-evening heavy and the many bars, including Poolorama, were rocking with Merle Haggard and Hank Williams in vocal duels with Patsy Cline and Tammy Wynette.

Country-western punctuated by slot machines.

Nick told Mitch to take the Beretta and they strolled into the pool hall. All the tables were occupied, as were most of the slots along the wall. The bar was fairly crowded but there was no sign of Angie at the office door in the rear wall, where he was usually stationed when Strozzi was in residence.

Nick was about to try knocking when Angie came out of the men's room and belligerently took up his station in front of the door.

Nick smiled pleasantly.

"Please inform Mr. Strozzi that Mr. Conti and Mr. Tanaka are in attendance and are requesting an audience."

Angie's lip twitched. There it was again. Every time Conti showed up he made some wise-ass comment to put him down. He hated the prick and vowed that one day he'd stuff his words up his ass. But for now he merely rapped his thick knuckles on the door, then waited the prescribed few seconds and opened it.

Strozzi was seated with his feet on the gray metal desk, and Fats was on the threadbare couch. His pudgy hands seemed permanently folded over his protruding belly, and the shoulder holster holding the .38 was smothered between his massive left arm and chest.

Strozzi gave Nick a menacing head-to-toe appraisal.

"Whaddaya want, Conti?"

Nick spread his hands, smiled warmly, and stepped toward the desk radiating amiability.

"Call it a negotiation."

Strozzi's eyes narrowed. He'd had a rough day. It'd gained him nothing and he wasn't in the mood for chit-chat.

"Get to the point, Conti. Whaddaya want?"

"It's more what you're going to want, Carlo."

"Yeah? What's that?"

"To stay out of death row."

Fats leaned forward and Angie moved a menacing step closer to Nick and Mitch. He stopped an arm's length away.

Strozzi jerked his feet off the desk, grabbed the arms of his chair, and glared.

"The hell are you talkin' about?"

"I know you paid Snuffy to torch my warehouse, I know you killed him, and I know Jason Pearl."

Strozzi glanced at Fats and Angie. His brain spun. How the hell could Conti know? Did Pearl rat him out? If so, he was dead.

Strozzi scoffed at the revelation.

"Bullshit. You know nothin'."

Nick placed the tape recorder on Strozzi's desk, hit play, and the sequence began. First the meaningless babble from Carlo, Fats, and Angie, followed by knocking and the door being answered. Then the voice of the disgraced doctor.

"Jason Pearl."

"Hi, Carlo, what's the problem?"

"It's on the couch."

"What happened to him?"

"That's what I want you to tell me."

Strozzi's eyes widened and then glazed in shock as he realized what he was listening to. Fats's jaw began to drop and Angie moved around Nick and Mitch. He stared down at the recorder as if it would make it less incriminating.

But it only got worse.

"He's a stuntman?"

"Yeah."

"This man's dead."

"What?"

"I only hit 'im a few times!"

That did it. Fats heard himself admit on tape that he'd murdered Snuffy, and he snapped. He bolted out of the chair screaming and lunged at Nick. His outstretched hands wrapped around Nick's throat.

"You cocksucker—you're dead!"

His charge drove Nick into the wall and Fats manically forced his thumbs into Nick's Adam's apple.

Mitch reacted in a split second and rabbit-punched Fats. It stunned him. He released Nick's neck and dropped to one knee. A normal human would have been out for a week.

A moment later Angie whirled around and joined the action by pinning Mitch's arms in a bear hug. Mitch was lifted off the floor and instantly felt the air being squeezed out of him. He was powerless in the crushing grip and his ribs were close to cracking.

Nick saw what was happening, leapt over Fats, and threw a right hook up and into Angie's armpit. He grunted and his arm went limp. Mitch dropped out of the vise and Nick threw a series of combinations into Angie's face and body. Angie was bloodied and staggered back into the desk but he didn't go down. Nick threw a final thundering roundhouse that spun Angie around and put him facedown on the desk—but his legs were still under him.

Nick was beginning to believe that both of these guys were super-human. He gave up on the ineffective punching, grabbed Angie's ponytail, jerked his head back, and put him in a choke hold.

Mitch recovered his breath and was about to aid Nick, but Fats got off his knee, shook out the cobwebs, and charged him. A mistake. The black belt deftly sidestepped, grabbed Fats's arm, and used the big man's momentum to run him headfirst into the opposite wall.

Fats again went down—this time for good.

Strozzi, who had been comatose from the first time he heard his voice on the tape, finally recovered. He pulled a gun out of his desk drawer and pointed it at Nick.

His hand was shaking.

"Hold it, you sonofabitch, or I'll blow your face off!"

Nick froze. He stared at the black hole of a .357 Magnum and, with no other alternative, slowly began to release his grip on Angie's neck. A moment later Mitch's calm and very soft voice cut the tension.

"Not a good idea, Carlo."

Mitch was pointing the Berretta at Strozzi's head. Strozzi's eyes darted from Nick to Mitch. It was a Mexican stand-off. He was still recovering from the shock of the tape—he'd seen his two protectors go down in seconds, and he knew if he pulled the trigger he'd be as dead as Conti.

He lowered the gun.

Nick pulled Angie back a few steps, hooked his leg behind Angie's calves, and tripped him. Angie toppled onto the couch like a disjoined puppet.

Nick turned and smiled at Strozzi.

"As I was saying, Carlo . . . What I believe you'll want is to stay out of death row . . . Here's how it works." He swiped the recorder off the desk. "I don't give this tape to the cops—you don't go anywhere near Pearl—and we both forget you ever tried to blackmail me."

Strozzi sunk into his chair. He slowly surveyed his damaged office and his two defeated thugs. He mentally reviewed his options and made the only possible decision.

He shook his head. It was over.

"Okay, Conti . . . you win. Forget the shakedown. But how do I know you still won't take that tape to the cops?"

Nick smiled and threw the words Strozzi had uttered two days earlier back at him.

"You don't. That's the beauty of our positions here. I got you by the balls, and all I gotta do is squeeze to make you squeal." He looked at Mitch. "Ain't that right?"

Mitch smiled. "That's right . . ."

CHAPTER SIXTY-FIVE

ALLIE POPPED TWO more antacid tablets into his mouth, angrily chewed, and swallowed. It was his third pair since the disaster at Papagayo and his stomach was still on fire. All he could think of was damage control—and revenge.

The bitch had defied and humiliated him and gotten him picked up by the goddamn cops. He was supposed to keep his affair with Conroy quiet and he'd tried, for chrissakes! He'd taken her all the way out to fucking Boulder City!

He'd paid off the rube from Des Moines, schmoozed the cop with a tip at Aqueduct, and was about to cover one last base.

Papagayo was still crowded when he parked and entered. Bernice was still at the cash register. She saw him as he walked in and frowned.

He gave her his best smile.

"Hello again, Bernice."

"You come back to start another fight?"

"Hardly . . . I came back to apologize and see if I could make it up to you."

Bernice noticed that the diners at a few nearby tables had recognized Allie and were whispering. The last thing she wanted was another disturbance.

She waved off his offer.

"Apology accepted, but I don't need anything else."

"How about a check to cover the dinner I ordered but didn't pay for."

"Not necessary. You didn't eat it."

Allie removed a checkbook and began writing.

"I insist . . ."

Bernice didn't want to argue; she wanted to get rid of him, so she let him write.

When he finished he handed her the check.

"For dinner, and a tip for your kindness."

Bernice looked at the check and her eyes popped.

"This is for two thousand dollars!"

Allie smiled.

"I know."

"I can't take this! It's—it's—I don't know what it is, but it's wrong." She thrust the check back at Allie.

He gently pushed her hand back toward her ample bust.

"Please . . ."

"But . . ."

"No buts . . . Take it—do something wonderful for yourself and forget about tonight." He left before she could object again and dropped his smile the second he was out the door.

Satisfied that there was nothing more he could do to cover the tracks he'd left in Boulder City, he headed back to the Tropicana to deal with the bitch.

CHAPTER SIXTY-SIX

NICK CALLED SAM from the car phone on the way
back to the hotel. He told him that Strozzi had been neutralized
but he still had the Hall problem and the second fire to deal
with. But at least the main threat had been taken out.

He told Mitch to have a second-unit director to replace Snuffy
flown in from L.A. first thing in the morning, and begged off having a nightcap in the lounge with him. Nick returned to his suite
and as usual his message light was blinking. The message was from
Erin.

She'd checked into the Desert Inn.

That couldn't be good. He knew she'd been out with Allie and
swore at himself for suggesting that she have dinner with him. The
number indicated that her room was in the Wimbledon and on his
floor.

He dialed it and she answered.

"Nick?"

"Yes . . . Are you all right?"

"I guess so . . . I mean yes, I'm not hurt, but the dinner was a nightmare . . ."

"I'm right down the hall."

"I know . . . I asked."

"Hang up, I'm answering the door."

Nick hung up and opened the door. A few seconds later he saw her coming toward him. Even though she'd obviously dressed down and was wearing slacks and flat-heeled shoes, there was no mistaking the sensuality she introduced to the simple act of walking.

In the last few steps she broke into a run, threw her arms around him, and began sobbing.

"Nick . . . It was awful . . ."

"It's okay, love, you're here now."

Nick led her to the couch and eased her down, but didn't sit. She looked up at him, stammering.

"I-it was terrible, Nico. He . . ."

"In a minute . . . You sound like you could use a drink first."

She removed a Kleenex from her purse and dabbed her eyes.

"I'm sure I look it, too."

Nick laughed, trying to break the mood.

"You? Never. You could pose for *Playboy* after a train wreck." He kissed her lightly and ruffled her hair.

She finally managed a smile.

"Make it scotch—neat—no ice."

Nick poured two tumblers of Chivas, returned to the couch, and sat. Erin took a sip and began telling him what had happened at Papagayo. Nick was sure Allie had taken her to Boulder City because of Nello's warning to keep his affair with Erin under wraps. What he couldn't figure out was why Allie had lost his cool.

And then she said Allie had been watching her suite. He knew they'd spent three hours together and wanted to know if she was fucking Nick.

It hadn't been Allie who'd lost it—it had been Erin. She bolted the restaurant—Allie dashed after her and turmoil ensued.

Nick took her hand and kissed it.

"I'll have it out with Allie tomorrow. I'll tell him to back off or I'll relate his little escapade at Papagayo to Nello, who'll relay it to Corky Civella. He can't let that happen—he'll back off."

She vigorously shook her head.

"He'll come looking for me tonight, Nico! This is the first place he'll think of."

"Fine—let him come. He'll find out tonight what I was going to tell him tomorrow."

"He's a violent man, Nick. You told me so yourself. He could be coming with a gun."

"Allie's imposing, violent, and arrogant—but he's not stupid. And that would be stupid. Too many people know he hates me. He was heard threatening me in my office. Julie knows. Mitch Tanaka knows. Stavros probably knows and Nello definitely knows . . . No—Allie won't be coming after me with a gun."

"You're sure . . ."

"I'm sure."

Erin reluctantly nodded acceptance and put down her drink.

"Can I stay with you tonight?"

"Tonight—and any other night . . ."

A beautifully warm smile crossed Erin's lips and Nick got up and held out his hand. She took it and he led her into the bedroom.

CHAPTER SIXTY-SEVEN

ALLIE FOUND NELLO backstage at the Tropicana. He was with Joe Agosto and they were watching a topless *Folies Bergere* performance from the wings. The girls were dancing to a lavish rendition of Porter's "It's De-Lovely." Donn Arden was watching with them, and Allie recognized the music and routine he'd seen the girls rehearsing the prior day.

No doubt Nello was carrying out his plan to "relax around the pool, see some shows, and jump a few broads." Agosto had suggested they kill two birds with one stone, and they were in the process of selecting a suitable subject to implement his wishes.

Because he was Corky Civella's envoy, the implementation of Nello's wishes in Corky's hotel was both automatic and mandatory.

Allie touched Nello's arm to get his attention, then jerked his head away from the stage to indicate he wanted to speak to him. Nello turned and looked more pissed off than usual at the intrusion. He took a last glance at the stage and whispered something in Agosto's ear. Agosto nodded and whispered in Arden's ear.

Subject selected—wishes implemented.

Nello followed Allie to a back corner of the stage.

"What the hell's the problem, Al?"

"The problem is that I had one tonight."

Nello was immediately wary. It couldn't be a little problem or Allie wouldn't have immediately sought him out. He would have waited until morning.

"What kind?"

Allie proceeded to tell him a sanitized version of what had happened at the restaurant, but included the major details.

"You stupid sonofabitch! And after I come here specifically to tell you to cool it with this broad!"

"I took her to Boulder City for chrissakes! Who the hell was gonna see us in Boulder City?"

"You just gave a fucking list of them!"

"I handled them all. I gave the cop a tip on a race, paid off the rube, and bribed the hostess."

Nello was barely able to control his temper.

"What about the broad? What'd you do about her?"

"Nothin' yet. She split while the rube and I were making a statement at the station."

"You're on record—what makes you think the cop's gonna keep his mouth shut?"

"He's a shit-kickin' cop in a rinky-dink town. But he's a big fan of Erin's. I told him it would really embarrass her if the story got out. He was grateful for the tip and said he'd clam up."

"If you've got an ounce of fucking brains in that thick head, you'll head for church, light a hundred candles, and pray you're right."

"I'm right—but I wanted you to hear what happened from me."

"What is it with you and this broad? Agosto told me you put eyes on her suite. They saw Conti go in and said they told you . . . What's the big fucking deal?"

"She's been fucking him."

"So what? You don't own her. She's free, white, and twenty-one!"

"She's my territory."

"Yours! She's a fucking star!" He twirled his fingers around his temple. "And you've gone *pazzo*!"

"Maybe . . . but I'm headed for Kansas City in the morning to straighten it all out with Corky."

Nello shook his head, too exasperated to say anything more. He just turned and walked back to the wings.

Allie went to a house phone and called Erin's suite. He let it ring ten times, got no answer, hung up, and tried again with the same result. He knew she'd had more than enough time to get back to the hotel. Either she wasn't there—or she was and wasn't answering the phone.

He wasn't about to stand for that bullshit.

He went back to the wings and picked up Agosto.

Agosto called the head of security and they took the elevator to the penthouse. The security chief opened Erin's suite with a passkey and they found it empty, but Allie noticed open drawers in the bedroom and checked the closet. A piece of the matched luggage she'd checked in with, along with her makeup case, was missing.

She'd been here and left.

It didn't take a genius to figure she'd run to the DI and Conti. He called, asked for Erin Conroy's room, and got it. After listening once again to ten rings he hung up. There was no question in his mind that she was in Conti's room, but a confrontation with him could lead to yet another major fuck-up, and one was enough for one night.

She was filming in the morning. He'd deal with her then—before he left for Kansas City, and when Conti wouldn't be around to interfere.

CHAPTER SIXTY-EIGHT

DAY FOUR

NELLO LET THE leggy dancer continue sleeping and put on a robe. Her face was rather plain without the ton of makeup she wore onstage, but her taut body, perky tits, and chalk-blonde hair had sealed the deal.

Hildigunn Jorgensen was his choice. Norwegian, and certainly an inventive bed partner, but he was getting paranoid about always winding up with women with weird names.

He answered the door to his suite and admitted room service with the breakfast he'd ordered before taking Hildi to bed. A continental for her, oatmeal for him.

His ulcer was acting up.

The waiter poured coffee while Nello sipped his milk and opened the complimentary newspaper on the serving cart.

He almost choked on the milk.

The banner headline splashed across the front page of the *Las Vegas Review Journal* read:

And there was a picture—a fucking picture! Allie running after Erin, probably taken by one of the customers.

The story was by Ned Day, a crusading crime reporter and investigative journalist for KLAS-TV. He'd been dogging the heels of the Vegas Mob since the late 1970s and was absolutely fearless. His documentary, *The Mob on the Run*, had revealed organized crime's hidden ownership of Vegas casinos and the depth of their partnership with public officials.

He had them literally shaking in their boots.

Nello read that Day had gotten the story from Bernice Logan, the cashier at Papagayo restaurant in Boulder City. She said that Erin Conroy, a star she loved, had come to her restaurant with a man she thought was very shady looking. They'd argued, Erin ran out, and he chased her. He'd almost killed a baby on the way and knocked down the baby's father.

Bernice called the police and they took away the shady culprit. But he returned and insulted her! The so-called tip he gave her was an obvious bribe to shut her up.

The story went on to say she'd called the newspaper and got Ned Day. He called the police and got a name. A name he knew very well—Alphonse Saltieri from Kansas City. He laid out Saltieri's connections to Corky Civella, the Tropicana, and Erin Conroy . . . who was staying in a high roller's suite.

Nello's ulcer singed his stomach.

Day had gone to Boulder City to interview Sergeant Janerone and Bernice. He then tried to reach Erin Conroy, but she wasn't answering his calls to the Tropicana. Faced with a deadline, he wrote the story without her—embellishing it with an abundance of lurid details.

Nello read and reread the entire story, put down the newspaper, and picked up the phone.

"Al Saltieri's room."

"Yessir."

A few moments passed, and then a second voice came on the line.

"Barnwell at the front desk, Mr. Marchetti . . . Mr. Saltieri just checked out."

"Did he order a limo?" Nello figured that if he'd left for the airport and was on his way to Kansas City, he was now Corky's problem.

"Yessir, but he hasn't left yet. He told us to give his luggage to the driver and have him wait out front. Mr. Saltieri walked out the rear doors to the parking lot." Nello slammed down the phone.

Allie was still his problem.

He dashed back into the bedroom and broke records getting dressed. If Allie had seen the morning paper, the fucking idiot might have gone berserk. Nello knew the wound-up bastard could be on his way to doing something stupid.

The clerk said he'd gone out to the parking lot—which was where the film company's vehicles were parked, including Erin Conroy's. If that's where he was headed, Nello had to stop him from doing something that would bring even more heat down on them.

Hildi woke up as Nello was leaving. She sat up in bed, revealing her wondrously perky tits, and greeted him in the accented, melodic, sing-song voice so characteristic of Scandinavians.

"Good morning, Nello . . . and how are you feeling this lovely sun-shiny morning?"

"Just fuckin' great."

He stormed out without looking at her.

CHAPTER SIXTY-NINE

ALLIE CROSSED THE parking lot and purposefully walked toward Erin's trailer with a set jaw. He had an hour before his eleven o'clock plane to Kansas City. Dressed casually for the flight in slacks, a sweater, a windbreaker, and a baseball cap, the attire also made him inconspicuous to the crew members that weren't filming inside the casino.

He spotted Trudy having coffee at the catering truck and walked over to his spy.

"Morning, Trudy . . . Is Erin in her trailer?"

"Nosir . . . But she has a ten o'clock call so she'll probably be here any minute."

"Good . . . I'll wait in her trailer—but don't tell her I'm here. I want it to be a surprise."

"Fine, Mr. Saltieri. I'll be out here in case she needs me."

Allie entered the lavish motor home with pop-out sides. The

expanded living area was followed by an ample kitchen and dining area—a hall led to a bath and bedroom in the rear.

Allie was still seething. He had read the complimentary newspaper when he got up and, as Nello predicted, had flown into a rage. *That goddamn fucking cashier?* And after he'd paid her off! He'd handle that bitch when he came back to Vegas. Right now he wanted to concentrate on the bitch that would be arriving any minute.

Allie wanted to beat the shit out of her. He would have, but she was too goddamned high profile. After what happened at Papagayo, the cops would believe her when she fingered him and he'd wind up doing five to ten for assault. Not worth it. But at least he would take a shot at giving her a heart attack.

He went into the bathroom, closed the door, and waited.

Nick had just pulled into the parking lot. He'd insisted on driving Erin to the set for her ten o'clock call. He wanted to ensure she was safely ensconced with the film crew before he went up to Allie's suite.

They were in the afterglow of their first full night together in two years. They'd enjoyed a leisurely morning of nostalgia in bed, love in the shower, and breakfast on the patio. Erin said she had only one scene to shoot and thought she'd be finished by midafternoon. They could have cocktails at five—with a predinner appetizer of each other.

As he drove up to Erin's motor home his car phone rang. It was Julie.

"Nick—two things. One—Johnny took Chrissie to San Diego last night and didn't get our message until this morning. They left La Costa at nine and should be in Vegas by four. And two—I just heard from Alfred. He's in the limo with Sam and Gwen . . . Cojo and Jake are driving *them* to Vegas."

Shit! Just what I need. "When'll they get here?"

"By one—they left at nine. They're booked into the Wimbledon."

"Okay—see you in half an hour."

Nick hung up and saw Trudy approaching from where she was waiting by the catering truck.

She was the smiling picture of innocence.

"Good morning, Ms. Conroy . . ."

"Morning, Trudy . . . I'll just run in to pick up my script and then I'll meet you in makeup and hair."

"Fine, Ms. Conroy . . . Can I get you coffee?"

"Sure . . ."

Trudy took off and Erin leaned over to kiss Nick.

"Be careful, Nico . . ."

"No problem . . . I'll see you for dinner."

Erin got out of the car and entered the motor home feeling relaxed and safe after an unforgettable night. It'd been two years since they'd spent an entire night together and she imagined she'd never get enough of them or him.

Allie heard Erin come in and tensed. He waited a few seconds, threw open the bathroom door so violently that it slammed into the adjoining wall, and stepped out.

Erin was at the desk and had just picked up her script. She whirled around and froze. She would have screamed if she hadn't been so shocked. Allie was standing five feet away and had an open straight razor in his hand.

She gasped and involuntarily tried to step back but was blocked by the desk. In two quick steps he was on her—his left arm embracing her—his left hand bringing the razor to her cheek.

His lips curled into a satanic grin and his voice was eerily calm.

"Good morning, bitch . . . Have a nice night?"

Erin felt the blood draining from her head and thought she was about to faint. Allie relished the terror in her eyes.

"You're not going to have a nice morning . . . your beautiful face isn't going to survive it . . ." He laid the flat of the blade against her cheek so that she could feel the cold steel.

Erin recovered enough to believe he'd use the razor no matter what she did or said. She'd played a heroine who'd gone down fighting on film—remembered the moves—and used them on Allie.

Her right foot crashed down on his instep and her left knee flew into his groin. More in shock than pain, he lurched back and dropped the razor.

At that moment Nello burst through her door, instantly absorbed the scene, and knew he'd guessed right. Erin was terrified, Allie's eyes were glazed, and he was bending down to swipe up a straight razor.

Nello stepped forward and pulled a snub-nosed revolver out of his waistband.

"That's enough, Allie!"

Allie looked at Nello—first surprised and then confused. He was totally immobile for several seconds and then seemed to register the futility of his situation. His fury slowly evaporated and he seemed to literally deflate. His hand opened and the razor dropped.

His voice was weak, almost apologetic.

"I wasn't going to cut her . . . I just wanted to scare the shit out of her."

Erin was still terrified but her voice was strong.

"Congratulations . . . You did one hell of a job."

Nello stepped aside and waved his gun at the door—his voice pure ice.

"Get out, Al . . . Get out and get on that fucking plane . . . Get on it and stay on it until you get where it's going and get yourself straightened out."

"Nello . . ."

"Now, Allie . . . Now."

Allie recovered a bit of his bravado and shot Erin an icy glare. "Be seeing you . . . Bet on it." Without looking at Nello, he stalked out.

Nello turned to Erin and slid the gun into his waistband.

"With all due respect, lady, someone like you should have a better class of friends."

Erin saw a smile on the man's face, even though he sounded irritated. "Who are you?"

"A friend of your friend . . . Tell Nick, Nello dropped by to play hero. He'll like that." Nello started out, stopped, and looked back. "You can also tell him he's got good taste."

CHAPTER SEVENTY

NICK WENT DIRECTLY to suite 2110 and used a credit card to slip the lock. Removing the Beretta from his waistband, he quietly opened Allie's door, entered, and listened. Absolute quiet.

Within minutes he determined that the suite and closets were empty, and after calling the front desk found that Allie had checked out.

He dialed Nello's suite and he picked up on the first ring.

"Marchetti . . ."

"Nick. When did Allie check out?"

"Where are you?"

"In his suite."

There were a few moments of silence before Nello spoke again.

"Meet me in the coffee shop."

Nick joined Nello at a quiet table five minutes later. He noticed Nello was drinking milk, and as usual he addressed Nick without preamble and in his permanently dyspeptic voice.

"You seen your girlfriend?"

Nick raised an eyebrow.

"Excuse me?"

"Conroy—the actress—the broad that's caused a shitstorm in the past three days—the one Allie tried to cut up a half hour ago."

The last comment shook Nick to his toes.

"The hell are you talking about?"

"Allie . . . I stopped him from using a razor on her."

Nick jumped up, but Nello grabbed his wrist before he could leave.

"Sit down. Allie's gone. On a plane back to KC. The girl's fine."

Nick reluctantly sat and Nello told him what had happened from the time he read the newspaper until he found Allie in Erin's motor home and ordered him out of town.

By the time Nello finished relating the events, Nick was a picture of barely controlled rage.

"I'm going to take that sonofabitch apart."

Nello shook his head.

"Don't . . . Whatever you think you might do to him, Nicolo, it's child's play compared to what Corky's gonna do when he reads that paper."

Nick considered for a few long moments and realized it was true.

"Okay, Nello, but if he doesn't, I will."

Nello hated Allie for the trouble he'd caused, for what he'd done, and for what he was. Attacking a woman, for chrissakes! He knew that if Nick eventually went after Allie, neither he nor Corky would stop him.

He nodded.

"Understood."

Nick thanked Nello and left for Erin's motor home. There was a small knot of crew members lingering around her door when he entered.

She was sitting on the couch. Stavros, Trudy, the assistant director, and script supervisor were crowded around her. Stavros was trying to talk her out of doing the scene he'd scheduled.

"Erin . . . I've plenty of other work I can do. You've had a helluva shock. We'll do your scene tomorrow. The best thing for you is to relax and recover."

Erin looked admirably calm after what she'd been through, and she was adamant.

"The best thing for me is to take my mind off what just happened." She saw Nick, her face lit up, and she held out her hand. "Hi . . . I guess you've heard . . ."

"I did." He took her hand and sat. "You sure you want to go to work right now?"

She nodded gently.

"I'm sure."

Stavros, who obviously had no idea who Nick was, pointed at him and looked questioningly at his coworkers. They all shrugged and shook their heads. They also had no idea who he was.

Stavros looked back at Nick.

"Excuse me. Who are you?"

Nick got up, stuck out his hand, and introduced himself.

"Nick Conti . . . I produce *The $trip.*"

"You're the guy from the television show." He said it with a filmmaker's obvious disdain for TV.

Nick disregarded the obvious disrespect and smiled.

"The same . . . Ms. Conroy and I are very old friends. And knowing her as well as I do—and as one professional to another—I'd advise you to honor her request and shoot her scene."

Stavros looked at his star. He saw Erin looking at Nick with something close to adoration and spun on his heels.

What he did next sounded like a bellow.

"First team!"

CHAPTER SEVENTY-ONE

NICK RETURNED TO his office hoping that he could pull off what he was planning, still find time to rewrite Lori's scenes, and have enough left over to see Erin—who still had to be in a state of shock, no matter what she said.

Julie got up to meet him as he entered.

"Brad Tilden called from the set. He wants to see you right away. He said it was urgent."

Nick was surprised by the message. Brad was not a costar like Johnny and Lori. He was a journeyman local actor, someone who was unlikely to leave a message asking for an urgent meeting with the executive producer.

"Did he say what it was about?"

"Only that it had something to do with the fire."

The fire? What the hell could Brad Tilden know about the fire? Nick had plenty to do but couldn't very well ignore such a provocative message.

"Okay, Julie, I'll take a run out there."

242

The second unit was on location at Nellis Air Force Base—no more than a twenty-minute drive. They were filming an action sequence for the current episode about an enlisted man who'd hired *The $trip*'s PI to find his seventeen-year-old sister. She'd come to visit him from Little Rock and disappeared, and he believed she'd become a prostitute.

Nick wryly noted that it was a plotline with something for everyone.

He found Brad, Lori, the replacement second-unit director, and the small ten-man crew on the flight line, where they were setting up a shot next to a row of F-16 Falcons. Lori was in the scene with Brad for a few glamour shots without dialogue because Nick had found an excuse for her to be out of the office.

Brad spotted Nick, walked over to greet him, and then led him away from the crew to the coffeepot on the snack table.

Nick opened the conversation.

"What's so urgent, Brad?"

Tilden looked around furtively to make sure no one was within earshot.

"I got a visit last night from a guy named Strozzi."

Nick's antennae went up. *Strozzi?* What the hell could Strozzi possibly want with Brad Tilden? He feigned innocence.

"Oh?"

"He wanted to know about the whereabouts of Snuffy the night of the big fire, and he'd heard I was with him."

Nick immediately knew why Strozzi wanted to know that—it was because he suspected Snuffy of setting the second fire and wanted to track his night. Acting as though the question meant nothing to him, he shrugged.

"What'd you tell him?"

"What I knew . . . but then I got to thinking. There've been a series of small 'incidents' on the set over the past week including a small fire, then a big fire . . . And then this guy who has Mob written all over him shows up with two thugs."

"How'd you figure that . . . ?"

"Hey, man . . ." He held out his hands as if it were obvious. "I was born and brought up in this town. I work as a dealer between acting gigs. I know wiseguys when I see them."

"Fair enough."

"Anyway . . . Strozzi wants to know about the second fire—not about all the incidents and the first fire . . ." Tilden waited for Nick's reaction but got none. Instead he got another question from Nick.

"And?"

"And so I think this is the guy behind all the incidents—and that Snuffy has something to do with them."

Nick quickly decided not to confirm or deny. He cocked an eyebrow.

"Really . . ."

Tilden smiled.

"Really. And I thought you might appreciate what I'm telling you but didn't tell anyone else."

Nick studied Tilden's face. Good-looking in an all-American way, and he wasn't a bad actor—he just wasn't overly talented. Nick had hired him for the minor part of the LVPD detective because he was a local and Nick saved the per diem and lodging he'd have to pay an actor from L.A.

He decided to waste no time.

"What is it you want, Brad?"

"Nothing . . . I mean, it'd be nice if maybe you could thank me by using me more . . . Maybe set up a buddy-buddy thing between me and Hank. And then maybe down the road I could even get billing as a costar . . ."

Christ! Nick almost couldn't believe it—but it was obvious. Actors!

A bigger part, more lines, better billing! The story never changed. But he had no time to argue, with everything else that was going on.

He smiled.

"Okay, Brad . . . I'll see what I can come up with."

Tilden broke into a smile that rivaled the sun.

"That's great, Nick! I really appreciate it. I won't let you down."

"No problem . . . and thanks for the heads-up. *I* appreciate it."

CHAPTER SEVENTY-TWO

TONY ACCARDO STEPPED out of the de Havilland Beaver onto a dock in Alberta, Canada. He was followed by a guide and Jerry Cellini, a young bodyguard. They were on a small lake east of Banff, staying at a very exclusive fishing lodge that catered to sportsmen who wanted complete privacy and security.

The Beaver was on floats and they'd just returned from an overnight trip two hundred miles to the north. The prior morning the pilot had put the Beaver down on a remote lake and they'd set up a fishing camp. This morning Accardo had hooked, fought, and landed a twenty-eight-pound lake trout—a huge trophy specimen he could mount and proudly display in his den. Ecstatic, he decided that anything after his half-hour battle with the fish would be anticlimatic and decided to return in triumph.

Charlie Johnson, the lodge manager, was waiting for them on the dock.

"Mr. Accardo, your wife called and left a message for you last night.

I told her you probably wouldn't get back until today . . . She said it was important and to please call as soon as you returned."

Accardo headed up to the lodge worrying that it had to be important for Clarice to call while he was on a fishing trip. She never had before. He'd met Clarice Pordzany, a Polish-American chorus girl, in 1934 and they'd been together ever since. It was a very strong marriage and Accardo had never been known to be unfaithful to her.

He dialed his home and Clarice picked up.

"It's me . . . Are you okay?"

"Fine, Tony . . . but Sidney called yesterday and said it was important for you to call him."

"Fine, Clarice—I'll be home in a couple of days."

Accardo hung up and checked his watch. Two o'clock—one on the West Coast. He dialed a number he knew by heart.

The Bistro.

Korshak was, as usual, in his "office." He was having lunch and picked up on the first low ring.

"Yes . . ."

"It's me."

Korshak instantly recognized the voice and waited for Accardo to follow with the agreed procedure when Korshak was called at the Bistro.

He gave Korshak a phone number. "Canada. 403-555-1666."

"Five minutes . . ." Korshak hung up, wrote down the number, and delicately dabbed his mouth. He told the waiter he'd be right back and left.

He walked to a phone booth two blocks away and took out the roll of quarters he always carried. He dialed the number and Accardo, who was waiting by the phone, picked up on the first ring.

"Sidney?"

"Yes . . . Is your phone safe?"

"I'm in the middle of nowhere and these people know how to sweep phones."

"Good . . . Here's what you should be aware of . . ."

Korshak related the conversation he'd had with Sam Altman. Accardo listened attentively, thanked Korshak, and hung up. He shook his head . . . Strozzi was apparently running a scam on his own. And the fucking kid was a cousin—distant, but a cousin nonetheless.

Accardo dialed a number in Chicago.

Joe Aiuppa picked up and once again the information that came from Sam Altman was relayed, along with instructions of what Accardo wanted done.

Aiuppa called Corky Civella in Kansas City, who called Nello Marchetti in Las Vegas. Corky then called back Aiuppa with confirmation from Nello that Strozzi was running a scam on Nick Conti and *The $trip*.

The whole process had taken less than two hours. The final call was made by Aiuppa.

It was to Skeets Travalino in Las Vegas.

CHAPTER SEVENTY-THREE

SAM AND GWEN arrived with their entourage at one o'clock and were put up in the Wimbledon's premier penthouse suite—a five-thousand-square-foot luxury complex with four bedrooms decorated with the best that money could buy. Sam and Gwen were in the master, with Alfred, Cojo, and Jake in the other three bedrooms.

Sam wasn't a high roller but he was *Sam Altman*. The publicity that his show generated brought hordes of fans who collectively dropped more cash at the tables than a whale.

He called Nick in his office as soon as they checked in and said he had to see him right away. Nick sighed, put aside the scenes he was rewriting for Lori Donner, and made his way up to the suite.

Sam's arrival in Vegas at a critical time was more than disturbing. The only reason he would have come was to interfere with something in which he had absolutely no expertise.

Not good.

Alfred answered the door in his customary black suit, winged collar, and bow tie. He looked a bit frazzled, and Nick assumed it was from the four-hour ride in the van carrying the luggage.

"Good afternoon, Mr. Conti. Mr. Altman is on the patio."

"Thanks, Alfred."

Nick crossed the massive living room toward a wall of glass. Before he reached the patio, Gwen came out of the master suite dressed to the nines for what he assumed was a lunch date. Her makeup and hair were impeccable and she didn't look the least bit frazzled from the trip.

Nick stopped and smiled.

"Good afternoon, Gwen."

"Is it?" She'd put every last ounce of venom into her answer and added a withering stare.

Nick knew she didn't like him and he knew why. It just didn't matter to him. But the attitude he was getting now wasn't dislike, it was hate.

He remained passive.

"I take it you're not having one."

"No—and yours is going to be worse."

She walked out without another word and Nick went out to the patio. It was an additional thousand square feet of terrazzo, half of which was covered by elaborate awnings—the other half exposed to the sun. There were several seating areas, both in and out of the shade, and a bar manned by a hotel employee.

Sam was on a chaise in the sun drinking his usual bourbon over ice. The sky was clear but the temperature was in the mid-sixties and Sam was wearing a shawl and pensively looking out over the golf course.

Nick sat across from him.

"Afternoon, Sam . . . How was the trip?"

"A pain in the ass as usual, but the trains aren't running yet. Next year, they tell me."

Sam never flew. There were a bunch of different stories as to why, but the prevailing tale was that a plane had crashed thirty-five years earlier, killing all aboard. He was supposed to be on it.

Nick flipped a thumb over his shoulder.

"I saw Gwen on the way in—she wasn't very friendly."

"She hates you."

"I can tell."

"She wants me to fire you—I told her I would."

Nick was taken aback by the comment although he couldn't really believe it—unless that was the reason for Sam's sudden visit. He studied Sam's face for a clue—a twitch, the beginning of a smile, a grimace—anything.

He saw nothing.

"Are you?"

"Of course not."

"Then why tell her that?"

"Manners told me Hall is in Vegas snooping around. He wants a tour of Hillside to back off. I initially said no, but now I figure it's the best way. Gwen said she'd allow it if I fired you. I said okay and brought her here to tell Hall herself so he would believe he'd get what he wanted."

"So what are you going to tell Gwen when you don't fire me?"

"What I heard this morning . . . it'll soften her up."

"Oh?"

Sam held out his hands in a hopeless gesture and shrugged.

"I've got throat cancer."

Sam said it so emotionlessly that Nick almost didn't react. When he did, his eyes narrowed as if to be sure he'd heard right.

"When did . . ."

"This morning. Kline came to the house—my ENT specialist. He used his juice to rush my biopsy. It was positive."

"Christ, Sam, I'm sorry . . . What now?"

Sam shook his head and rotated his hand.

"Chemotherapy, radiation, operation—who knows? I'll get there when I get there. The worst part is no cigars."

"When are you going to tell Gwen?"

"As soon as you leave."

"Anything I can do . . ."

"You can get Hall up here to meet with Gwen and we'll put out at least one fire."

CHAPTER SEVENTY-FOUR

NICK WENT BACK to his office and told Julie to call Hall. He wasn't in his room so she tried the set—maybe he was still trying to ferret information from the cast and crew. No one had seen him. She left a second message with the hotel operator.

Nick again began rewriting Lori's scenes.

An hour later a man sauntered into the production office and made his way to Julie's deck. He was lanky, middle-aged, wearing a turtleneck sweater, slacks, and a sport jacket. He had a battered trench coat draped over his arm, but the thing that fascinated Julie was his shiny bald head—and the cigarette dangling out of the corner of his mouth. He looked like a film-noir private eye.

The man handed her a card.

"Benjamin Hall to see Nick Conti."

Julie took the card and got up.

"He's expecting you, Mr. Hall." Hall followed Julie into Nick's office. "Mr. Hall to see you."

Nick got up and extended his hand.

"Nick Conti . . ."

"Ben Hall . . ." He took Nick's hand. "L.A. *Times.*"

"Nice to meet you, Mr. Hall."

"Ben's fine."

"So's Nick." He asked Julie to get them both coffee and they sat: Hall in one of the captain's chairs, Nick at his desk.

"What can I do for you, Ben?"

"You can tell me what really happened to Johnny Johansen."

Nick cocked an eyebrow. Hall was as abrupt as Nello, but without the pissed-off attitude. In fact he was smiling. Nick decided to casually repeat the party line.

"He had a motorcycle accident."

"I don't think so."

"Oh? Why not?"

"Because I went to see him where you had him holed up in La Costa."

"Holed up?"

"Uh-huh . . . Why not here or in L.A.? Why La Costa? One of our stringers saw him check in—got suspicious when he was fed the motorcycle line and called here to confirm it. No one has ever heard of any accident."

"It didn't happen on the set."

"No one off the set ever heard about it. Cops, hospitals—you know, the usual."

Nick admired Hall's determination but still made an effort to dissuade him.

"We didn't inform them. It wasn't serious."

Hall smiled and Nick's effort went down like a cement kite.

"Then why did you send Kulakowsky and Siegel to threaten our guy and then bribe him to keep his mouth shut?"

Nick leaned back in his chair and lit a cigarette. There was no way to explain that. When Cojo and Jake showed up, no matter what the excuse, it was an obvious attempt to cover up something far more serious than a motorcycle accident, and Hall knew it. Nick inhaled and slowly let it out.

"Sam Altman just arrived. He wants to see you."

Hall's eyebrows rose.

"Oh?"

"He's in the Wimbledon. I'll take you to him."

Nick got up and walked out, followed by Hall. Julie called out and stopped them as they reached the front entrance. She cupped the phone she was holding.

"Nick . . . Nello's on the line."

Nick excused himself, walked back to Julie's desk, and took the phone.

"Nello?"

"I've got some bad news . . . I just heard from Corky. You sittin' down?"

"Go . . ."

"Allie never got off the plane in Kansas City."

Nick couldn't control an outburst.

"What?"

"Corky had two of our guys there meet the plane when it landed. Allie didn't get off . . . Which means he never got on."

CHAPTER SEVENTY-FIVE

"**C**ALL OUR SECURITY people. I want someone with Erin twenty-four seven. She's on the set—stay with her and bring her back to my suite as soon as she wraps."

Nick's orders to Julie were sotto voce because Hall was lingering by the front entrance. But her face automatically registered concern.

"What's wrong?"

"Allie's still in town. Call Stavros and tell him what we're doing. I'll be with Sam."

Nick spun around and walked back to Hall. He'd heard Nick's outburst and seen Julie's reaction.

"Something wrong?"

"A problem with a guest star we hired out of L.A. He missed his plane."

Hall no more believed that than he believed in the tooth fairy, but he let it go. He was more interested in what Altman had to say.

Alfred answered the door and greeted them in his clipped English accent.

"Good afternoon, Mr. Conti . . . Mr. and Mrs. Altman are waiting for you in the salon."

Hall cocked an eyebrow. He knew Sam and Gwen's background. The Jewish tailor's son from Odessa and the used-car dealer's daughter from Yorba Linda suddenly had a butler who sounded like Rex Harrison and a salon instead of a living room.

Only in America.

The Altmans were on a couch in one of three seating areas in the massive living room. Sam was wearing his signature suede track suit and Mephisto sneakers, both in chocolate brown. Gwen had changed into an exquisitely embroidered silk caftan—emerald green with a gold sash. Simple loop earrings and an array of matching bracelets, also in gold, completed the picture.

The lady of the manor at home.

But Nick thought she looked pale in spite of her makeup—undoubtedly a reaction to the news Sam had given her about his condition. Nonetheless she retained the glare Nick thought was permanently reserved for him.

Sam got up and extended his hand to Hall.

"Sam Altman . . ." He indicated Gwen. "And my wife, Gwen."

"Benjamin Hall . . . Call me Ben."

Gwen nodded and they all sat. Sam signaled Alfred.

"Bourbon—rocks. Ben—Nick?"

Nick held up his hand. Ben answered.

"No, thanks . . ." Again demonstrating his abrupt style, he went straight to the issue. "What can I do for you, Sam?"

Gwen frowned. She considered him an interloper, and now he'd added rudeness to his profile.

Sam smiled. He appreciated directness.

"It's what we can do for you, Ben . . . Norman Manners said you'd like to visit Hilltop with your family. You know we normally don't allow such visits, but I've spoken to Gwen and she's agreed . . ." He turned to her. "Gwen?"

She assumed an imperious attitude and addressed him.

"Mr. Hall . . ."

The salutation was tinged with distaste, and everyone noted that she had pointedly refused to refer to him by his first name.

"My husband has asked me to honor your request for a visit to my home . . ."

Again everyone noticed that the reference was to *my* home as opposed to *our* home.

"And I've agreed. Did you have a particular date in mind?"

"No . . . as a matter of fact, I didn't."

"Well . . . when you do . . ." Gwen's tone was as haughty as she could make it. "Call Alfred and he'll make the arrangements."

"I don't think that will be necessary, Gwen." She had been introduced to him as Gwen, so he took pleasure in using it and watching her frown. "I won't be visiting."

In the silence that followed, a dropped pin would have sounded like a falling anvil. But neither would have matched the drop of Gwen's jaw.

Sam spoke first.

"You're not coming?"

"No."

Sam was aghast.

"But you told Manners . . ."

Nick was studying Hall's face. He was enjoying himself, but Nick knew there was more to it than that. Hall was turning down a visit to Hillside because he wanted something more . . . and that could only mean one thing. It took five seconds to verify the thought.

"I know what I told Manners. At the time it seemed important. But now I find there's something I want more. If you'll excuse me . . ."

Hall got up, tipped an imaginary hat, and headed for the door.

CHAPTER SEVENTY-SIX

NICK RETRIEVED THE card the *Folies* showgirl had left on his bedside table. The girl whose name was Brie. He dialed the number and a throaty voice answered—very sexy. Nick remembered that.

"Hello . . ."

"Brie?"

"Yes . . ."

"Nick Conti."

"From *The $trip?*" Her voice rose with each of the three words. She was obviously happy with the call.

"The same."

"Nice to hear from you." She was definitely happy.

"Glad to be calling . . . I have a job for you."

"Acting on the show?" She went from happy to thrilled in four words.

"Acting—but not on the show."

"Oh . . ." The sudden disappointment was unmistakable.

"But if you can carry off the part I have in mind, I assure you I'll see to it that you'll be on the show."

"What do I have to do?" Her mood again changed—for the better—but she sounded wary.

"Dress in something sexy that shows off that fabulous figure and come over to my suite as soon as you can get here."

"Is this . . ."

She clearly thought something kinky was on the agenda. He already knew what her figure looked like. Did that mean he was dressing her for someone else?

Nick caught the hesitation in her voice and reassured her in his most authoritative voice.

"No—it's not what you think. Your 'something sexy' stays on."

There was a slight pause before she answered.

"Okay . . . I can be there in about twenty minutes. Is that okay?"

"Just fine . . . and there's just one more thing I want you to bring."

Nick told her what it was, thanked her, hung up, and called Julie.

"Is Johnny back yet?"

"A half hour ago with Chrissie. They're here with Mitch."

"I'm in my suite. Tell Mitch to bring them over."

Five minutes later Mitch showed up with Johnny and Chrissie. Johnny looked marginally better but was still not ready for a prime-time camera. Chrissie, on the other hand, looked ready for another *Playboy* shoot and Nick began to doubt whether his plan was viable.

Until Brie got there.

She was wearing a *Folies* costume used in their *Jungle Queens* extravaganza. It was a leopard-skin leotard V-cut to the navel. Her endless legs were shod in four-inch spikes, and a glittering tiara crowned hair that was braided in a long ponytail. During the number it could be whipped around her head like a vicious lash. She wore less than her normal stage makeup but retained the catlike mascara that swept up from the corners of her eyes. It completed the feline image as effectively as a set of claws.

She was devastating.

CHAPTER SEVENTY-SEVEN

SKEETS TRAVALINO OPERATED his liquor-distribution business out of a warehouse adjacent to the North Las Vegas air terminal. Desert Distributors was a legally licensed company that dealt with all the major distillers and whose clients included all the major hotels.

What made Skeets's operation infinitely more profitable than a normal distributorship were hundreds of cases of hijacked whiskey that arrived by truck from up and down the entire West Coast. He cleverly mingled the hijacked booze with the legitimate purchases he made from major distillers and then sold the whiskey to customers all over Las Vegas. This, of course, more than tripled the profits in an industry that was already very lucrative.

It was beautiful.

And naturally, 25 percent of the profits was kicked upstairs to Accardo and the boys in Chicago.

His partner was Leo Carlin, and, in addition to their distribution

company, the dynamic duo had a second source of illegal income de-
rived from home invasion.

They'd hired a three-man team of wannabe wiseguys who would
stake out likely targets and report back. Skeets and Leo would then determine the best method of avoiding whatever security systems were
in place and Leo, who once worked for a company that installed such
systems, would disable them. The two partners would then burglarize
the house, fence the swag in L.A., and split up the cash.

Again—it was beautiful.

They also had a third source of income. It was the reason Accardo
had called and why Skeets had to get Leo back to town immediately.

Not easy.

Leo was a fishing nut. He had a houseboat on Lake Mead and bolted
to it every chance he got. He was more interested in bass than bur-
glary. For Skeets it was a constant pain in the ass keeping Leo's head in
the simple task of "takin' care of business." Part of his problem was their
ultimate boss in Chicago, who was also a fishing nut. Leo claimed the Big
Tuna loved him—and they were cut more slack—because when he was
in town they enjoyed regaling each other with stories of "the one that
got away."

It was bullshit and Skeets knew it. They were cut slack because they
were great earners.

Skeets was paged to pick up a phone call while he was on the warehouse floor checking inventory. It was a six-thousand-square-foot facil-
ity with liquor cases stacked eight feet high in rows wide enough for
forklifts to navigate the aisles. Three wide roll-up doors led to a loading dock where trucks were on-loaded with deliveries or off-loaded
with legally purchased as well as hijacked booze.

He went to a wall phone and picked up the call. It was Accardo. As
usual, Skeets was instructed to call back from a phone booth within
ten minutes—which he did—to get his instructions.

He called Leo as soon as he hung up.

"Get your ass back here. We got a job to do."

"I'll be back in the morning."

"Not the morning. Now!"

Leo was clearly miffed.

"What's the big hurry? They're bitin'. I'm on a roll out here."

"The big guy called. We got a job to do."

"What kind?"

"Not on the phone. Get your ass back here or I'll be fishing for you."

It was four o'clock by the time Leo got to Skeets's office. He still had on a straw fedora covered with flies and was still annoyed that he'd been abruptly taken away from his favorite pastime.

"Okay—I'm here. What's up?"

"That ridiculous fuckin' hat. Take it off."

"What the hell's eatin' you?"

"Like I said—I got a call from Tuna."

"He comin' to town?"

"No. He's got a job for us."

"What kind?"

Skeets told him.

CHAPTER SEVENTY-EIGHT

NICK LAID OUT his plan to Mitch, Johnny, Chrissie, and Brie. They listened attentively, but when he finished they were silent and exchanged skeptical glances.

Mitch was the first to speak.

"You really think it'll work?"

Nick nodded.

"I do." He went to the phone and called Hall.

The reporter had left word for Nick after he'd left Sam's suite, and Nick knew he'd be waiting for the call.

He picked up on the first ring.

"Hall . . ."

"Okay, Ben . . . I'm ready to tell you what really happened."

Hall sounded shocked.

"An honest man?"

"And you can have interviews with everyone involved."

A few seconds passed before he answered. "Okay, Nick . . . But if it's a con—you're toast."

Ten minutes later Nick let Hall into the suite. He was carrying his trench coat and had a signature cigarette hanging out of the corner of his mouth. He looked around and was startled when he saw Brie in costume, but was even more surprised to see Johnny and Chrissie.

He smiled at them.

"So . . . we meet again."

Johnny and Chrissie were a bit nervous, but Johnny managed a greeting.

"Nice to see you again, Mr. Hall."

Nick introduced Hall to Mitch and Brie and asked them all to sit down. Hall looked around, trying to get a handle on what was going on, and addressed Nick archly.

"Why, may I ask, did you bring these people to our meeting?"

Nick nodded at Johnny. He appeared tearful and contrite.

"I never had a motorcycle accident . . . I got hurt because I got drunk and was where I shouldn't have been."

Chrissie vehemently echoed his sentiments.

"You sure as hell shouldn't have!"

She glanced at Brie, who jumped in on cue.

"I'll say . . . He attacked me!"

Hall sat forward and squinted. He looked from Chrissie to Johnny to Brie. The costumed girl whom Johnny had supposedly attacked was over six feet two in her spiked heels, had a perfectly formed body, and resembled a very capable cat. She didn't look all that attackable.

He smiled.

"I beg your pardon? He attacked you?"

Brie ignored his obvious disbelief and forged on. She was playing her part to the hilt.

"Damned right he did. We had a date after the late show and went

266

back to my apartment. Johnny had a lot to drink. He wanted to jump my bones and I said no."

Now it was Chrissie's turn to glare at Johnny. He seemed to wilt, and Brie continued.

"But he insisted, and when he grabbed me I hit him."

Hall almost laughed. He wasn't buying a bit of it. Brie was gorgeous but so was Chrissie. Why in the hell would Johnny take a chance on getting busted for assault when he had her in his crib? Added to that was the fact that Johnny was a very well-built young man.

He scoffed at the notion.

"You hit him—blackened his eye, lacerated his face, and chipped his tooth? What'd you use, your purse?"

"No. My scepter."

"Your what?"

"My scepter." Brie reached behind her on the couch and produced an ornate, faux-gold scepter that might be seen in the hands of a king—or queen. When Nick had told her to bring it, she'd decided on the whole costume for "something sexy." "They're a prop we use in our Jungle Queens routine." She wielded the scepter like an ax. "I used it on Johnny."

Hall shook his head and looked at Nick.

"You expect me to believe this bullshit?"

"Believe what you want—but the story your stringer told Cojo and Jake was true. Johnny didn't want Chrissie to find out about how he got banged up and asked me to make up a story about a motorcycle accident . . ." He turned to Chrissie and cued her. "Chrissie?"

She was glaring at Johnny with all her considerable power. Nick suppressed a smile.

Another wannabe actress auditioning.

Chrissie thrust her finger into Johnny's chest.

"The cheating bastard confessed after you came to see us at La Costa. I wanted to beat up the other side of his face."

Hall shifted his gaze to Brie.

"And you didn't press charges for attempted rape because . . ." He paused and left the question hanging.

Brie shrugged.

"Hell—there was no harm done and I told him I'd keep quiet if he'd speak to Mr. Conti and ask him to help me with my career."

Nick added the final dagger.

"I know you're skeptical, Ben, but Johnny, Chrissie, Brie, and I will swear that that's what happened. You can print the story if you like—but I think it's beneath you. It would be a big deal if you were writing for the *National Inquirer* but not the L.A. *Times* . . . and there's still the option of a visit to Hilltop. Sam can still see to it that it happens."

Hall lit a second cigarette from the one already burning. He snubbed out the old one in an ashtray, shook his head, and smiled respectfully at Nick.

"I've got to hand it to you, Nick . . . Everyone in this room knows this story is bullshit, but you figured out a way to make it fly, and I admire that. But it's no deal."

Nick was surprised. "You're going to print the story?"

"I am . . . unless I have a better reason not to. What's the quid pro quo, Nick?"

Nick thought about it for a moment. He lit a cigarette and looked around the room at his collaborators, got up, took Hall's arm, and led him to the patio.

"Excuse us."

When they were outside, Nick closed the door and faced Hall. "How would you like to be the investigative reporter who exposes the biggest coke and loan-shark operation in Vegas? The dealers, their marks, and their bosses."

Hall squinted and said nothing for a few moments. He was skepti-cal. "What guarantee do I have that you've got the story?"

"None . . . except if you're not happy with what I give you, you can always print what you originally intended to."

Hall hesitated a few more seconds, smiled, and stuck out his hand.

"Okay, Nick, but like I said—if it's a con, you're toast."

CHAPTER SEVENTY-NINE

TILDEN AND LORI wrapped at four thirty and Lori headed for her motor home. *The $trip* had four—one for the director and one each for Hank, Johnny, and Lori. All four were much smaller and far less lavish than those employed on *Seven-Eleven*, but that was a major feature film and *The $trip* was a TV show.

Their budgets were exponentially different.

Tilden stopped her as she arrived at the door.

"Lori . . ." He eased closer to her and furtively looked around. "How'd you like to share some primo uncut blow like we had with Snuffy two nights ago?"

She was instantly attentive.

"You have some?"

"I can get it."

Lori wasn't so sure. His stash had always been average—it was Snuffy who came up with the real thing. Also, she'd agreed to see Mitch for "dinner" later that evening. But with a few hours to kill and the prospect of some world-class coke in the offing, she couldn't resist the temptation.

She smiled and patted his cheek.

"Love to."

Tilden drove them to Fremont Street and parked in front of Poolorama. Lori immediately recognized it as the place Snuffy had scored the uncut two nights earlier.

She beamed when he pulled up in front, her dimples blossoming like a pair of inverted jewels.

"You know Snuffy's supplier?"

Tilden crossed his index and middle fingers and held them up.

"Like that . . . Be right back."

Lori nodded vigorously and Tilden dashed into the bar. Ten minutes later he returned displaying an A-OK with his fingers.

"As Snuffy would say—Voilà! Let's party!"

They returned to Tilden's apartment; he made them a drink and spread two lines of coke on his glass coffee table. Lori rolled a pair of dollar bills into tubes and they got on their knees facing each other. With exaggerated gestures they gleefully placed one end of the tubed bills in their nostrils, bent over, and sucked up the lines in one long inhale. Tilden spread out two more lines and they repeated the action with their other nostrils.

Lori leaned back against the couch, Tilden leaned back against an opposing chair, and Lori cooed like a contented dove.

"Wow . . . now that's what I call a magnum hit . . ."

Tilden leaned forward in a mock bow and swept his arm across his body.

"Your pleasure is my desire, madame."

They went through two more lines and Tilden downed a few more drinks in the next hour. Lori didn't drink—she was happy with the buzz she got from the coke. At some point Tilden made his way to the other side of the coffee table and got cozy.

Lori really didn't mind. He was a nice-looking guy, he'd provided her with some fabulous coke, and she was always ready to feed her overactive libido.

He led her into the bedroom and she didn't resist.

They both stripped and got into bed. But as expert as Lori was in the art of copulation, she couldn't get him up. He tried, but he couldn't perform. He was too ripped.

"I'm sorry, baby . . . I'll be okay in a while."

Lori caressed his cheek and soothed him.

"Not to worry—you're a champ."

"No—but I will be . . . real soon . . . a *real* champ . . ." He giggled—truly ripped. "I talked to Nick . . ."

Lori was suddenly more attentive. Nick was going to make him some sort of a champ? What the hell did that mean? She figured that if it had to do with Nick, it had to do with the show, and that meant it had to do with her.

She again caressed his cheek.

"Really . . . And what did you talk about?"

"Me . . . He's going to give me a bigger part."

"He said that?"

"Yep . . . He owes me . . ." He giggled again. He was reliving his moment of triumph and enjoying the thrill through the buzz of cocaine. "I gave him some information about the fires and he was very grateful."

"Really . . ."

"Uh-huh . . ."

"What kind of information?"

Tilden told her—and more.

CHAPTER EIGHTY

THE SCENE ERIN was shooting in the Tropicana casino was taking much longer than anticipated. They were in the baccarat pit—actually not a pit at all, more a very plush, raised lounge, three steps above the main floor. The area was roped off over thirty feet from the pit but it was still difficult to control the starstruck crowd of lookie-loos who strained to see the action up close. And it was almost impossible to keep them quiet during a take.

There were nine players at the table. All the men as well as the croupier and the two dealers wore tuxedos—all the women wore gowns and a glittering array of jewelry. Erin's gown was a dazzling white, off-shoulder Dior with a plunging neckline. An authentic Cartier diamond necklace worth over a half million dollars hovered over her cleavage.

Anyone unfamiliar with the game would wonder how any of the male players could possibly have kept their minds on their cards. Fortunately, once a hand is dealt, baccarat is devoid of decisions. The cumulative total of the cards dealt to each hand determines the action.

The scene Stavros was filming involved Erin in a head-to-head confrontation with the villain of the film in an obvious homage to James Bond in *Casino Royale.* They were at the end of the last shot he needed to complete the sequence, and the dealer dealt each payer two cards.

Erin flipped hers over.

"Nine."

The perfect hand.

The players gasped and the camera pushed in toward Erin. She reacted with a Mona Lisa smile, and a few moments later Stavros's voice rang out.

"Cut and print!" He nodded to his assistant, who put a bullhorn to his mouth.

"That's a wrap!"

A representative of Cartier immediately walked over to Erin, accompanied by an armed guard. She removed the diamond necklace, thanked him, and blew a kiss to Stavros. The security man Nick had hired appeared, took her arm, and led her off the set behind a phalanx of assistants.

Shouts of autograph hunters and admirers followed them to the exit, where a limo was waiting to whisk her back to Nick's suite. Her security man called Nick from the limo's phone to say they were on their way back to the Wimbledon.

Nick met them at the entrance and watched Erin's perfect leg precede her out of the limo. Her gown was slit up the side and fell open clear to her upper thigh. Nick just smiled and shook his head. It didn't matter what she wore, the effect was always the same.

He took her hand and helped her out.

"How'd it go?"

"Fine . . . but I could use a hug and a drink."

"In that order?"

"Actually, the reverse. The hug would eliminate the possibility of a drink."

They went up to the suite and while Nick prepared a pair of Rob Roys with his back to her, she unzipped the back of the gown and let it fall to the floor. Nick turned around, placed the drinks on the bar, and stared.

Minipanties and heels—no bra.

Erin smiled.

"It's a six-thousand-dollar Dior gown, and your record of removing clothes is abysmal. You ruined my bikini."

She took a sip of her drink. Nick ignored his and walked around the bar. He picked her up, took her into the bedroom, and they wantonly released the pent-up emotions of a trying day . . . until the phone rang.

It was Dan Dietrich.

"Nick—I just picked up on something you should know . . ."

"Go, Dan . . ."

"We finished checking out your entire crew and didn't come up with anything hinky . . ."

"That's okay, pal." *So much for uncovering Snuffy with that method.* "I think we found out who . . ."

Dan interrupted him.

"But just for the hell of it, I began checking the cast."

"Oh?"

"Yeah. You're using a local named Brad Tilden. It doesn't really connect, but LVPD once picked him up for reckless driving. He was high, couldn't pass a sobriety test, and they found coke on him . . . That, and I also found out he spent some time in a sanitarium—treated as a manic-depressive—maybe the reason he uses coke."

Nick thought about it.

"You're right, Dan—it doesn't really connect, but thanks for the heads-up."

CHAPTER EIGHTY-ONE

JOE AGOSTO WENT through his cursory inspection of the Tropicana's backstage area and dressing rooms, stopping occasionally to chat with a few stagehands and *Folies* girls arriving for the early show.

Most of the showgirls were statuesque and buxom, while most of the dancers were average height with flatter chests. All were young and attractive, but without their elaborate stage makeup there were some that were downright plain.

Joe smiled to himself.

It's all an illusion . . . including his backstage tours that were designed to register his presence for the benefit of anyone who asked— primarily the feds and the gaming commission. It had to appear that he was employed by the Tropicana to run *Les Folies Bergere* while he was actually running the casino and the skim for Corky Civella and the Kansas City Mob.

But the cosmetic cover-up had its benefits. As far as the girls were

276

concerned, Joe was the boss and they worked for him. The showgirls and dancers were, for the most part, pragmatic, so when it came to Joe . . .

There were many, and they were willing.

Agosto strolled through the casino noting that it was humming as a result of all the starstruck yokels who had remained behind to gamble after *Seven-Eleven* had wrapped for the day.

Hell of a deal . . . He'd have to figure out a way to attract a TV show into the hotel like the Desert Inn had done. *Seven-Eleven* was a one-shot. *The $trip* would be in town for years.

He entered his office, saw who was seated behind his desk, and stopped cold before he'd shut the door. Allie Saltieri was in his swivel chair. He was leaned back with his feet up and his hands folded at his waist—the picture of contented relaxation.

"Hello, Joe."

Agosto was shocked because he'd heard what had happened that morning in Erin's trailer and knew Nello Marchetti had ordered him out of town.

He closed the door and apprehensively started forward.

"Allie . . . I thought you left town."

"I did . . . as far as anyone is concerned. But I've got some unfinished business I've got to take care of."

"Oh?"

"And I need some heat."

From all he'd heard, Agosto immediately knew the unfinished business had to be about Nick Conti. A friend of Nello Marchetti's.

Not good.

He hesitated, and Allie caught his uncertainty.

"Joe . . . What's wrong? I said I need a piece."

"Right . . ." Agosto quickly recovered and went to his safe. "You got it . . . but I don't think you should do somethin' stupid, Allie."

"Not to worry. The gun's wardrobe. I feel naked without one."

277

Agosto wasn't buying it.

"Allie . . . If Conti gets iced and you don't show up in KC, everyone's gonna put the finger on you."

"Not really . . . I've got that covered."

Typically, Allie's ego allowed him to believe he could outsmart anyone. Joe was an old friend and admirer and he couldn't resist crowing. He righted himself, leaned forward, folded his hands on the desk, and smiled.

"I picked up one of our dealers before I left for the airport. I gave him five grand and bought him a ticket to L.A. with my credit card. When he gets there he's gonna call Corky and leave a message like it's from me. It'll say I had to wrap up some business on the coast and I'll be back in KC in the morning."

"What happens when he finds out Conti's dead?"

"Nothin'. When Conti gets whacked I'll already be back in Kansas City."

"So who's gonna do Conti?"

Allie got up and walked around the desk.

"A hitter I met from Chicago . . . Strozzi . . . Which is why I need a twenty-five-grand loan."

"Jesus Christ, Allie!" Agosto knew who Strozzi was—one of the Chicago guys who'd done some wet work in the past. "How am I gonna hide it?"

"You won't have to. When I get to Kansas City tomorrow I'll wire you the twenty-five large and you put it back before anyone's the wiser."

Agosto began to sweat, but he removed a nine-millimeter automatic from the safe and handed it to Allie. He then removed twenty-five thousand dollars in banded hundreds, put them in a briefcase, and held it out.

"Be careful, Allie . . . This could turn to shit in a hurry."

Allie patted Agosto's cheek.

"Not to worry, Joe . . . I got it all figured."

Allie left and Joe sat. Completely dejected, he put his elbows on the desk and his head in his hands. He had a huge problem.

Allie was an old and good friend, and Joe had meant it when he told him to be careful. But he was about to buy a hit on Nick Conti—a friend of Nello Marchetti's—and Nello was not only senior to Allie in the Kansas City hierarchy, he was Corky Civella's fair-haired boy.

Allie was already in deep shit with Corky. And if Nello and Corky found out that he knew Allie's plan and didn't tell them, he'd be fish bait.

Agosto sighed and picked up the phone.

CHAPTER EIGHTY-TWO

LORI LEFT TILDEN'S apartment and took a cab back to Nellis. The coke was wearing off and she wanted to pick up her motor home. She needed to talk to Nick and then grab a shower and change. She had a date with Mitch and was looking forward to it.

The teamster driver took her back to the DI and she stopped by the production office, where she expected to find Nick. He wasn't there, but she overheard Julie making arrangements on the phone for security guards at the Wimbledon. She'd been at Nellis all day and knew nothing about the altercation between Allie and Erin.

She was about to question Julie when Mitch came in and was surprised to find her there. He thought she looked a tad frazzled.

She gave him a dimpled smile but appeared concerned.

"Hey there, Mitch . . ."

"Hi, Lori . . . everything okay?"

"I'm not sure. I have to talk to Nick."

Mitch took her arm and led her into Nick's office.

"He's on his way. He called and told me to meet him here."

"If it's okay, I'll wait with you . . . We still on for tonight?"

"Sure . . . What's up?"

Mitch started to respond, but Nick arrived. He didn't expect to see Lori and repeated Mitch's question.

"Lori . . . everything okay?"

"Like I just said to Mitch . . . I'm not sure, but I had a drink with Brad after we wrapped and he said some things that didn't make sense. Can I have a glass of water?"

"Sure . . . Have a seat."

Mitch and Lori took the seats in front of the desk. Nick retrieved bottled water from his fridge, poured her a glass, and handed it to her.

"What did he say?"

Nick sat behind his desk while Lori drank half the glass before she began.

"Well, he had too much to drink and was pretty out of it, but for one thing he said that you were going to give him a bigger part in the show . . ."

Nick suppressed a sigh. His immediate thought was that Lori was concerned because a bigger part for Tilden could mean a smaller part for her. There were only so many lines to go around. He exchanged a glance with Mitch, who couldn't suppress a smile and shrugged.

Nick couldn't think of a reason to deny what he'd told Tilden.

"As a matter of fact, I did tell him that."

Lori's eyes widened.

"Why? He's not that good an actor."

"Perhaps not, but he did me a favor and I'm just doing something for him in return. Is that what's bothering you?"

"No . . . It's what he said after that." Lori paused dramatically and looked from Nick to Mitch to Nick as if she was waiting to be prompted.

Nick obliged her.

"And that was . . ."

"He said he told you about a man named Strozzi."

Nick felt a slight stomach twinge. *Why the hell would Tilden bring up Strozzi to Lori?* The only way he could find out was to acknowledge the fact.

"That's right . . . He told me Strozzi had come to see him."

Lori continued as if she were leading a witness.

"And that the reason he came was to ask Brad about the fires."

Nick's slight stomach twinge got sharper, but again he had to find out where this was leading.

"Again, correct. That's what he said."

"And finally . . ." She paused to gather the thought. "He said that he'd figured out that Strozzi was probably blackmailing you . . ."

Shit . . . now Lori was in the goddamn loop. The last thing Nick needed was the extortion story being spread all over town by a pair of damn actors who had no idea of the repercussions.

He tried to wave the notion off by lying about the final revelation.

"Lori . . . Brad never said that to me. You said Brad was pretty out of it . . . What he said to you was either pure speculation on his part, or—" He then threw in a shot of flattery to take her mind away from the issue. "—because you're a very beautiful, talented, and desirable young lady . . . He was just trying to impress you."

Lori weighed the comment but wasn't convinced.

"Maybe . . . but why would he keep saying that he felt that all this Strozzi person wanted to know was who set the second fire?"

Nick obviously knew but had no intention of offering even a bogus explanation.

"I have no idea."

"But Brad did. He was laughing about it because he said he knew who set the second fire."

Nick again shot a glance in Mitch's direction before looking at Lori with narrowed eyes.

"I beg your pardon?"

"He told me he knew who set the second fire."

"Who?"

"Him."

CHAPTER EIGHTY-THREE

ALLIE PAID THE cab driver and strolled into Poolorama. He surveyed the room and winced at the blaring sounds of the Charlie Daniels Band. He hated country-western music. He'd removed his suit jacket and tie and put on a windbreaker and baseball cap, but he was still out of place amid the jeans, embroidered shirts, and boots of the shitkicker clientele.

He ignored several questioning looks at his briefcase as he made his way to the bar and took a seat. The female bartender with big hair and bigger tits came by and he ordered a straight rye whiskey. She thought he was darkly handsome, so she leaned over and gave him a come-on smile.

"New in town, big fella?"

"No. I'm here to see Strozzi."

She dropped the smile like a hot horseshoe and leaned back.

"I don't think he's in yet. But his office door is on the rear wall. You can go knock if you want."

Allie nodded and made his way past busy pool tables to the room's back wall. He knocked on the only door, waited, and knocked again.

No one answered.

A pool player at a nearby table stepped toward him and called out.

"He's not in there. If he was, Angie would be standing by the door."

Allie knew who Angie was—he'd seen him at Maxi's with Strozzi. He nodded his thanks and went back to sit at the bar and wait.

Strozzi, Fats, and Angie entered the office from the alley door. Poolorama was their first and last stop on their nightly rounds. They included cash pickups from their loan sharks and cocaine drop-offs to their dealers around the city. Strozzi went to the safe to retrieve the coke he intended to distribute that night and waved a hand at Fats.

"Fats—check the bar and see if we got any messages."

Fats nodded and left. Angie sat on the couch with a bag of Fritos and began his perpetual munching.

The phone rang and Strozzi picked it up.

"Carlo? Skeets."

"Yeah, Skeets, how ya doin'?"

"Great. You gonna be at Maxi's tonight?"

"Yeah. Why?"

"Me and Leo got somethin' goin' and we need a partner. It's not the kinda thing we can handle alone."

"Yeah? What is it?"

"Meet us at Maxi's and I'll lay it out. What time you gonna be there?"

"In about an hour."

"Great—see ya then."

At the bar, Fats was told that there were no messages but the female bartender pointed out the guy who'd said he wanted to see Carlo. Fats walked down the bar and thought he recognized the man, but couldn't place from where.

He tapped him on the shoulder.

"You want to see Carlo?"

Allie turned and smiled.

"I do . . ." he stuck out his hand. "Allie from Kansas City. We met at Maxi's the other night."

"Oh yeah . . . right. Yeah . . . Come on back. We just got in."

Fats led Allie back to the office door, rapped twice, waited a few seconds, and entered. Allie followed him and looked around. The place was a toilet. Strozzi was at a dented metal desk, there was a makeshift plywood rear door, and Angie was munching Fritos on a threadbare couch. Allie considered himself a sophisticate and his sensibilities were affronted, but he swallowed his revulsion.

He thrust out his hand in his best version of a Hail fellow well met and smiled.

"Carlo . . . good to see you again—we met at Maxi's."

"Yeah, I remember—it's on our rounds. A little business, a little pleasure . . ."

Allie winked conspiratorially.

Strozzi smiled.

"What can I do for you?"

Allie laid the briefcase on the desk, popped the latches, and opened it. He grinned and turned the briefcase around so that it faced Strozzi.

"It's what you can do for me . . . for twenty-five large."

It took less than two minutes for Strozzi to agree to the hit on Nick. He knew there was no chance that his original scam would ever work, and less chance of finding out who set the second fire. His business with Conti was done. Not only that—he hated the arrogant sonofabitch. Killing him would be a pleasure.

He snapped the briefcase shut, put it in his safe, and turned back to Allie.

"Why's it so important it happens tomorrow night?"

"Because I'm leaving in the morning and I'll be in KC by tomorrow afternoon."

Strozzi nodded his understanding.

"I get it . . . And you got it."

CHAPTER EIGHTY-FOUR

I T T O O K N I C K a few seconds to digest Lori's revelation, and then he asked her if Tilden had said why he set the fire. She said she tried asking but he was babbling and passed out before he'd given her a reason.

Nick bounced out of his chair and waved at Mitch.

"We're outta here."

Mitch got up, kissed Lori on the cheek, and quickly switched their dinner date to a midnight snack. He dashed out after Nick and two minutes later they were in Nick's Firebird, speeding toward Tilden's house.

Nick was furious, driving recklessly, and determined to find out Tilden's motivation even if he had to beat it out of the fucked-up actor.

"I get Snuffy—he got paid to do a job—but why the hell would Tilden set a goddamn fire?"

Mitch shrugged.

"Dan said he was on coke and was a manic-depressive. You think that might have something to do with it?"

"We're sure as hell gonna find out."

Mitch remained silent several seconds, and then broached a sub-ject that had been bothering him since they'd listened to the Strozzi tape.

"You thought anymore about what we're going to do about Snuffy?"

"You mean about his work with Strozzi?"

"Yeah . . . At the end of the day Snuffy turned out to be bent. But he'd been one of ours for a long time . . ."

Mitch let the thought hang there, and Nick waited for him to go on. When he didn't, Nick prompted him.

"And . . . ?"

"And I hate to see people get away with murder—especially people like that sawed-off prick Strozzi."

Nick gave him a thin smile.

"Relax, Mitch . . . Strozzi's going down. We're taking that tape to the DA as soon as we put this thing to bed."

"We're going to burn Pearl?"

"Why not? He's a Mob doctor and an abortionist . . . but he'll prob-ably cut a deal for his testimony and skate."

Mitch smiled and nodded knowingly.

"That was your plan since you heard the tape."

"It was."

They pulled up in front of a small bungalow on the far east side of town and got out of the car. It was in a row of similar structures on both sides of the street. Nick pounded on the door several times but got no response.

Mitch peeked through a front window.

"I can't see anything."

"Lori said he was ripped. Maybe he's still out."

"You want me to do my number?"

"Why not?"

Mitch positioned himself in front of the door and lashed out with his foot. For the second time in as many days, a door was ripped out of its frame and they entered.

The front room and a combination dining room and kitchen were empty. They found Tilden in the back bedroom. He was sprawled across the bed naked and dead to the world.

Nick grabbed one of his arms.

"Take his other arm—we need to get his attention."

They hauled Tilden off the bed and dragged him into the bathroom. Mitch spun the shower's cold-water faucet to the limit and they dumped him on the floor.

Seconds later Tilden stirred, raised a hand to ward off the icy deluge, and then struggled to rise. Mitch shut off the water, hauled him out, and slammed him on the toilet seat. His legs splayed, his arms dangled, and his eyes tried to focus.

Nick's hand shot out and gripped his jaw. When they were face-to-face, he roared.

"Why'd you set the fire?"

Tilden's eyes tried to focus. When they did, he recognized Nick and they bulged. He was terrified.

"N-Nick . . . ?"

Nick squeezed Tilden's jaw tighter and he shouted louder.

"Who paid you?"

"N-no one . . ."

"Then why? Why did you do it?"

Tilden began shaking, suddenly burst into tears, and began moaning. He was coming apart. Nick released the grip on Tilden's jaw and stepped away. Tilden rocked back and his head wound up on the toilet tank.

He was blubbering.

"Lori . . . It was Lori . . ."

Nick and Mitch stared at him and then at each other, aghast. Nick managed only one word.

"Lori?"

"Yes! Yes—yes—yes!" Tears streamed and spittle was running from his mouth. Between the coke, the liquor, and finally having been discovered, he continued to unravel. "I love her . . . I wanted her to have more time for me . . . For me!" He started laughing hysterically. "I was happy when it seemed the show would have to be shut down . . . I was happy! Happy about the sabotage! Don't you see? If we weren't working, she'd have more time . . ." He wailed, raised his clasped hands, and rocked on the toilet seat. "Time for *meee* . . ." He was shaking so hard it looked like he was vibrating. "I set the second fire to make *suuure* . . ."

The last two utterances came out like plaintive wails.

Nick looked at Mitch and shook his head. The motivation was so ridiculous that it could only mean Tilden was mentally ill and no one had realized it.

Mitch asked an obvious question in a compassionate voice.

"It was you who attacked me the other night after I left Lori . . ."

"Yes . . . I was following her . . ." He looked at Nick. "I saw her go to your suite two nights ago . . ." He looked back at Mitch. "And then his last night . . . Neither of you care . . ." He sobbed. "But I love her . . ."

Nick gently took Tilden's arm.

"Let's get some clothes on him."

Mitch took his other arm and they lifted him off the toilet. Tilden stopped sobbing a moment and stared up at Nick.

"What're you going to do?"

"Get you some help."

They eased him back into the bedroom, but before they could put him on the bed he jerked free, collapsed to the floor, and rolled around, wailing.

They let him be and Nick picked up the phone.

CHAPTER EIGHTY-FIVE

S KEETS SCREWED SILENCERS into the barrels of two .22-caliber revolvers and again went over the plan for Leo. They were in his office at the warehouse, and Skeets was exasperated because he thought his plan was the model of simplicity.

Leo wasn't so sure.

"Strozzi's gonna have his two gorillas with him."

Skeets held up the two guns.

"Which is the reason for these."

Skeets had explained his plan twice. They were going to park their car in the parking lot behind Maxi's and go in to wait for Strozzi. When he got there they would say they'd gotten their hands on half a million in counterfeit hundreds. Then they'd point out that they had no "retail outlet" to spread around the queer cash. But Strozzi put loan-shark money on the street and could palm it off through the suckers that came to him daily.

The funny money cost them next to nothing to manufacture once they had the plates. But when the loans, plus the vig, were paid back by the clueless marks, they would be repaid in real cash.

Beautiful. But they'd say that since Strozzi was doing all the work, they'd split the half million seventy-thirty in his favor.

Leo nodded tentatively.

"He'll probably buy that, but it's the parking lot I worry about."

Skeets threw up his hands and couldn't help shouting.

"That's where the money is! In the trunk of our car!" He was convinced the only goddamn thing Leo was ever confident about was the selection of bass lure. "Christ, Leo—don't you see? He's gotta come out there to get it!"

"Right—but suppose Fats and Angie don't let me hang back behind 'im when we get to the car?"

Skeets sighed.

"When I open the trunk, all three of them are gonna be lookin' in to see a half million in hundreds. It's human nature. That's when you give 'em one slug each. Pop, pop—back of the gorillas' heads. Quick—no hesitation. Pop, pop, and they're done. I'll take care of Strozzi when he turns to see why his guys collapsed like two sacks of shit."

"Why don't I open the trunk and you do the pop-pop?"

Skeets again threw up his hands and yelled.

"Because you're not a schmoozer! *I'm* the schmoozer! And it's *me* who's gonna be keeping their minds off *you*!"

Leo shook his head—still unconvinced.

"I dunno, Skeets . . ."

"Of course you don't! You never do—I do! Now get your ass in the car and let's get this fucking thing done."

They drove to Maxi's in Skeets's Cadillac, parked it in the back lot, and went in. Strozzi hadn't arrived yet.

As usual, the smoke-filled room was rocking with raucous patrons and thundering disco. "Up, Up and Away" was rattling the speakers and the two dancers onstage were gyrating to the beat. Their routine was an erotic pas de deux of lesbian sex.

A little something different for the cognoscenti.

In spite of Skeets's desire to witness their act up close and personal, he led Leo to a quieter table in the rear. A topless waitress in net stockings and four-inch spikes arrived to take their order and they lit cigarettes, adding to the smoke-filled, eye-watering air.

Ten minutes later, Strozzi entered with Fats and Angie.

Skeets winced.

Allie Saltieri was with them.

CHAPTER EIGHTY-SIX

NICK AND MITCH waited until an ambulance arrived, told the attendants Tilden was a manic-depressive, and asked that he be taken to the psychiatric ward for examination.

When they got back to the car, the phone was ringing. It was Julie.

"Nello called. He wants you to call him at the Tropicana."

Nick hung up, dialed the Trop, and asked for Nello's room. Nello had left a message saying he could be reached in Agosto's office, and Nick was transferred.

"Nello? Nick. I just got your message."

"Where are you?"

"On the east side, why?"

"Get over here right now—don't ask questions and don't stop for nothin'!"

Nello hung up before Nick could ask him why.

They found Nello waiting in Agosto's office, but Agosto wasn't with him. Nello had obviously commandeered the premises. Nick could tell by his face that he was in a darker mood than usual.

The observation was confirmed when he pointed his finger at Mitch and growled.

"Who's he?"

"Mitch Tanaka . . . my producer, a friend, and Rambo in a pinch."

"He know what's goin' on?"

"From the beginning. He knows what I know."

Typically, Nello spelled out the situation without preamble.

"Okay . . . Allie's gonna put a hit on you. He's contractin' Strozzi to take you out."

Nick felt his pulse jump. He thought Allie was borderline psycho and probably should have figured he might go for the final solution.

"How do you know?"

"Agosto. Allie came back here and asked him for a piece and a loan. If you give a shit, your ass is worth twenty-five G's to him."

"I should be flattered."

Nello looked as if he agreed, but went on.

"I called Corky and gave him a heads-up. He went batshit and said Allie was a loose cannon who's outlived his usefulness."

Nick was surprised. He knew Civella would want to teach Allie a very strong lesson, but thought he'd stop short of killing him.

"Corky wants him taken out?"

"Yeah . . . by me." He eased back the lapel of his suit coat and revealed a shoulder holster.

It figured. Nello was there, experienced, and as good as anyone in the business. Anyone who'd ever gotten in his crosshairs was history.

"You know where he is?"

"I know where he went. To hire Strozzi. He owns a joint on Fremont—Poolorama. I find Strozzi, I find him."

"You know what he looks like?"

"I got a description: short, wiry, with a pinched face and a sneer. How many of those own a joint called Poolorama?"

"Suppose he's not there?"

"I'll find him."

"Maybe . . . but I'm going with you."

Nello recoiled.

"What? You're a fuckin' civilian, fer chrissakes!"

"Strozzi hangs with a pair of goons named Fats Arnheim and Angie Angelino. They're big and they're tough. Three to one are long odds even for you."

Nello shook his head and snickered.

"You've been out of our thing since you were a kid . . . Now you're gonna let a broad and your little head take over your big one?"

"Put it any way you want . . . but Mitch and I are gonna back you up."

Nello hadn't heard about Strozzi's two goons and he wasn't stupid enough to go three on one if he didn't have to. He sighed, smiled respectfully, and nodded.

"Okay, *Nicolo* . . . You and your friend just bought some action."

Ten minutes later Nick and Nello dropped off Mitch in the alley behind Poolorama. They wanted Mitch guarding Strozzi's rear door with his Beretta in case Strozzi was warned when they entered the bar from the front and tried to rabbit. Nello had a gun to protect himself and Nick.

Nick and Nello parked out front and entered to the familiar racket of clacking pool balls and country-western music. Apparently a tournament had begun, and most of the clientele were crowded around the tables watching the elimination matches. There was a crowd of uninterested drinkers at the bar, and Nick elbowed their way into an opening.

The female bartender, always on the lookout for good-looking men, sauntered over with her chest out.

"Whatcha havin', handsome?"

"I'm looking for Carlo. He in yet?"

She grimaced.

"Christ—he's more popular than Elvis tonight." She gave him her best come-on smile and added a compliment. "You're the second stud that's come lookin' for 'im."

Nick grabbed at the thin straw.

"Ah! My brother? Handsome guy—looks like George Raft?"

"Yeah . . . that's him." She broke into a wide grin. "You boys new in town?"

"We are . . ."

"Carlo's been here and gone—maybe a half hour ago. What's your poison?"

"A quick rain check, gorgeous. We'll be back."

They left and drove back into the alley to pick up Mitch. When they pulled up he held out Dan's cassette.

"No Strozzi, but I remembered the tape. Think it might tell us something?"

Nick put the cassette into the Firebird's tape deck and, after a few rounds of dialogue and a phone call, they heard Allie enter. They listened to him hire Strozzi for the hit on Nick . . . but they already knew that. What got their attention was the phone call—and in particular a three-sentence exchange between Strozzi and the caller.

"Meet us at Maxi's and I'll lay it out. What time you gonna be there?"

"In about an hour."

"Great—see ya then."

Nello looked at Nick and smiled.

CHAPTER EIGHTY-SEVEN

STROZZI PAUSED INSIDE the entrance to Maxi's and briefly watched the dancers performing their simulated-sex routine. Unlike Fats and Angie, he wasn't particularly intrigued by the girl-girl scene. Allie, however, was smiling and seemed fascinated. He'd concluded his business, had nothing better to do until his plane left the following morning, and was happy he'd joined them.

Strozzi spotted Skeets and Leo at the rear table and started toward them—but found only Allie had followed him. Fats and Angie were still staring at the dancers. He turned back, whacked them on their arms, and they reluctantly followed. But their eyes never left the stage.

Skeets got up when the threesome approached. He grinned and stuck out his hand.

"Carlo! You're lookin' good. How's tricks?"

"Makin' a livin'."

Leo got up and shook hands with Fats and Angie. Wanting to echo his partner's flattery, he offered them what he thought was a compliment.

"You're all lookin' good. You guys lose some weight?"

Fats grimaced. He hadn't, and wondered if he'd just gotten a back-handed shot. Angie had actually gained weight. He frowned and his harelip twitched.

After a moment of silent tension, Skeets extended his hand to Allie.

"Allie! From Kansas City, right? We met the other night."

"We did . . . I appreciated the info."

They all sat, but Skeets's brain was in overdrive. Allie's presence completely fucked up his plan. If he remained behind when they lured Strozzi, Fats, and Angie out to the parking lot, he'd realize something was up when they didn't come back. If for some reason he came with them, he'd witness the hit. Either way they were screwed.

Unless . . .

Allie was Kansas City, and KC reported to Chicago. His orders came straight from Accardo—the very *top* of Chicago—and the Tuna wanted Strozzi and his boys dead. If Allie got in the way, that was his tough shit. They'd take him out, and Accardo would straighten it out later with Corky Civella.

The topless waitress in net stockings and four-inch spikes arrived, and they ordered a round of drinks.

Skeets leaned closer to Strozzi.

"You got a problem discussin' our business in front of Allie?"

Strozzi almost laughed. He'd just contracted with Allie to do a hit for him. What the hell difference would it make if he were witness to a scam?

"Allie's cool . . . Whaddaya got?"

"A half million in queer hundreds. First-class stuff."

Strozzi reacted. A half million was a big number.

"Where'd it come from?"

"The top . . . Tuna. The word is he's got ten million he's sendin' out in half-million batches—everywhere west of Chicago. We got ours, but no good way to spread it. You could palm it off to the suckers in your loan-shark operation. It's a no-brainer."

Strozzi took a few seconds to think about it and concluded Skeets was right.

"What's the cut?"

"Sixty-forty . . . you on the fat end."

Strozzi's response was automatic.

"Seventy-thirty."

Skeets had to counter or risk raising suspicion.

"Sixty-five–thirty-five."

Strozzi stuck out his hand.

"Done." Skeets shook the hand to seal the deal.

The topless waitress arrived with their round of drinks and tab. Skeets dropped a fifty on her tray. She cooed at the tip, kissed him on the cheek, and bunny-dipped away.

He raised his drink.

"Salut!"

The group all answered the toast and drank.

Strozzi put down his glass and asked the question Skeets was waiting for.

"Where's the stuff?"

Skeets smiled.

"In my car."

CHAPTER EIGHTY-EIGHT

NICK PULLED INTO the crowded front lot of Maxi's and finally found a space in the far corner. They got out of the car and started toward the entrance, but Nick suddenly put out his hand and stopped them.

Exiting the building were five men: Strozzi, Fats, Angie, and two others Nick didn't recognize. Strozzi and one of the unidentified men seemed to be chatting amiably while the other three followed.

Nello saw the man that matched Strozzi's description.

"That him?"

Nick nodded.

"Yeah . . . with Fats and Angie. But I don't know who the other two are."

Mitch stated the obvious.

"Allie's not with them. Now what?"

Nello, who was responsible for the hit, made the decision. He removed a nine-millimeter Glock from his shoulder holster.

"We ask Strozzi where he is."

Nick held out his hand to Mitch.

"Let me have it."

Mitch took the Beretta out of his waistband and handed it over.

Skeets was waving his hands to emphasize whatever he was saying to Strozzi as the group disappeared around the side of the building and headed for the rear parking lot.

As they proceeded, he continued to bullshit for all he was worth.

"So I says to Tuna . . . Tuna, I says . . . we got a lot of friends out here—he don't know it, but I'm talkin' you and your boys—and we can handle more than the half million . . . I know you're tryin' to spread it thin and far, I says, so's not to let it bunch up in one spot and attract attention, but Vegas is hot . . . know what I mean? And he says, 'Yeah, I know what ya mean . . . '"

The five men reached the car and Skeets circled to the trunk, where he made a production out of removing the key. As predicted, Strozzi, Fats, and Angie were looking over his shoulder when he inserted it.

Leo dropped back behind them.

Inside Maxi's, Allie felt the call of nature and made his way to the men's room in the rear of the establishment. He was smiling to himself over the funny-money scam and made a note to figure out how he might become a part of it in Kansas City. He entered the empty men's room, walked up to a urinal, and unzipped his fly.

Outside, Nick, Nello, and Mitch had rounded the building's rear corner and spotted their quarries as Skeets opened the trunk. They watched as the unidentified man who was standing behind Fats and Angie suddenly pulled a gun and fired a shot into the back of Angie's head.

There was no more sound than the pop of a champagne cork. Angie's head jerked, his ponytail whipped up, and he dropped on the spot.

Strozzi's head turned and he looked down. A second later the assassin fired a second shot into the back of Fats's head. The result was the same. The big man's head jerked and he went down like a dropped anvil.

Strozzi's street-smart brain instantly processed the information his senses were feeding him. A pop—cordite—Angie down—a second pop—more cordite—Fats down.

He pulled his .38.

Skeets let go of the trunk lid, pulled his .22, and spun toward Strozzi. It was in his waistband, but because of the long silencer it took a split second longer to get it out.

It cost him his life.

Strozzi fired a shot under his arm and through his heart. The boom of the unsilenced .38 reverberated across the lot.

Skeets went down and Strozzi turned toward Leo.

Inside, Allie heard the unmistakable sound of a gunshot. The men's-room wall faced the back lot and the shoulder-high window was open. He dashed to the window, raining piss across the floor.

He was in time to see Leo fire a silenced shot into Strozzi. He hit him in the chest, but Strozzi didn't go down. The .22 was good for a head shot but had little stopping power.

Strozzi returned fire with another booming shot.

Leo went down.

Allie stuffed his dick into his pants and ran out the door zipping up his fly. *Shit! What the hell was going down? He'd just hired Strozzi to take out Conti, and his goddamn hit man was in a shoot-out with two guys he's just made a deal with!* He'd seen Strozzi staggering and had to get out there and help him.

He had an investment to protect.

CHAPTER EIGHTY-NINE

ICK, NELLO, AND Mitch were running toward the bodies when Allie dashed out of Maxi's rear door. The first thing he noticed was that Strozzi was down, but he'd taken less than five steps when he saw Nello, Conti, and the Asian he remembered seeing in Conti's office. He jerked to a stop—stunned. Nello and Conti were packing! He was even more confused than he'd been a few seconds earlier when he'd witnessed the shoot-out.

Nello and Conti were part of this? Nothing was making any sense! He had less than two seconds for further thought. They'd spotted him. He skidded to a halt and everything seemed to unravel in slow motion.

Nello unhurriedly raised his gun.

Allie reached for the gun in his hip holster.

Nello calmly took a bead on Allie.

Allie's gun came out and he began to raise it.

Nello fired.

Allie flew backward like he'd been snatched by a bungee.

Nello rushed forward with Nick and Mitch right behind him.

Even though Nello was sure Allie was dead, he was a professional and he dropped to one knee beside the sprawled body. A brief look at the hole in the center of Allie's chest confirmed it was over.

He grabbed one of Allie's arms.

"Nick—get his other arm—we've got to get him out of here. Mitch—get the car."

Mitch's head popped forward in a quick nod.

"Right—what about the other ones?"

"See if they're dead and forget 'em. Let the cops sort it out. Allie's the only one we have to worry about."

Mitch quickly checked them out. "They're history." He took off running.

Nick realized Nello was right. When the five other bodies were discovered, it would look like exactly what it was—a double assassination gone wrong that ended in a shoot-out between the three remaining men. And when ballistics confirmed their initial conclusion and the bodies were identified, they'd have a plausible reason. All five were suspected or known Mob associates, and the cops would write it up as a gangland shootout.

But Allie Saltieri was a different matter.

He was connected to the Tropicana and the Kansas City Mob, he'd been seen with Erin Conroy, and he'd been all over the news because of the altercation in Boulder City.

His shooting would create a whirlwind.

Nick and Nello started to drag Allie's body toward the front lot when two men appeared at Maxi's back door. They'd probably been in the office in the rear of the building and heard one or both of the unsilenced shots. No one out front could have heard them above the pounding din of the music. One of the men reacted, pointed, and started toward them.

Nello unhesitatingly fired two shots over their heads.

The men dove to the ground and scrambled back into the building. They undoubtedly would be on the phone to the police within minutes.

Nick and Nello redoubled their efforts and reached the front corner of the building when Mitch skidded up. He jumped out, popped the trunk, and Allie's body was unceremoniously thrown in.

CHAPTER NINETY

MITCH DROVE THE Firebird to their warehouse and went in alone. He told the guard he'd forgotten to leave a set of keys the prop man would need first thing in the morning and was dropping them off in the truck parked out back.

He left by a rear door, didn't go anywhere near the prop truck, retrieved what he needed, and returned to the car without reentering the building.

Twenty minutes later they were on an isolated road a few miles south of town. Low dunes and sagebrush lined both sides of the two-lane blacktop and a three-quarter moon bathed the area in silver.

Nello indicated a dirt trail a short distance ahead.

"Pull in there."

Mitch did as instructed, and a hundred yards later Nello again held up his hand.

"Stop here."

Nello knew the area because he'd been there before—eleven years earlier, when he first came to Las Vegas. Most of the Mob guys knew it. The remote, endless stretches of low dunes and soft sand had been a Mob burial ground for over three decades. They didn't know it, but they were within a half mile of where Strozzi had buried Snuffy.

They got out of the car, opened the trunk, and removed the body along with the shovels Mitch had taken from the toolshed behind the warehouse.

Nick and Mitch dug the grave. Nello stripped the body. Allie's clothes would go into an incinerator when they got back to town.

When the hole was almost five feet deep, Nick and Mitch rolled the body into it. Nello went back to the trunk and retrieved a two-gallon jug of water and the sack of lime that also came from the shed. He poured the lime over the body and the water over the lime. Nick and Mitch refilled the hole.

It wouldn't be long before all traces of Big Allie Saltieri disappeared.

Nello held out his hands and swiped them as if they were a pair of cymbals.

"*Arrivederci*, asshole . . ."

CHAPTER NINETY-ONE

NICK DROVE BACK to the Tropicana and Nello led them to the Havana Hideaway for a celebratory drink. He loved the relaxed, intimate atmosphere, with leather sofas and cushioned chairs, and was a fan of the muted jazz playing in the background.

When the thirty-year-old Napoleon cognac he ordered was delivered, he raised his glass.

"Salut."

Nick raised his.

"*Cent'anni.*"

Mitch followed.

"*Kanpai!*"

They all drank, and Nick regarded Nello with renewed admiration. He was fascinated by how a man as abrupt and gruff as Nello could become instantly serene after the surprise appearance of Allie, coolly kill him, and then calmly engineer the disappearance of the body.

It was a bravura performance and Nick smiled at him respectfully.

"When are you headed back?"

"Tomorrow . . . My business here is done."

Nick nodded.

"It might have ended differently if I hadn't been involved with Erin . . ."

Nello waved away the comment. "Bullshit. The way Allie was going, he was a walkin' train wreck. Corky ordered him to knock off the shitstorm that was causin' all that publicity. He didn't. He's dead."

So much for the life and times of Big Allie Saltieri.

Nick and Mitch exchanged warm abrazos with Nello and said goodbye. When they returned to the Wimbledon it was well after midnight and Nick wondered if Mitch was going to prolong the evening.

"You still plan on your midnight snack with Lori?"

"Why not? She's beautiful, talented, and intelligent, uncovered Tilden, gave him to us, and deserves a thank-you . . ."

"Very gallant . . ."

". . . and she's the eighth wonder of the world in bed."

Nick laughed, entered his suite, and found Erin fast asleep. It had been a long, tough day, and exhaustion had undoubtedly taken over. He undressed and slipped into bed without waking her.

Nick was asleep as soon as his head hit the pillow and slept until he was jolted awake.

CHAPTER NINETY-TWO
DAY FIVE

H E WAS STARING into Erin's eyes. It was morning; she was on top of him and began to slowly kiss her way down his body. His attempt to remain motionless lasted about ten seconds before he was all over and into her.

Good morning, world!

Nick thought love in the morning was the world's most underrated sexual activity. Unlike an afternoon quickie or a late-night snoozer, you were fresh and literally beginning the day with a bang.

They showered, dressed, and were having breakfast on the patio when the chimes rang. Nick answered the door and Mitch entered with a folded morning paper.

He held it out.

"First page."

Nick unfolded it. Anyone could have predicted the *Sun Times* headline.

Nick scanned the story that gave the names of the five dead men. It speculated that it was a gangland shoot-out, but the police had no idea about a motive.

He refolded the paper and tossed it onto the sofa.

"As we thought—thank God. Want some coffee?"

"Had some with Lori—I'm headed for the set."

"Talk to you later. I'll be in the office."

They finished breakfast and Nick drove Erin to *Seven-Eleven*'s base camp at the Tropicana. They were shooting at Boulder Dam, and her motor home would take her to the location.

On the way back to his office Julie called with a message from Sam.

He was leaving.

CHAPTER NINETY-THREE

ALFRED ANSWERED THE suite's door, and Nick saw what looked like an entire luggage department stacked in the inner hallway. The luggage would go in a van and Alfred would go in Sam's stretch limo. But the butler wasn't dressed comfortably for the long ride home. No—he was, as always, in his black suit, with a winged collar and bow tie.

Another of Gwen's pretensions of pomp? Probably.

"Good morning, Mr. Conti . . . Mr. Altman is having breakfast on the patio. Would you care for anything?"

"Just coffee will be fine, Alfred . . ."

Sam was seated alone and reading the *Sun Times* when Nick walked up. He looked up and indicated the headline.

"You have anything to do with this?"

"Certainly not."

"One of the dead guys is Strozzi."

"I saw that."

"He's the one you said was trying to blackmail us."

"True."

"And now he winds up dead."

"Also true."

"And you had nothing to do with it . . ."

"Three trues in a row. You hit a trifecta."

"And you're fulla shit."

"Possibly. How's Gwen?"

"Don't change the subject."

"I won't. Where's Gwen?"

"In the bedroom. She heard you were coming."

"She remains a fan."

Sam grunted, threw aside the paper, and sipped his coffee. Alfred arrived, handed Nick his coffee, and left. Nick sat across from Sam and smiled.

"How do you feel?"

"Shitty. I'm probably dying."

"You're too mean to die."

"You're probably right . . . Can I assume our recent problems in Vegas are over?"

"You can."

"And things will go back to normal."

"They will."

Sam nodded. He sipped his coffee and stared out over the golf course. He looked thoughtful and solemn, and Nick wondered if he might be contemplating his mortality.

"Nick . . ."

"Yes, Sam?"

"There's something you should know . . ."

"Yes . . . ?"

"I really like you . . ."

Nick nodded.

"I know that, Sam."

Nick got up, patted Sam on the shoulder, and left. Neither had said another word.

CHAPTER NINETY-FOUR

NICK PUT THE top down on the Firebird and called Julie as he drove out of the parking lot. It was a chamber-of-commerce day, and a blazing sun was keeping the high desert in the low sixties.

"I'm on my way to Boulder Dam—having lunch with Erin. Forward the important calls and leave the others on the spindle."

"Have you read the morning paper?"

"I have . . ."

"Wow! That'll sure be the flavor of the day for a while . . ."

"It will—but some new sensation will knock it off the front page in no time. Publishers can always find something to keep people buying papers."

Within a couple of weeks Nick's prediction would come true. The five dead wiseguys who were shot in Maxi's parking lot were to become a fading memory because Vegas was about to experience an event that would make headlines all over the world.

The MGM Grand Hotel and Casino would go up in flames.

On November 21 at seven thirty in the morning, a fire broke out in a delicatessen. There were about 5,000 people in the twenty-six-story resort at the time. Smoke and fire spread through the building, and 84 people were killed; 785 more were injured. Most of the fire was in the casino and adjacent areas, but most of the deaths were caused by smoke inhalation on the upper floors.

It would be the worst disaster in Nevada history.

But not on this glorious day.

As Nick drove to Boulder Dam the air was clean, the sun was out, and all was right in the world. He slipped a cassette of *Charlie Parker with Strings* into the tape deck and the virtuoso jazz saxophonist began "Stella by Starlight," backed by a full concert orchestra.

Lush and mesmerizing.

Two nights earlier Nick had slipped a cassette into the same tape deck and learned that Snuffy was dead. Within forty-eight hours Strozzi, Skeets, and Saltieri were dead and he was listening to "Stella by Starlight" by a saxophonist who was also dead . . . seven S's.

Meaningful? Probably not.

Boulder Dam is thirty miles southeast of Vegas. It's over seven hundred feet high and almost a quarter mile long—a massive concrete arch blocking the Colorado River in Black Canyon. Lake Mead, formed by the dam, is an oasis of recreational boating, fishing, camping, and all manner of water sports.

But the surrounding countryside is a barren wilderness.

Stavros had set up the sequence he was filming opposite the lake to take advantage of the desolation—overlooking the precipitous drop to the canyon floor.

Nick arrived as the cast and crew broke for lunch.

Erin saw him drive up and hurried toward the car. She was wearing a silk blouse, heels, and a billowing skirt that caught the wind as she rushed up with a lunch basket.

"Roast beef or turkey with hard-boiled eggs, salad, fruit, and cook-ies from the caterer . . . I added caviar and champagne from the hotel." She hopped into the car, kissed Nick, and sidled up next to him.

Nick cocked an eyebrow.

"No oysters?"

"My body couldn't deal with the reputed consequences."

Nick put his arm around her and they drove along the top of the dam toward Arizona. There was a brisk wind blowing up the canyon and her fiery red hair billowed out behind her.

She nuzzled closer to him without looking up.

"I saw the morning paper . . ."

"Oh . . . ?"

"All five of those men who were killed were affiliated with the Mob."

Nick nodded.

"I read that."

"So is Allie . . ."

"Yes."

They remained silent for several seconds before she asked the ques-tion that had made her bring up the subject.

"Will we ever see him again?"

"No."

She was again silent for several seconds.

"I love you, Nick."

Nick smiled and remembered the last words he spoke to Sam Alt-man.

"I know that."

They reached the Arizona side of the dam and Nick turned south on a little-used access road. Unlike the Nevada side, which had a mu-seum, gift shop, café, and huge parking structure, the Arizona side was comparatively barren, with only a camper trailer sitting on a dirt lot, selling bottled water.

Nick followed the access road to its end and parked. They were a thousand feet over Black Canyon and the Colorado River. The entire area was devoid of vegetation, but the rugged hills and sheer drop of the cliffs had an unmatched beauty of their own. A mile to the north the dam's towering white wall of concrete rose like an impossible master-piece of engineering.

It felt as if they were alone at the top of the world.

The lunch basket was on the seat beside Erin, and Nick reached over and took out the champagne.

"Do we have flutes?"

"*Certainement!*" She fished out two paper cups. "Voilà!"

"Disposable . . . Ingenious."

Nick popped the champagne, poured, and faced her.

"Do you have a toast?"

"Only clichés. Do you?"

"Maybe . . . It depends."

"Do hurry, my sweet, I'm thirsty."

"In that case, how would you like to star in a Nick Conti produc-tion?"

She looked surprised.

"Television?"

"No."

"What?"

"Life."

The realization of what was coming slowly crossed her face, and she smiled expectantly.

"What would be my billing?"

"Mrs. Nick Conti."

She threw her arms around him and the two paper cups flew out of their hands. Champagne filled the air along with a whoop of delight.

It echoed off the canyon walls.

ACKNOWLEDGMENTS

Once again I am indebted to Ed Snider, Herb Simon, Jimmy Argyropoulos, Mike Bonsignore, Jeff Barbakow, and Gene Montesano (the *boyus*), and to the incomparable Ed Victor, my literary agent, for pushing me to create a novel out of the many stories I related on the subject of the Las Vegas casinos, the Mob, and filming a television series in the city between 1977 and 1982.

To my brilliant young editor, Ben Adams of Bloomsbury, my deepest thanks for an outstanding job that not only made the process thoroughly enjoyable but added significantly to the end product.

And finally to "the Hens," my supportive, unwavering wife and the love of my life.